Carlton Hill

a novel

Lukas Eberhard

Lukas Eberhard
Carlton Hill - a novel
1. Edition August 2025
Copyright © 2025 by Lukas Eberhard
Cover Design Copyright © 2025 Lukas Eberhard
ISBN: 9798296368850

All rights reserved. All trademarks, product names and trade names portrayed are the property of their registered owners.

This is a work of fiction and should be regarded as such. The characters, names, places and incidents in this work are entirely fictional and imaginary or used in a fictionalized way. They do not portray any actual persons, parties or events, historical or not. Resemblance to real persons, either living or dead, events or locations is completely coincidental and not intended.

This book, or sections of it, may not be reproduced or copied in any form without permission

To Ellie

1

The evening light tinted her features in the most beautiful red, yellow and orange. Lying behind her, he looked at her back, her legs, not slim but not beefy either, the dark blonde hair, falling like waves breaking on cliff. The shape was reminiscent to Arthur's Seat, at least to his eyes. But not the rough, rocky contours, formed by force and time. When he looked at her, he was reminded of one cold but beautiful day in winter, some years back, and the snow-capped Arthur's Seat's appearance from the lake at Holyrood Park.

From Waverley Hotel, you had a nice view over Old Town, hanging to the hills in levels. But you could also see Arthur's Seat to the left. And Carlton Hill, in the corner of your left eye. Almost like an afterthought. She yawned, the beautiful thing, breaking whatever thought had crossed his mind when he looked at the town that was home to so many memories, both his and others'.

"Are you tired?" Duke Arrowsmith asked, stroking her temple, running his fingers through her hair like he would through patches of golden wheat in summer. Eyes closed, he could smell it, too. The scent of harvesting season, producing the best wheat and barley for beer and whiskey. But in February, harvesting season seemed like it was an eternity away.

"What were you looking at?" Rachel asked back, discarding his question before she pulled a deep breath, probably fighting the urge to yawn.

"At you, gorgeous," Duke said and kissed her neck. Gently, but also forcefully, protracting the process. It was one of his specialties. Rachel moaned. And even though he could still only see the back of her head, he knew she was closing her eyes, holding her breath firmly.

"Liar. Think I'll tip you generously just for bluntly lying to me?"

"Well, I was hoping for it."

"Well, then you're wrong, little schoolboy," she went and turned around, looking right into his eyes, drowning.

"You're beautiful," he said and meant it.

"You're more beautiful. So beautiful and still youthful."

"I'm a full-grown man."

"Yes, you are."

She ran a hand down his belly, tight with hints of a six-pack but not excessively muscular, down further, solidifying her grip.

"All the girls are jealous of you."

"For knowing how to keep you around?"

"For your beauty. You don't look your age."

"And yet, I am my age."

"You don't look a day older than thirty-five."

"Thirty-five?" she asked in good fun, raising an eyebrow. "I should give you a good whippin' for saying that."

"Please go ahead."

Their eyes met. They stopped. Both of them. Whatever it was between them was strong and fragile and all at the same time. As much as neither of the two would ever say it, they were both aware of it.

"There's something I dislike about seeing you this way," Rachel said with a smack of disappointment swinging in her voice.

"It figures."

"You know what it is?"

"I have my theory. But please, tell me."

"It's the fact of the matter. The realization that all we've had, that we've shared for these sweet hours, was only a fleeting apparition."

"Like a sparrow in an apple tree."

"You could never have it. Nobody could."

"To hell with those that ever tried."

"It's a¬– "

"Crime?"

"Pity," Rachel replied after a moment's consideration.

"And yet, I prefer a fleeting apparition over the dull, gray bleakness of our existence."

"No wonder. You built a career on it."

"Hm."

"I'm sorry," Rachel said and rolled over to the edge of the bed, breaking free from Duke's embrace.

"You don't need to."

"But I had no right saying that," she calmly explained. Whatever remorse she felt, it wasn't tormenting her, at least not to the surface she'd turned to the outside world. No, Rachel had been through plenty of regretful encounters, situations and human relationships, so she was simply too experienced to show how she took it to heart.

As she sat on the edge of the bed, slipping on her stockings, she still looked gorgeous. Duke blinked twice. The sight of her aroused, yet also appalled him. It was something he still had to come to terms with.

"You can say whatever you want," Duke said and embraced her from behind, making sure he could smell her hair. Rachel took his right hand and put it to her cheek.

"There's no way to be mad at anything for too long in your presence. How do you do that?"

"Chemistry, I supposed when I was younger."

"What would you suppose now?"

"Magic."

That had her smiling.

"I'd call you Magic but I'm afraid that nickname is already taken."

"More than once, certainly."

"You're smart."

"No, I'm not."

"Anyway, I think you're smart. It's a sign of intelligence to know who you are, what you're good at and what you're bad at. A quality I know nothing about."

"Care for coffee?"

"Hm," she began and Duke knew the answer.

Ever since they first met, he'd continuously asked the very same question, disregarding society's daytime restrictions on drinking coffee. And even though it was about the best time to go for coffee and soak up the last light of day, Duke knew the answer already.

"Maybe next time," he answered to himself and jumped out of bed.

That ended it. A simple act but it felt like turning off the tap. The flow had stopped.

Silent at first, they both dressed, straightened the clothes so carelessly stripped and tossed to the thick-carpeted floor, arranged their hair. To look presentable and innocent as well. After a while, when Duke wound up his wristwatch and Rachel replaced the red lipstick she'd smeared over both of them, they fell back to the business-like small talk no intelligent human being could ever find enjoyable.

"If that watch didn't look so stylish on you," Rachel repeated a comment made already months back, "I'd advise you to get a new one. Why'd anyone go at such length these days and remember winding up a wristwatch?"

"Because it's a pleasure. I like mechanical things."

"For their simplicity?"

"Nothing's simple about mechanics. It's because they have a tendency of working splendidly for decades without ever giving me a headache."

"That's nice," she replied. Duke could tell from the undertone that she wasn't really interested anymore. He could relate. For Rachel, reality hit much harder than it should've every time their pleasures came to an end.

"So, what're your plans for the evening?" he asked to change the subject. "Any appointments?"

"Dinner with my daughter."

"What about Charles?"

"Charles will join us. If work permits."

"I see."

"No," she said and finished a delicate line under her left eye to accentuate the tasteful makeup she'd applied. "No, you don't."

When they left the room, it looked like nobody had ever been there. Only the bed was deranged, but someone would take care of that. Someone always did. Some person with no voice, no face, no identity in society. Making sure the cogwheels of this enormous machinery would keep spinning and clicking in place. Only the slightest disturbance would bring it all down in a tumble, Duke thought when he peered into the room, then pulled the door shut. Another clicking of the machinery.

They wouldn't talk much on their way down to the parking garage, moving swiftly and casually, raising no suspicion. Nobody really took notice of them. But it seemed that Duke turned more heads.

"You must've been so cocky back in school, Rachel," Duke said very charmingly.

"I was. But so were you. Obviously."

"Don't give me that, I lacked all confidence and was a pitiable mess back in school, routine."

"It was worse than that."

"You're still driving that old thing?" she asked when she spotted Duke's car, parked right next to her brand-new Jaguar.

"It's got class and I like the feel of it."

"That's not what cars are about. It doesn't suit you."

"It's all I have," Duke said and ran a hand along the subtle rear wing.

The car was a Lotus Excel SE, built in 92, running the 2.2-liter Lotus 912 engine. Red paintjob, red interior, a rare combination for sure. Duke kept it in pristine condition. To him, it was the most beautiful thing he'd ever seen. What he appreciated the most was how much he felt connected to the road through the car. With its thin glass-fiber body, Duke felt sure he'd get killed instantly, should he ever hit a tree in it.

"You got a lot more than that," Rachel said, threw her arms around him, then pressed her lips on his'.

"Mind your makeup," Duke reminded her but she didn't reply. Neither did she care.

"Why do you make me feel that way?"

"Ask God."

"God is dead."

"Ask a scientist, then."

"I don't know any scientists," she said enjoying one last kiss to the fullest before slipping an envelope in Duke's coat pocket.

"Thank you."

"Thank you, Mr. Arrowsmith."

Without saying goodbye, she got into the car, backed it up and rolled off without ever looking back at Duke. She always did that. What got him was the smell of the car. Or lack thereof. It was a hybrid, making a buzzing sound instead of explosions.

When he started the car, he reached for the seatbelt, then changed his mind and got back out. Exhaust fumes were rising like cigarette smoke from the back of the car. They smelled just right. The engine was humming its typical, carbureted sound. A fire door banged shut, spoiling the mirage. But Duke had had plenty. As he sped up the ramp, he rolled down the window, listening to the stainless-steel, iron and aluminum orchestra.

Behind the wheel of the Lotus, the 912 buzzing like a bumblebee at work, Duke never felt any hurry. Nothing ever worried him. The world even looked brighter through the windows, so he barely ever rolled them down. Edinburgh looked like it hadn't changed in the past three-hundred years when you walked down the street. But whenever Duke took the Excel out on a stroll, it looked a bit better. Like anything he could ever imagine.

The asphalt was glistering, a sign of cold rolling in from the ocean. It had been a while since he'd been out there, standing at the pier, scent of salt in his nose, soon getting him hungry and yearning for fish and chips and a cold beer on a chilly day. Before he knew, he was in Stockbridge, where he was familiar with every street and alley. A couple of years back, people would've watched and turned their heads when a handsome man in a car like that drove by. But those times were past and gone. Behind the wheel of the red Excel, Duke wouldn't leave no impression on the world.

In front of a small café, he spotted a parking spot and effortlessly backed the car into it. Nobody took notice. Only the girl behind the counter was eyeballing him through as he crossed the sidewalk.

She was a real treat to the eyes. Tall, slender and beautiful. From the sidewalk, through the fogged-up window, her hair looked a shade or two too dark. From up close, you could tell it was the sweetest of honey blonde. The leather apron they made her wear like anyone else working at the café did nothing to diminish her attractiveness.

"Hi there," she went to greet Duke, trying in vain to make it sound casual.

"Good afternoon."

"Is it that late already?"

"Uh-huh. The weather's playing tricks on your perception that time of year."

"Had someone asked me, I'd have sworn it wasn't much past midday."

"Working long hours?"

She smiled as she poured foamed milk into thick espresso, attempting to put a leaf on top but failing miserably.

"What can you do? I'm strapped for cash."

"Most are."

"Not all of us," she said and stopped before saying anything further. Duke smiled.

"What's your specialty?"

"Barely not flunking out of college?"

"Funny."

"Why aren't you laughing, then?" she asked and handed the cappuccino to an overweight waitress, huffing and puffing, making her way across the small shop floor.

"I don't look good when I'm laughing."

"Bad liar, eh?" she said blinking for emphasis.

"Keep hearing that."

"Maybe it's true, then. My specialty is what they call Angel Stain."

"What's that?" Duke asked even though he knew.

And she went at some length explaining how Angel Stain, in essence, was the thickest of espressos, wrung from the most aromatic beans, roasted to perfection, how it was invented in Japan and caught on in small cafés all the way across the globe, and how she'd never been there, yet wished to go to Osaka someday.

"So," she said in closing, checking that nobody was impatiently waiting on coffee while she was chatting, "that's my specialty. Even though I, technically, don't know what it's supposed to taste like."

"Because you've never been there."

"Right."

"But you wish to go."

"I do."

"At some point, when there's no courses you're trying not to flunk."

Using his coy smile on her, Duke got her blushing just some. It put off a stud well in his thirties, sitting at a small table with his back to the brick wall so he could watch her while mustering the courage his career and paycheck should've provided him with and finally hit on her.

"That's a long shot, still," she said and some deeper emotion appeared around the lines of her eyes. It looked like grief but there was no definitiveness in telling what other people were feeling.

"What about that Angel Stain?"

"I'll get you one."

"Wonderful. I'll sit over there."

Duke pointed at the table facing to the street, closest to the salaryman looking for his own courage. When Duke walked back there, their eyes met but the poor slob looked away. Another faux lion, Duke thought with some amusement, who should rather go see the Wizard of Oz.

There was the always pressing urge to check his phone as he waited, a very post-post-modern angst Duke could relate to but still held in check. Just peering at life going on in the streets outside of the café felt more compelling. With his face so close to the fogged window, it seemed like a zoo. Only he couldn't tell if he was within or without the enclosure.

"There you go," gorgeous blonde said and placed the world's smallest cup in front of him, turning it slightly so it was positioned perfectly. The cups and saucers were beautiful, art déco and much too tasteful for a contemporary café, cranking out almond milk latté like it was the end of the world by midnight.

"What a scent," Duke said, inhaling some more, wishing it was burning high-octane fuel.

"Go ahead, try it."

"Can't curb your curiosity?"

"Taste it already," she told him and smiled her million-dollar smile.

The scent was more intense and as thick as the texture of the coffee as Duke lifted it to his nose. He could've gulped it all down at once it was such a small shot. But he remembered good manners and took a tiny sip.

"It's amazing," he lied.

"Aw, thank you."

"Nice flavors of dark chocolate for starters, then a hint of Madagascan vanilla, raisins to wrap it up."

"I knew you'd like it."

"Thank you very much."

"You're welcome. It's on me this time."

"Lovely," Duke said instead of insisting on paying and tipping her generously and sneakily. "Are you applying the drug-dealer marketing scheme?"

"Like giving out free trials and getting people addicted? Got me."

"I call it dedication."

She blinked at him, then turned to start off. Duke stopped her, gently taking her wrist.

"Say, you mind if I make it up to you some time?"

You could tell she was hooked when she paused for a moment's consideration. Just for good measure.

"Sure, why not?"

"Will you be back at university some time tonight?"

"I'll be down there soon, once I wrap up my shift."

"I'll have some business to attend to at the Meadows. You care to meet me there at, say, nine?"

"I can do nine."

"It's decided then. I haven't even introduced myself. I'm Duke."

"Emily," she said and shook his hand, not checking if Duke was a legal first name, nickname, or alias to a wanted criminal. Her eyes were fixed on his'.

"It was really nice meeting you, Emily."

"It's been a pleasure."

"I gotta run now."

"Where will we meet? Meadows is huge."

"You'll find me hanging with my kind. Maybe on top of the Range Rover."

Emily nodded and laughed, wishing him a fine afternoon. This time, it was Duke blinking at her as he walked out. In the corner of his eye, he spotted the gutless lion in the back of the place, eating his heart out, probably cursing a man going by the name of Duke.

2

The Meadows wasn't a long drive from Stockbridge, ten minutes if things went well. Crossing the bridge giving the name to the quarter, Duke looked down at the waters, running their course so relentlessly. Something made him uneasy. There was still time. Should he be late, there was no hell to pay. With his smile, he could maneuver himself out of any jam.

There was a strong urge pulling him towards his favorite place. Even if he decided to go, it wouldn't prove to be very satisfying. Chances were slim he'd find any kind of solitude up there at this time of day.

Still, he decided to steer the car towards North Bridge. Just in case he changed his mind. As the traffic light switched on Princes Street, fortune shifted him in a different direction. Most cars were rolling east, giving way to Carlton Hill. A firm believer in good fortune, Duke followed along.

The steps looked so familiar. They felt homely, like meeting an old friend. Fresh air entered his lungs. This was almost the center of town but you always had the feeling of being somewhere entirely different. Turning his head, Duke checked just how far up from the ground he'd made it already. Down there, the Excel, looking like a beacon surrounded by all the new and blank and anonymous cars people drove these days.

Some years back, he would've been panting by this time, with cigarettes and beer having taken their toll on him. But almost no damage was irrevocable. The steep and seemingly endless steps had not much of an effect on him anymore. Neither had all the filth and latex evidence of close, anonymous chance encounters, enjoyed in questionable anonymity.

Whenever he could spot the tips of the structures atop Carlton Hill, Duke had a feeling of accomplishment. Even though he'd seen them time and again, like an abundance of people in history had before him, and will after him, the feeling couldn't be taken away from him. What he felt was triumphant in its own right, something hard to capture. And Duke felt no need to ever capture and harness it, like stalking and trapping a beautiful man-eating beast.

The cold was much fiercer this far up from regular street level. A strong wind was blowing, deranging his hair. Little did he care. It only reminded him of the deranged sheets of the bed back at the hotel. Has anyone taken care of that already, he wondered.

There was the typical flock of tourists, snapping pictures and selfies to post wherever it was people put out their redundance. It had been years since Duke had cut ties with that reality. The world he now lived in was more like a shadow.

Which made him something like a ghostly apparition. For better or for worse, at some point, Duke had pulled the pin from that grenade, still holding it in his hand, pressing, the safety switch. Hands buried in his coat's pockets Duke wandered the hilltop like he'd done so many times before. The cold was sharp as a knife, as if it was trying to rip the flesh off his bones.

A couple from Japan was walking past him, the girl meeting Duke's gaze. But his eyes were empty. She looked away. Basic Japanese in college wouldn't really pay in moments like that. All he understood was gibberish, the type of talk between two young fools thinking they were in love.

The feeling of solitude wouldn't hit this time. It was the same disappointment Duke had assumed it would be. The idea bored him as much as it made perfect sense. Sometimes, all of Edinburgh just wasn't big or small or spacious enough for Duke to be what he would aspire to be.

"Excuse me," a bloke in his late twenties went and almost right away shoved his phone in Duke's face, "would you take a picture of me and my girl with the city in the background?"

"It's a town," Duke said with disinterest, taking the phone.

"Can you get the castle in the frame?" the bloke asked without acknowledging Duke's comment.

"Why, sure," it came back in Duke's best, thick, Scottish accent. It was phony and sounded just right to tourists.

They were laughing and enjoying themselves and shivering some as they posed against the mighty castle that had defended Scotland before but couldn't anymore. When it was done, Duke wished them a nice trip. He even made sure to recommend the best place for deep-fried chocolate candy bars.

The cold was creeping under his skin, deeper and deeper. Lips feeling dry and cracked, Duke knew it was time to go. It had been a vain endeavor anyway. As he climbed back down, he looked at Arthur's Seat not far in the distance. The top was crawling with people, looking like rainbow ants in their fashionable clothes from all over the world. Duke shook his head but thought nothing, really.

Only when the door clicked shut, he felt his spirits rising back up again. Going up there had been foolish. The ride to the Meadows cheered him up, though. It did him a world of good. Not even when someone blew the horn at him for overtaking when the street was two-wide did Duke feel any anger.

3

Cold Czech beer warmed him from the inside out as he glanced across the spacious room. Staropramen had always been one of his favorite brews, regardless of what anyone else was saying. Whenever he drank at university, Duke felt like foreign matter. What he saw seemed familiar but felt alien. Too much time has passed. Too many amends had been made. Only the beer tasted the way he remembered.

The walls were lined with books, some of them so old they looked like they would be falling to pieces, would anyone ever mind blowing the dust off of them. Would the words still have the same meaning since the day they were printed on paper mechanically? Seeing an array of laptops and smartphones and tablet computers rendered the question doubtful. It was only human to be looking down on the past.

"Can you get me another one?" he asked the bartender, a slender guy fresh out of school, dressed like the next guy, crew cut but nails painted black.

"Another Staropramen?"

"Uh-huh," Duke said and when he counted out the money plus tip, the bartender looked at him just as baffled as he'd done the first time.

"Say," he went as he drew another one, "how come a guy like you's still paying cash?"

"Guy like me?"

"I mean, a man like you."

"I wasn't going after that."

"Okay," he said expressing his increasing bafflement.

"A guy like me wouldn't concern himself too much with trends. Or the zeitgeist, if you will."

"Uh-huh."

"A guy like me goes about things the way he feels fit."

"And what does that involve?"

"Minding your own fuckin' business, mostly."

With that, Duke took his pint and retreated to the seat at the helm of a bookshelf as spacious as a cruise ship, books behind glass panes like anonymous passengers. He checked his wristwatch, not wanting the beer anymore.

But the first sip off his second Staropramen was even better, cold and smooth and delicious. For an instant, he pictured himself sitting at a café in Prague in summer, nice view of the castle to his left, gorgeous girls walking by, chit-chatting and giggling as they checked him out. Duke had never been to Prague, least so in summer.

Almost half the pint was finished. Something was telling him it was time to go. Even if that dictated wandering the quarter in the cold for some time. The door swung open, ancient glass rattling, on the verge of shattering. One glance and Duke knew his instinct had been right. There was no point trying to hide his face anywhere. As much as he felt disregarding people was bad form and generally despicable, he was in no mood for talking. Neal Briggs had already spotted him.

Duke took another sip, making sure not to finish his beer, while Neal said something to the flock of young, female students he'd waltzed in the place with.

"Son of a gun!" the Texan uttered in full disregard of British and European chicness, an attitude he'd adopted rather quickly after crossing the pond.

"Mr. Briggs."

"Look at you, Mr. Arrowsmith. Been working out?"

"You can tell."

"Built like a brick shithouse, that for sure."

"Wish I could say the same about you," Duke said and tapped what sign of a pot belly Neal couldn't conceal even with clever fashion choices.

"Body's decomposing into a carcass for some time now, Duke."

"Is it any wonder? You're not twenty anymore."

"Exactly," Neal said and fingered a cigarette from the pack in his chest pocket, popping it into his mouth before remembering anti-smoking restrictions and repocketing it. "World's a jungle, Duke. It's always been."

"Difference is, it's digital now."

"That's right," Neal said and signaled the bartender. The place was no service but he got a nod and the bartender went to work.

"What's he gonna get you?"

"Carling."

"Hm."

"Can it already, will you?"

"No shame being a country boy."

"No shame chewin' tobacco an' spittin' it on me feet, pickin' the five-string banjo on me porch."

"Horrible. You don't even sound Texan anymore."

"It's horrible, I know."

"I mean, you'd pass for Shreveport. Or Texarkana."

"Screw you. There's nothing bad about Shreveport or Texarkana."

"Oklahoma, maybe."

"Hold it right there, Sir."

"How's everything going?"

The Carling arrived and the bartender put another Staropramen in front of Duke. It was hard on Duke not to repeat Neal's opening line.

"How'd Waterloo go," Neal said and took a big gulp of his beer.

"Depends on who you're asking," Duke replied. If anything, he'd have expected Neal to hoot and toot on how everything was beautiful, smell of roses, taste of peaches and cream. It was common for the academic staff to boast about creative influx from brilliant young minds, a bit misled and radical, unpolished diamonds with a bright future ahead of them just around the corner.

"Ask me. And cheers."

"Cheers."

"That's good."

"What's the trouble?"

"What world are we living in?"

"You shouldn't answer a question with another question. As a respected professor of American Literature, you should know."

"The sacred cows are dead, Mr. Arrowsmith."

"Some posh girl ranted on Papa Hemingway?"

Another big gulp of beer and Professor Briggs went into further detail. It was all so presumptuous, ill-informed and riding the tide of the zeitgeist. Duke didn't feel like contesting or weighing in on the soliloquy. What he listened to was yet another example of why he couldn't be bothered with the academic world anymore.

"Know what really did it for me, Duke?"

"Tell me."

"It's that they got the brass neck sitting there, spending daddy's money, hating on everyone and everything they dislike purely out of personal taste."

"They confuse taste with argumentation."

"Exactly," Neal said and pointed his almost empty glass at Duke. "They have the nerve criticizing history."

"Which is foolish."

"True again."

"And you wouldn't say they got the brass neck back in Texas, would you?"

"I'm more interested in that gorgeous sweetheart over there, devouring you with her eyes."

"Who're you talking about?"

When he checked he knew right away. There she was, sitting at a small bar table by the door all by herself.

"I'll go tell her to bludgeon you over the head next time she's after your attention."

"Never mind, she's an acquaintance."

"Liar."

"I never lie. I merely stick to the American virtue of plausible deniability."

"Look what it did to Tricky Ricky."

"If they really mean to screw you over, they'll always find ways. If you pardon my French."

"You're acquitted. And dismissed."

"Thanks for the beer. It was nice seeing you."

"You're welcome."

Duke got up to leave when Neal took a hold of his wrist. A smile appeared around Duke's mouth. Subtle, but speaking volumes.

"You never told me why you left."

"I did."

"Yeah, you did. Technically. But that was hogwash."

"It's only hogwash if you decided to question the validity of my statement."

"What a well-spoken man. I wonder where you learned. And where you're putting it to good use now."

"Hush-hush."

"Get outta here," Neal this time said in legitimate Texan, dismissing class definitely for the day.

They said their goodbyes, somewhat harsher than it should've been, and Duke walked off.

From afar, she was beautiful. From up close, a lesser man would've gasped for air. Dark blonde hair, prettiest of faces. Body to die for. A table of fraternity boys was picking up volume, though neither of them would've had the heart to hit on her, even though they boasted about it.

"When did you come in, Natalie?" Duke asked and gave her a half embrace and a kiss on the corner of her beautiful mouth.

"It couldn't have been more than five minutes."

"And you've already been served."

A glass of Martini, much out of place, remained untouched in the farthest corner of the small, high-legged table.

"Bartender's crushing on me, I assume."

"Who's not?"

"You."

"Oh, my."

"Too real?"

She smiled, looking even prettier. You could tell that, with more maturity, she would develop crinkles underneath her eyes, accentuating the class she oozed. And how much she would hate them once it was time, for they stood testament to a fact of life. Nobody, not even the prettiest females, would remain young forever.

"What gave me away?" Duke asked, chiming into the banter.

"I'm not sure."

"Give me your best guess."

Natalie leaned forward, meeting his gaze first, then grasping his hand, making sure the entire pub would see. Once the establishing shot was done, she stroked his cheek.

"It's because you can't be had. Not an inch of you."

"You've had me."

"I'm not so sure about that."

"Believe me."

"Nobody will ever have you."

"You think that's definitive? So much I couldn't be crushing on you?"

"I don't like being turned down."

"Who'd ever turn you down?"

"I always get what I want."

"Only a chosen few ever do."

"At least for now."

Before he could say anything else, she forced her lips on his', biting him, pushing her tongue into his mouth. Duke could feel the sets of eyes of jealous men on his back. The target hanging there weighed heavy.

It was short, but intense, terminated when Natalie withdrew and whipped a pocket mirror out of her purse. To touch up her makeup. But also, to put emphasis on whatever it was for her she wanted to clarify.

"How was dinner with your mother?" Duke asked.

"Oh, don't mention it. French place in Haymarket I hate. And how come you know I went for dinner with my mother?"

"Just an uneducated guess, really. You want to go?"

"Desperately so. I feel like chopped liver on a plate in this place."

As they walked out of the pub, the bartender crushing on Natalie was eating his heart out in all secrecy and anonymity.

"Who were you drinking with?" she asked, clinging on to Duke's arm walking towards her apartment somewhat off campus.

"Someone I know."

She laughed.

"What's so funny?"

"Of course he's someone you know."

"And that's funny?"

"The fact that you're a professional at evading every question is funny."

"Funny as in gallows humor."

"That clarifies it."

"Your maturity astounds me."

"It's the expensive clothes and jewelry."

"I wish it was."

Suddenly, a shudder went right through her. Duke saw it. He felt it vibrating in his arm as well.

"I didn't ask you how your day went, Mr. Arrowsmith."

"What's troubling you?"

"You're again–"

"Please, I can tell when something isn't right."

Natalie wouldn't say a word for what felt like the longest of time. Being a gentleman, Duke wouldn't push her. Sirens howled somewhere around the quarter. Nothing out of the ordinary. They made Natalie cringe some more.

"Gosh," she finally said and broke the silence, "I wish they'd change the tune of their sirens already."

"Are you sure you don't want to talk about it?"

"Well, if it turns out to be a bad, very distasteful joke, then I'll certainly feel like a fool for telling you."

"What if it's nothing but the truth?"

When they crossed the street, the evening was illuminated by a poorly-choreographed ballet of red and blue. Police cruisers were lining the block that didn't look like anything out of the ordinary. Georgian Edinburgh architecture.

"Come on," she said and pulled at his arm, "let's get out of here."

"Would you please tell me what's going on?"

"At the apartment," she replied and rushed him some more, trying not to glance at the police doing whatever it was they did. Duke couldn't help but look. Even though he held a strong disdain towards anyone attracted by the spectacular. And then he saw a detective about to climb the stairs into an apartment building as generic as the next on the block. Their eyes met.

It was hard making out her features against the dark, alternately discolored in red and blue, with the night throwing itself upon the land like a black silk scarf. But he noticed how beautiful she was. What he noticed next was her delicate but well-developed build, the standard-issue semi-automatic on her belt looking so terribly out of proportion.

"Excuse me, I didn't catch that," he said when their gaze was broken by the sharp edge of a brick wall.

4

The call had been a punch in the gut after a calm weekend off duty, the first in a while. Though it wasn't really too bad getting away from the desk, writing reports and catching up on whatever was kicking around with slim chances of ever getting done. Communication over the radio had been vague and inconsistent, and while she hadn't really taken it seriously, thinking it for a fluke or some greenhorn overblowing what was daily business in every big town, she'd decided to go and see for herself.

The street looked like an American state fair. Only the lights weren't thrill rides and snack shacks selling deep-fried cool-aid. Even when she climbed the stairs to the very inconspicuous building, she was convinced they'd come for nothing. Fuss. And then she spotted a man, walking with a young posh darling. Their eyes met. Gosh, she thought, what a handsome man. Much too classy for a girl like that. Too mature.

"Move it, Joe," Francis called out when he almost bumped into her.

"See that guy over there?"

"What guy?"

"That guy. Down the street."

"Another yuppie, so what?"

"That's no yuppie."

"What's he instead?"

"Good question."

"Would you knock it off already?"

Had anyone had the nerve talking to her like that, Josephine would've given him a good dressing down. But after almost a decade on the squad together, their banter was little more than small talk.

"Interesting guy."

"If you need to get laid, be my guest."

"Screw you."

As the handsome gentleman and his escort she didn't care for disappeared around the corner, Joe managed to collect her senses.

On the way upstairs, Francis provided all kinds of information that shed some more darkness on an already shady case. If there is a case at all, Joe thought.

"What is this," she went to no one in particular upon seeing the apartment crawling with new brass, "freshman course in college?"

It was a three-room, not very spacious. A typical student's apartment. It would've been nice after the war but nobody had really cared making improvements since then. The carpet used to be thick but was crinkly and ugly now. It was made even more obscene by the flashing of a camera. The kitchen seemed like a bunch of boards hammered into an alcove. Worse, an unknown officer was interviewing a girl there. She couldn't have been older than nineteen. They'd handed her a glass of tap water with limescale floating in it and thrown a police issue blanket over her shoulders.

"They look like we did back then," Francis commented. "Cut them some slack."

"They ever cut us any slack?"

"When did you pick up the Old Testament, hot shot?"

"Who's the lady, questioning our eye witness?"

"Jerry Lundin."

"Doesn't ring a bell."

"New brass on the squad. Fresh import from Manchester or something, don't recall."

"Can't stand her already."

"Want to chase her away?"

"No, let's see the crime scene first."

Whatever pessimism she'd retained to that point was quickly waning when they were led in the small room adjacent the combined living room and kitchen.

"What a mess," Francis summed it up when they stepped inside. The room was small and poorly-lit and smelled of stale air. There was a dried-up plant in an ugly pot at the window sill. All that constituted to a basic level of smell. On top of that was a layer of iron-like blood smell.

Joe said nothing. What first crossed her mind was common sense. Someone got murdered in this room. The bed was deranged, sheets torn, smeared with what seemed like two gallons of blood. The walls were sprinkled, too. It was one of those cheap beds. Joe thought it must've made a hell of a racket when someone was having fun in it.

The photographers packed up their gear, now that they'd banned the scene on digital film to the ends of time. The final flashlight gave Joe the faint idea of a very bad headache. As if someone had thrust an ice pick right into her left orbit. She rubbed her temple, trying to ease it off some.

"Lead me through this, Franny. What do you see?"

Francis looked at the scene, a small desk to the wall that could merely hold a laptop that was still there, some scribbled notes on crinkly paper, a narrow wardrobe built like a forest stalker, and the bed of pressed pine dust that looked like it would collapse the second a feather landed on it.

"Young girl living here, just started college. She goes out, meets someone, they talk. Casually first, then about their courses. She takes a liking in him. He's experienced. She's not. He talks her into taking her home. Turns her on. Pushes the right buttons. But he's an animal. She turns him down when he's whispering nasty things in her ear while licking her earlobe."

"Nasty like what?"

"Like taking the back door. Spanking her. Using that belt of his on her. Strap first, then the buckle. Or worse."

"Go ahead."

Francis kneeled down at the bed, making sure not to hit any puddles where the blood hadn't dried yet. Whatever he'd hoped was there, some evidence – any evidence – was omitted. It was all guess work.

"She's coy about it first, telling him she doesn't like it that way. When he's trying to talk her into it, she starts getting scared. Only there's nothing she could do. She feels powerless all of a sudden. Against him. Against his advances."

"She could've sent him away."

"She wouldn't dare. He's muscular. Not as strong as he looks by any means but she thinks more than a handful for her."

"And she wouldn't play along?"

"Maybe she tried. Giving him what he's asking for so he's satisfied. Only he's playing it rough, hurting her."

"And she's telling him it hurts."

"Yes."

"And she's telling him to stop."

"She's imploring him. Close to tears."

"But the guy discovers that he likes it rough. Her fear is giving him another rush of blood to his head."

"His heart's pumping like crazy. Adrenaline and testo, right to the processor."

"The more she's scared, the more he likes it."

"Turns him on. Big time."

"Then he draws the first blood. How?"

"Could've been the buckle."

"A belt buckle can draw blood."

"If you care about hitting hard enough. Very hard. Much harder than any remotely sane person would ever feel comfortable with. Even enraged."

"Now she's in real pain, fearing for her life. What would she do, push him away?"

"She's trying but in vain."

"What's next? Scream for help?"

"That does it for him. Smacks her in the face."

"Splitting her lip."

"It bleeds like crazy."

"Hm," Joe said touching her lips, tracing the fine lines of flesh with her fingertips.

"Numbed with pain, she's swallowing her blood."

"Makes it hard to scream."

"But she does scream, magnifying his rage."

"Nobody would really care if a girl screamed once or twice in this part of town."

"No, I don't think so."

"What we got now is a suspect as crazy as a shithouse rat, who's seriously injured a girl. He could stop now, right at this point, pull himself together, do some sweet talking, limit the damage. And pray that she wouldn't press any charges."

"That's not what's crossing his mind."
"What is it instead?"
"If she talks, I'm chopped liver on rye."
"There's hell to pay."
"Prison sentence, maybe being registered as sex offender, financial compensation."
"Still something you'd get out of as if nothing had ever happened after a couple of years of being a good boy."
"His reasoning wouldn't go that far."
"He needs to silence her."
"There's the belt in his hands. He's feeling the weight of it."
"Smacks her right in the face again. But she won't stop crying."
"And she wouldn't stop crying for help. He's losing it."
"And then he starts strangling her."
"All while telling her to shush it up. To stop it already. To shut her mouth. Never tell anyone about it."
"He doesn't notice her face turning blue."
"No."
"He doesn't notice her eyes turning up, the expression fading from them."
"No."
"When he finally releases the grip on the belt, muscles shaking, aching with pain, she's dead."
"Dead for minutes already."
"Must've been a shock."
"Not any more than realizing he might find himself at the receiving end of some serious retribution."

Images were running through Joe's head, flicking like the first motion pictures, patched together from single frames. Like a bad movie, trying to lure a simple-minded audience in with gore. When she understood that it made her sick to her stomach as if she was on the squad for only a couple of months, Joe tried pushing the images away. It was the first time in countless years a crime scene touched her on a personal level.

"Maybe he's feeling remorse and guilt now," she continued to end the uncomfortable silence, "but that's all beside the point. The point is, there's no body."
"He's taken her somewhere, obviously."
"He didn't dismember her. Don't need no coroner telling me that. It looks like a lot of blood but far from an abattoir."
"I second that. He carried her away."
"How?"

For over half an hour, they examined the staircase, the backyard, every possible route out of the building. The most conceivable explanation was that the suspect hastily cleaned the body, put clothes on her and carried her downstairs. There were yet no traces of blood or any other physical evidence to be found. And they concluded the suspect must've had a car parked somewhere nearby. Otherwise, there was no way taking a body through the streets of town and going unnoticed.

"You really think he told unsuspecting witnesses she was drunk and he was taking her home?" Joe asked when they were on their way back upstairs.

"I think he got lucky and didn't run into anyone. But I also think he'd be doing alright saying that if the body was prepared well enough."

"Plenty of people look like carcasses after passing out on parties."

"Exactly."

"One more thing," Joe said while they were entering the apartment: "Why would you think our suspect is male?"

It took Joe about five seconds of consideration to discard Inspector Lundin's work. Much to the new gun's dismay. They were about getting into a fight when Francis broke it off and did some of his sweet talking. It relieved the heat, if only momentarily.

Their only witness was way in over her head. Questioning her again seemed like pushing it. But Joe felt it necessary. She wanted to cut it short. A farmer's daughter. Good grades had gotten her a scholarship and paid the price of the ticket to formal education. Yet the grades had been bought by constant studying. Somehow, she was a defiance to the system, striking Joe as a halfwit. A cheat to society. Someone who could perform in education but ultimately good for nothing. Other than eating up tax money. A farmer's daughter, nothing more, Joe thought wondering where her disdain was coming from.

"Let's cut this short, Hailey," she said for starters. "We all want to go home. Tell me what you know."

"Can I have a cigarette?"

"I don't carry any," Joe lied.

"Help yourself," Francis said and offered his pack. Turkish tobacco, no filter. After he lit the cigarette for her, it bludgeoned her over the head like a sledgehammer.

"Thank you."

"Back to business," Joe said.

Staring at the floor, she exhaled some fine, odorous smoke. And then she willingly repeated her statement. How Agnieszka was from Kraków, intelligent but shy, a pretty girl always smiling even though she had no money. Two jobs on the side, one regularly at a call center, the other occasionally at a night club.

"What night club?" Joe asked.

"I don't really remember. Didn't ring a bell when she said it. Something like Nite Owl or anything along those lines. Or Red Tiger, maybe."

"Go ahead."

An abundance of insignificant facts wouldn't bear much information, so Joe asked blatantly if Agnieszka was seeing any boys.

"Angie? No. Not that I know of. I mean, boys seemed to notice her. At least the intelligent ones."

"She doesn't look posh or anything?"

"No. She could never afford to. Not even the fashion jewelry."

"The brass and nickel crap that stings on your skin."

"It's not her style anyway."

"But she's pretty. Not an ounce of fat where it don't belong?"

"Yes."

As she took as last drag from the cigarette, small beads of sweat in her temples, Joe could tell she was on the verge of crying. Keeping her occupied was the best way of avoiding that, at least for now.

"She never brought any boys back to the apartment?"

"No."

"What did she do at the night club?"

"Waiting tables, working the bar. I don' know, really."

"Have you ever been there?"

Pause. It was the end of the rope. Joe realized there was no point in pushing further. It was characteristic of her. To overstay her welcome.

"If you remember anything of help," Francis jumped in, "you can call us any time. We really appreciate your cooperation."

He handed her a business card with contact information. It was crumpled and looking terrible, as if it had been printed some twenty years back. Hailey took it, now close to tears again.

"Is she dead?"

Neither of the two said anything on the way back downstairs. Their steps were dampened by the thick, stained carpet that must've been there for fifty years. Only when Francis stopped on the sidewalk, the uncanniness turned manageable.

"Poor girl," Francis said.

"Poor country girl in the big city."

"Edinburgh's not a big city."

"If you're from the Highlands or the Hebrides or Shetland, it might as well be New York City."

"You put the screws on her for no reason."

"I know. I pushed too hard."

"She'll manage."

"It's not giving her any choices."

"There's a place called The Hooting Owl in New Town. But I don't know any place that's called The Red Cat or anything."

"Red Tiger."

"You know the place?"

"No. But I bet you a thousand quid it's not listed in the tour guides."

"One of those private clubs?"

"It figures."

"You think our suspect is not your regular college bloke going rampage?"

"Right now, I don't think anything."

"Typical Joe. Hungry?"

"I could use something."

Whenever Joe said she could use something, she was referring to fast food, usually burgers. Her eating habits were peculiar. They fit the bill.

"What about falafel or kebab for a change? We got plenty to digest already tonight."

"You take the wheel."

The apartment block grew smaller in the rearview mirror. Much less suspicious with every turn of the wheels. But it didn't do anything to take the stress off of Joe's thinking. She handled a fresh case like anything else in her life. It needed to get settled. And that right away.

5

The night was cold, like running ice cubes over your skin, and when he exhaled, it looked like his lungs were a steam engine. Something thoroughly mechanical. Not human. Natalie had fallen sound asleep, like she always did when Duke played his A-game. That hadn't been an exception.

The city was silent, right to his feet, the Meadows more like a Victorian wonderland than its actual self. In summer, it would've been different. Far from peaceful. Farther from silent, even at midnight.

Something disturbed Duke. It interrupted his sleep as much as his inner peace. The warmth of the bed made him uneasy. The silk sheets scratched his skin. There was nothing there for him. Leaving was an option but he hesitated.

For a lack of anything else to do, he checked his phone. Too many messages. He could fork through them now but they wouldn't just turn to dust anyway. No, he could do that in the afternoon, once he'd spent some time with himself. All he could do for the time being was staring at the night in the cold.

"Duke," he heard a soft voice that seemed unfamiliar. "What're you doing out here? It's cold. And you're cold to the touch too. Why didn't you get slippers?"

"I'm good, Natalie."

"Why wouldn't you sleep then?"

"To much energy, I assume. What about you?"

"I was exhausted but my head started racing again. You want a cigarette?"

"No, thank you."

"There's no need for acting the disciplined athlete when we're alone. I know a front from a real face."

When she put her cheek to his shoulder, she jerked right back.

"What's wrong?"

"Your skin's as cold as if you've been left in the ice box for too long."

"Let me have that cigarette. It's going to heat me up."

The tobacco did what it always did to Duke. It made him sweat, his muscles turning to steel cords. He was getting a headache, too.

"You're much warmer already. Your shoulder feels nice to my cheek."

"What bothered you so much earlier? And why did the cops give you the shivers?"

"I don't want to talk about it."

"I think you do. It's why you can't sleep."

"Maybe you're right. But I feel like a fool for letting gossip rob my sleep."

"It didn't look like the cops were breaking up a house party. Looked like a crime happened. The worst kind of crime."

Natalie said nothing.

"You heard about it on campus," Duke continued. "Sounded like hogwash. At first. But the more you think about it, the more it figures."

"A distasteful joke, nothing more."

"Police lining the block for a joke?"

"Been fooled as well."

Her hand started trembling, creating the strangest of smoke patterns.

"Did you know her?"

Natalie took another quick drag.

"Maybe."

"You knew her."

"She was kind of adorable in her naivety, okay?"

"What did you hear?"

"Her roommate came back to the apartment and her tiny broom closet of a room looked like an abattoir. That's what I heard."

"Where's the punchline? You're not laughing."

"It's not funny."

"You're right. It certainly isn't."

"At the same time, it's so typical. Naïve girl from Poland, barely keeping her head over the water. It's only a matter of time until someone's going to pick on her."

"Bad world. Mad world."

"It is what it is."

"Eat or die. Know who said that?"

"Shakespeare?"

"Where did you get to know her? Campus? Classes? Nightclub?"

Natalie flicked the cigarette butt over the balustrade, smiling hawkishly.

"I never knew you were a police inspector. Check the dresser when you see yourself out."

With that she left him stranded on the balcony, burning cigarette pinched between two fingers that would smell bad for days. Duke never wanted the cigarette but finished it anyway.

Walking felt like a good distraction for whatever reason, clothes still cold on his skin, cigarette taste in his mouth somewhat spoiling it all. The park lay in utter darkness. Only a few people were walking around, a couple making out by a tree. Up front were the silhouettes of 24 lions, with one even prettier silhouette mingled between them.

"I thought you weren't coming," Emily said when she saw him, hearing the clicking of his wingtips on asphalt.

"Been held up. My apologies. God, you must be cold."

"I'm alright."

"It's a cold night and you're not wearing gloves."

"Should've brought a heavier jacket."

"Here, take my gloves. But let me warm your hands first."

As he gently rubbed her cold, delicate hands, Emily looked at his features, illuminated by the moon's grayish light.

"You looked good in daylight, Duke."

"What about the moonlight?"
"I'll keep that my secret."
"I'm sorry for being late."
"I accepted your apology the first time."
"You shouldn't have waited on me in the cold. It's unacceptable."
"Hadn't I waited on you, you'd have slipped out of my life as quickly and swiftly as you'd slipped in. I wanted to see you again."
"Here, put on the gloves. They'll warm you."

Duke handed them to her. Black moleskin. Stylish and elegant. Even though taking proper care of moleskin was a pain, they were in pristine condition. Emily looked at them.

"They're nice."
"They'll run large but you should be okay. My hands aren't that big either."
"Your hands are very masculine."
"I've only heard that on rare occasions."

When she slipped the gloves over her hands, they almost looked like a parody, making her laugh.

"It's funny. I don't eat meat but putting a dead animal's skin over my hands to warm them wouldn't stir any emotion in me whatsoever."
"Are you hungry?"
"Skipped dinner because I put in some more extra time at the café and then I wasn't sure I could make it here on time."
"I definitely owe you dinner," Duke said making sure not to apologize again.
"You don't owe me nothing."
"Would you have a very late dinner with me?"
"I'd be my pleasure."
"My car's parked around the corner. We need to get you out of the cold and that rather soon."

It was natural when she reached for his arm as they started walking, clinging on to Duke, then gently putting her head to his shoulder. He wouldn't mind, yet asked what she thought of the 24 lions and the Range Rover and what they did against climate change and facing imminent extinction. The moment she saw the Lotus, Emily jumped with joy and excitement. She had no idea what it was, what it had taken to develop and build it. She also wondered if cars running on internal combustion engines were still appropriate. But something about the car spoke directly to her senses, not her sensibility. As the engine roared to life, she was having goosebumps. The hair on her neck was standing up for the entire ride.

The burger shacks in the center of town were buzzing with all kinds of people, both good and bad but mostly a nuisance, so they drove farther out to the outskirts of town. Apart from a mid-aged man eating his burger menu in solitude and three teenagers that should've been home for a while sitting around a single cup of cola, they were to themselves. Emily did the majority of the talking, how she was studying German literature with no clear career path in mind. Writing for money. Or doing something else if need be. Duke told her it was tough getting into journalism, and even tougher finding appropriate compensation. But also to follow your heart, not your pay check.

"You seem like an experienced person," Emily said and smiled, trying to conceal it.

"What makes you laugh?"

"Oh, I don't know."

"It's cruel asking that, I'm sorry."

"Why is it cruel?"

"It's part of a game I play by default and can't help it."

"Got me hooked," she said and leaned closer across the small table.

"I learned how to analyze. Everything and everyone. All the time. Can't unlearn it. It's within me."

"Where did you learn?"

"Studying literature."

"Literature?"

"In its broader sense. Film. TV shows. Novels. Non-fiction. Graffiti. Anything, really."

"What's your specialty?"

"American Literature. The Modernists."

"Like Fitzgerald."

"Hemingway, rather."

"You analyzed me."

"Not really you. What I think is you."

"Okay, that's a nice puzzle right there."

"You've been hurt, not long ago. But you're trying not to show. It's there anyway. Not far behind the front."

"Front," she repeated rather than asking for clarification.

"I didn't mean to bug you. I shouldn't have started acting like Freud in the first place, I'm sorry."

"You shouldn't say you're sorry all the time. It's just that, hearing it from someone who shouldn't know or surmise is startling."

"You mean, it's startling realizing that someone cares enough to pay attention."

"Right."

"He cheated on you."

"Yes."

"How did he vindicate it?"

"That he'd been crushing on her since thirteen and never made it happen and when they stumbled upon each other at a party and she got a bit tipsy and said she'd never noticed how cute he was, it wasn't really giving him any choices."

"Did he say that?"

"Maybe I'm paraphrasing."

"There's only one aspect that speaks for him."

"Is there?"

"He didn't lie to you."

"Are all men that vicious?"

"I speak for myself. It's not necessarily viciousness. All men are susceptive to that line of reasoning."

"Meaning that all men have equal thoughts in a comparable scenario."

"Yes."

"Oh, dear."

"There's a flip side to it."

"And I was expecting you to acquit all men of their sins tonight."

That had Duke smiling.

"Consider this. If you were having these images in your head, virtually all the time, and you're good-looking or attractive for whatever reason, it takes discipline not falling for it."

"Women find other men attractive, too."

"It's also women, making up half of the equation. There's no cheating without opportunity."

"Which implies it's the women's fault."

"Hear me out."

"Okay."

She was more than curious by that point.

"You can be attractive and faithful but eventually, you're going to fall. A single opportunity. Like meeting your teenage crush and wondering what she would look like without clothes on, that stinging in your groin. And her, playing along."

"It's all it takes."

"To seduce a boy. But a real man won't follow the same route, no matter how hard the stinging."

"Or how much she's presenting herself to him."

"Don't judge his yearning, because we all feel it. Judge his being a boy about it."

Emily dipped a fry in yellow, gooey sauce, unaware of what to say next.

"It won't relieve the pain," Duke added. "I know."

"It certainly won't. It's not that I feel like contradicting you. I mean, I follow your reasoning."

"But it's so dissatisfying, isn't it?"

Starch and gooey sauce didn't feel right in her mouth. For the night, her hunger was satisfied.

"It's late."

"Got courses in the morning?"

"At ten. Not crazy early."

"Want me to drive you home?"

Thinking of home, Emily felt a bleakness, a staleness in her mouth.

"Home is a dorm room with nobody waiting anymore," she spoke her mind clearly.

"You can come to my place. It's a fifteen-minute drive."

Back in the car, they wouldn't speak. The roads were clear. Only a fox crossed between the shrubs and residential homes, looking at them with glistering eyes and that foxish smile. Emily rolled down the window, letting in some of the cold night air, tilting her head out some. Duke could see her in the rearview mirror, the beautiful lines of her face, honey-blonde hair like ocean waves, playing in the wind. He was to tell her to be careful and not catch a cold but made up his mind.

The house was on the outskirts, somewhat detached from everything. The real estate agent had called it a craftsman's dream. Fortunate factory worker's reality would've been much closer to the truth. But it fit the bill for Duke, who appreciated the spacious garage and the single-floor layout. All the lights in the quarter had been extinguished already.

"That's a nice little house," Emily said waking from her semi-sleep.

"You're the first to say that."

"What did the other ones say?"

"Meh. Come on, let's put you to bed."

There was nothing to be ashamed of, even though Duke hadn't expected anyone. It wasn't a typical men's house. Everything was tidy and clean. The few pieces of furniture were mid-century modern off flea markets and antique shops. Not the best quality but also not the worst and in fair shape. No dirty dishes in the sink, attracting flies even in winter. None of this occurred to Emily.

Duke showed her the small bathroom, unwrapped a new toothbrush, handed her a towel, then fixed the bed while she washed herself.

"Hope you appreciate a sturdy mattress," Duke said, then turned around to see her emerge from the bathroom with only a borrowed t-shirt and her underpants on.

"I could sleep on a rock and cuddle with a snake tonight."

"There's a glass of water on the night stand."

"Thank you," she said, yawned and snuck into bed.

At the sink, Duke looked at himself in the small and somewhat faded bathroom mirror. Whatever dissatisfaction had bothered him from the inside out emerge to full effect. It was too hard to look. The only thing he felt fit was staring right through the reflection of himself and turn off the lights.

Thinking that she was sound asleep already, Duke flicked the switch and lay down on the old Chesterfield sofa, leather creaking and cold to the touch.

"What're you doing over there," a soft voice asked through the darkness.

"Sleep by myself."

"A sofa's not for sleeping."

"I'm good."

"Your bed is big enough. And I'm cold."

Maneuvering through the dark, he almost bumped into the coffee table. The edge of the bed was still unoccupied, the very spot where Duke preferred to sleep. Little warmth rose when he lifted the blanket and tucked himself in, his back to the far side of the bed. Within the instant, Emily slid up on him, pressing right to the small of his back, wrapping an arm around his waist. Duke lay still, waiting for sleep to come.

It wasn't the scent of freshly-brewed breakfast tea that woke Emily around seven in the morning. It was the lack of warmth she felt to her body. When she opened her eyes, it took her a moment to realize where she was. It was what dreamless sleep did to her. A brief moment of desolation. Until she remembered. Remembered it all.

"Duke?" she asked into the room. "Duke? Where are you?"

The house had seemed inviting with its stylish furniture and tasteful trimmings hours before but the early morning desolation gave it a certain uncanniness. It looked like a movie stage to Emily. Deserted. Lifeless. False. It gave her the bad kind of goosebumps.

The borrowed t-shirt had a car print on it, some make and model she'd never seen before. It made her feel vulnerable. Foolish, she reminded herself. Waking from dreamless sleep had always rivaled nightmares to her. Taking a deep breath, she adjusted herself to the situation. In the kitchen, she checked the teapot, decided it was good, and poured herself a cup. Even without milk, and she liked tea with a cloud of milk in it, it was delicious. Then she warmed her hands against the cup, feeling the relief of a fine print on the porcelain. A kangaroo, made up of flowers.

"Beautiful," she said to herself.

Back against the kitchen top, alternating between takings sips of breakfast tea and admiring the artful print on the cup, the morning gradually started losing its terror. Eyes closed, she suddenly picked up a strange sound she couldn't place. It came from the vicinity of the front door, where she noticed a small, hidden door built into the wood paneling. It led to the garage.

Duke was using a Japanese pull saw, not noticing that Emily had stepped into the garage. It was much more spacious than it had looked from the outside. The front was a shop floor, one side for car repairs and mechanical work. The other side was for woodworking. The back of the garage was dedicated to a home gym. Nothing flamboyant. A bench, lat-pull tower and Olympic weights for deadlifting.

"That's nice," Emily said when she rounded the workbench, taking a look at the work piece clamped in a wood vise.

"Did I wake you up?"

"No, you didn't."

"The neighbors never complain when I'm using power tools, not even this early or late in the day. But I had to hand-saw this piece anyway and thought I'd try not disturbing you."

"You didn't disturb me."

"How do you like the tea?"

"Delicious."

"I can get you some."

"No, thank you. I'd rather have it when I'm visiting."

"Any time."

"What is this?"

"It's a cherry wood picture frame. Used a contour routing bit here, cut a recess on the table saw, ripped to width and did some hand sanding."

"Why wouldn't you cut the angles on the table saw as well?"

"It's not as accurate as I'd like it to be that way."

"I've never seen a saw like this before."

"It's Japanese. They call it Ryoba. It's got a cross-cutting and a ripping blade."

"And it won't bother you that your gym is always covered in dust?"

"Not really. I got proper dust extraction and I vacuum the garage regularly."

It turned out Duke had built some of the pieces of furniture around the house by himself. And he'd also built some for friends and even some commission pieces. Working on wood and cars and bicycles was his way of relaxing. He rarely ever went on vacation, not disliking but also not embracing the experience either.

"You're a lot more complex than I thought," Emily confided him in her thoughts. "I like that."

"What about you?"

"I'm not complex," she said sipping her tea and gazing around the garage, sometimes pulling out a power tool, revving it up, or tracing polished wood with her fingertips. "I'm complicated. That's the bad sibling of complex."

"If you care about making class on time, we should go."

"It's not that I desperately want to make classes today. I rather should be making class. Studying starts feeling like a grind."

"The feeling will pass. If it won't, at least if you hang in there and graduate, you got the means to do something else afterwards."

"How come you always say these things and I like them?" she asked and threw her arms around his shoulders, head resting against his neck. Duke never moved a muscle.

"It's my finest quality. Deceiving people."

"You're not deceiving me."

Traffic was thick that morning but the car made it manageable. This time, there was no silence between them. It wasn't a soliloquy, either. By the time Duke pulled the car into a parking spot at university campus, it seemed like they knew each other for years, not hours.

"Here we are," Duke said.

"I'd rather spend the day with you. Drive out to the ocean."

"Or go bird watching at Holyrood Park."

"Right."

"I'm not going to kick you out."

"You don't have to. Are you free tonight?"

"Need to check my schedule, first."

"Okay."

"There's a good chance I'll be free for dinner."

"Dinner sounds great."

"I'll try and make it happen."

"Don't rush anything," she said and got out. Duke rolled down the electric window, she leaned in.

"Tell me about your classes tonight. I'm curious."

"Liar."

"And don't let anyone hit on you and invite you out for dinner."

"I won't."

"Take care, Emily."

"Just one more thing."

"Hm?"

"What're you doing for a living?"

"If I told you, I'd have to liquidate you."

"I knew you was going to say that."

"I'll text you once I know when to meet."

"Goodbye, Mr. Arrowsmith."

With a smile, she sent him on his way, but it was a forced smile. In the rearview mirror, as the window was still rolling back up, Duke could see her gazing after the car. When he turned the corner, she was still standing there, watching.

6

The TV in the kitchen was tuned to some breakfast show, muted and, in her opinion, much too big at 50-something inches wide. The marble kitchen top was twinkling in the early morning light, almost blinding her. The maid had polished it the day before. Rachel was staring down the abyss of a cup of organic fair-trade coffee that cost an arm and a leg and was so acidy and bitter and all at the same time her stomach was revolting, as it always did when she had it.

Pacing the living room, her husband was talking on the phone. Using the wireless in-ear headphones, he looked like he was talking to himself. If it hadn't been for the hand-tailored silken suit he'd bought on their last trip to Venice, right next to Rialto Bridge, and the expensive interior trim work and furniture, you could've mistaken him for a patient at a mental clinic. The haircut also suggested otherwise.

The night before, he'd shown up for dinner almost two hours late, only to take another phone call during dessert, then giving Rachel and their daughter a kiss before starting off to an emergency meeting at the office. The sound of running water in the shower had woken Rachel when he finally made it home. She hadn't dared checking the time. And when he entered the bedroom, she'd pretended to be asleep. While he'd been sleeping like a rock instantly, Rachel hadn't been able to find enough inner peace to do likewise.

Whatever it was her husband was discussing on the phone was beyond her. Many years back, she'd tried developing an interest in his profession so they had something to talk about. But only once had she tried weighing in on the discussion, with Charles' protégée in attendance, soon finding her opinions negated. It wasn't just the fact they didn't share her sentiment. It was the fact they wouldn't even appreciate her bringing up the argument, and ridiculing anyone not having received the equal of their formal training.

After that unpleasant episode, Rachel had turned to being the good, luxurious housewife she was supposed to be. Her main responsibility, apart from looking fashionable and maintaining good physical shape, was having taste that represented their status. That said, Charles never trusted her enough in that regard to let her roam free and purchase anything without the consent of a conscripted professional.

There were experts for everything. Furniture. Decoration. Wallpaper. Whoever you hired charged generously for seconding your decisions and suggesting the most lackluster pieces of trendy crap to be put up in the living room. In the end, the result looked like a mishmash of cheap Victorian reproductions, Scandinavian modern and white and silver and gold plastic bathroom appliances. Like a post-post-modern princess' bedroom.

Next to being a housewife, Rachel's role was that of a manager. She managed the homely assets on her husband's behalf. Even though her knowledge on arts and style was quite profound, having majored in arts history, a fact Charles had forgotten since the day they'd met at the country club, he a rich kid socializing with the likes of him, her working as waitress trying to keep her head over water, her decisions came down to saying yes or no. A fact that, if she cared for alleviating her status, made her equal to a Roman emperor, judging over the fate of defeated gladiators. Whenever that thought crossed her mind, she laughed almost hawkishly.

With her daughter out of the house, there was even less to do. And her husband's increasing absence had led to the inevitable. Does he suspecting anything, Rachel wondered. Two weeks back she'd stopped by the office after a shopping spree and drinking way too much coffee in bad company for much too long. With the office interior all glass, she'd spotted Charles from some thirty yards away, explaining business to a student about their daughter's age while caressing her buttocks underneath her skirt. It was evidence pointing at the obvious, and when Rachel had looked at her left hand, the rather modest ring he'd put on her finger, she'd waited for tears to come. But they never came.

Lost in thought, it had taken her a moment to realize Charles had stopped talking on the phone.

"Charlie? Charlie? Charles!"

"Did you say something?" he asked staring in his phone.

"What're your plans for lunch?"

And he went to town, telling her about all the things that needed to be addressed, and how he wouldn't make lunch break until probably four in the afternoon, after his workout with his personal trainer, and how he would have to head straight back to the desk once that was done with. The little bit of fun in his day.

"Did you notice how Natalie was behaving herself yesterday?" Rachel asked.

"College is doing her a world of good."

"To me, she seemed kind of upset."

"Just a period of readjustment."

"She's been through that back in school. When she was about fourteen."

"Yes."

"To me it seemed like she'd made some very bad experience. I simply didn't know what to make of it."

"Can you say that again?" he asked after a pause.

"I asked if you could give me some cash."

"Can't you go to the ATM?"

"I'm a bit pressed for time today."

"Of course, you are," he said with his eyes on the display, whipping out his wallet and handing her a nice bundle of cash.

With Charles gone for the office soon after, the house fell into a different silence, one Rachel wasn't quite sure she preferred or despised. For a lack of anything else to do, she called Elisabeth on the phone, chatting for a while about all those things she didn't care for, and never would care for. Elisabeth had no time to go out for coffee. New carpets and matching curtains had to be picked out, the key element to the ongoing restorations at their house.

There was an interesting film showing, and when she was just about to leave, Rachel realized how foolish it was for her to go see a movie alone. Then she tried talking herself into it, that there was nothing to it. Only it was to no avail. In conclusion, she found it foolish. With nothing else on her mind, she took the Jaguar out to Princess Street, rounding the blocks for over half an hour in search for a parking spot. Paying for a parking garage was not on her mind.

All the clothes she liked when window shopping seemed just fine, until the moment she saw her reflection in the glass, surprisingly similar to the mannequins she'd been eyeballing. She sighed, but only a beggar took notice, asking for change. When Rachel apologized for not having any, he insulted her in the thickest Glaswegian accent she'd ever heard.

Turning towards Waverley Station, she checked her phone. No text messages, only a voice mail from another rich housewife she listened to for five seconds before she turned it off. The day had been hard enough on her mental health already and she didn't feel fit to deal with any more.

The walking did her some good, so she crossed the bridge and kept on going all the way to Old Town, headed for the Red Elephant. People were going there because of a famous children's book that had, in part, been written there. Or so they said. It had been years since Rachel had been there. Halfway down the road, she remembered the place had burned out. The idea made her wonder if red elephant meat would char just the same. She shook her head, calling herself a fool again.

The Grassmarket intersection was as busy as always, tourists buying cheap souvenirs. Rachel scanned the shops and cafés and pubs. So many options. Too many options. None of which seemed very appealing. The only thing she felt was appropriate was getting out of the cold, and she walked into one of the less touristy places. A working man's pub. First thing she did was order a Heineken, then check the menu.

"What can I get you to eat?" the young waiter asked when he brought the lager in a tall glass.

"What's the soup of the day?"

"Today that's–"

"Never mind, I'll have one. And Scottish pie to go with it."

"Very well," he said instead of commenting on her peculiar choices. But then, it was peculiar enough already when a lady like her walked in. If they knew how I was brought up and what I did to survive in college, Rachel thought and took a big sip off the beer. It was good but didn't taste Scottish, something she lamented.

The soup turned out to be something very traditional, tasting great but the name being lost on her. The real keeper was the Scottish pie. Dough, essentially of flour, water and lard, filled with ground meat and onions, big serving of baked beans poured over it, fries with gravy as side. A simple, yet very elegant dish. Rachel downed the lager, then ordered another one.

"Can you get me a Scottish beer this time?" she asked the young waiter on his trip to the bar from the back of the pub.

"We got Tennent's on tap."

"Sold."

It had been years, decades really, she found with astonishment, since her last Tennent's Lager. The brew was frowned upon as working class, cheaply-produced industrial beer. But it tasted well just the same, like the very thing Rachel had been looking for. With the pie gone, her appetite and thirst subdued, Rachel had time to think again. Something she'd so pleasantly avoided since walking into the pub and mingling with people so much not considered her kind.

She settled the check, congratulating the waiter and bartender on their splendid work, tipped them generously, then walked out. Skies a bleak gray, tourists everywhere and the sound of a bagpipe rolling in from the castle all the way down the Lawnmarket, starting a slight melancholy, she headed for the Meadows. But when she dialed her daughter's number, she stopped. Walking towards someone you didn't even know had time for you or wanted to see you was foolish.

Self-evidently, Natalie didn't pick up the phone. Within the instant, a text message came back, stating the obvious. She was busy and couldn't talk. Nothing more. Turning on her heels, Rachel wanted to head back to the car but made up her mind. There was someone she could call.

"This is Duke," he said picking up on the first ring.

"_ "

"Hello?"

"Duke, hey. This is Rachel."

"Hi, Rachel. How are you doing?"

"Lovely. Had Scottish pie and two lagers."

"No soup of the day?"

"You bet I had it."

"Wish I were you right now."

"Am I holding you up?"

"No, you don't. You never do. I'm at the gym."

"And I'm not holding you up when you're working out?"

"Had to catch my breath after deadlifting anyway, so this is alright. I'm done for the day."

"I was wondering if you were free this afternoon."

"Let me check this. Hm. Right away would be an option."

"Oh, that's great."

"Where are you?"

"Lawnmarket."

"Want me to come down, pick you up?"

"I'm not sure."

"Don't say you don't want anyone to see you riding in my car," Duke joked. It was exactly what Rachel was afraid of. He knew it. Darn well, he knew it.

"Let's meet at the National Museum," she said for no particular reason. "Walking will help me digest lunch."

"I can make it in about half an hour. Main entrance?"

"Yes."

"Don't wait for me outside, go get yourself a coffee. It's on me."

"See you there."

When she put the phone away, Rachel felt a blast of joy going right through her body.

7

Joe was looking at the screen but it was more like she was staring right through it. As if there was nothing there. Somehow, she was wary of all those digital gizmos, buzzing and ringing all the time. A pen and paper seemed more appealing. Thinking of fighting windmills was a bummer. And it was a stupid idea in the first place. It took her a second to imagine what life would've been like in the Middle Ages. How much harder everything would've been. Or was that true? Maybe there was a certain appeal to the simplicity the digital age lacked. At least it was pretty to imagine that every time you felt like throwing the towel.

None of their leads had produced anything of substance so far. That wasn't all that uncommon. The regularity of the pattern was as discouraging as it had always been. Now, she could've applied everything she'd learned. Through basic training. Through advanced training, eating up her weekends. Through experience. But experience dictated something else. To not care about stipulations, all the rules and regulations. Even less so to adhere to the text books she'd never believed in to begin with.

But breaking habits was tough. Being independent and responsible for one's actions even more so. Get dinner, she thought. Think things over at home. It was time to go home. Turn off the computer. Control the urge to throw the office chair right at it.

"Calling it for today?" Francis asked.

"Had plenty for one day."

"Word in the street is nothing. As if she never existed."

"Maybe that's true."

"What do you mean?"

"If someone never really existed in the realm they're exposing themselves to, for who they are and what the rest of their limited environment thought of them, wouldn't it be easy to destroy them?"

Francis let that sink in. It didn't help. The idea was too alienating.

"Maybe you go talk to a philosopher. Someone who's read Nietzsche and Marx and all those jerks."

"I'll let you know once the concept has straightened out in my mind."

"Call when the starship has returned to Earth."

"I could kiss you, know that?"

"Screw you, Joe."

"Ready for night shift?"

"Screw you, Joe."
"We're too old for the graveyard shift."
"You can say that again."
"Call if you need me."
"Thanks."
She was already on her way out when Francis called after her.
"Joe?"
"Huh?"
"Don't take it to heart. I've said that before. This time, I mean it."

Words were unspoken between them, with no way of expressing them. Not then. Not now. Not ever. Had she ever believed in the shrinks putting words in their mouths when they were compelled to see them, Joe would've hit one of them up just for the hell of shaking the tree.

On her way home, she stopped at a fast food joint, eating the same menu she always had. It was the kind of stability she needed in her life, and she was fully aware of it. The staleness and the tastelessness of two thin slices of gray beef were more than welcome on a night like that.

If you cared to take a look from the outside, you might have wondered what a woman like Joe was doing at a fast food restaurant. At night, the majority of the customers were young and as loud as they were stupid. And you could tell she wasn't really partaking in it. As much as she sometimes felt the nuisance of those people, guys in particular, would need some reining in, she never went forward to the execution.

This time, she noticed something, a guy of about twenty looking at her from across a table on the other side of the restaurant. He seemed to blend in perfectly. It wasn't true. He was eating alone, isolated at a table for four that hadn't been cleaned, chunks of cold burger and fries scattered about. At the ready, he had a paperback the size of a phone book. History book, Joe thought. Those are big enough to bludgeon someone to death even in paperback. Whenever she glanced in his direction, he sought eye contact, then looked away.

It wasn't the first time she'd experienced something just like this, and Joe had never taken any action either. The plan was wolfing down the rest of the burger, which she greatly enjoyed, then leave for home.

"Excuse me," she heard a voice asking gently, and when she looked up, sure enough, it was the young man with the book tucked underneath his arm, paper cup in the other hand.

"Hm?" Joe went.

"Mind if I sit here? Table over there's not exactly tidy."

Pointing at the mess for emphasize, he smiled at her. Twenty, about six-foot tall, one-hundred and ninety pounds. Athletic. Dark blonde hair. Blue eyes. Beautiful face. Something Joe had always felt the majority of men were lacking.

"Please go ahead," she said and smiled when she saw him noticing the gun on her belt.

"Thank you."

"What're you reading?"

"What am I trying to read would be a more appropriate question."

"What're you trying to read?"

"It's called A People and a Nation."
"Title's very ambiguous."
"American history."
"Know that old joke? What's the shortest books in history?"
"No."
"German Tolerance. British Cuisine. American History."
"That's funny."
"You're not laughing."
"Not slap your thigh funny."
"Bad book?"
"Very bad."
"Why?"
"Lots of academic gibberish. I wish they'd get to the point already. I have too many reading assignments for one week."
"I hate when people are messing around."
"Makes us two," he said, smiling and slurping some more of his strawberry milkshake.
"At your age, you may still be nonchalant about having a milkshake."
"What would you think my age is?"
"Twenty."
"Nailed it. What's yours? I know I shouldn't be asking."
"Why wouldn't you?"
"It's a cultural thing."
"Culture is dead. I'm a bit more than twice your age."
"How's culture dead?"
"Take a look around."

When he did, it was interesting to see. Joe wondered what he saw when he glanced around the fast food restaurant. Was it the same mess she saw? Or something entirely different?

"I know you want me to contest your statement, but I'd rather ask you a question."
"You're asking a lot of questions."
"I'm not trying to annoy you."
"You don't. I didn't make myself clear. I think it's beneficial to ask questions and listen, instead of doing the talking when you have no idea what you're talking about. Which is a generalization, nothing directed at you."
"Sounds fair."
"Stop pleasing me, it's not going to get you far."

Waiting for a comment, Joe looked at the young man again. It annoyed her when she found her heart racing after noticing his strong forearms, exposed by rolled-up sleeves.

"What was it that made you so tough?" he asked.
"That's another story. And none of your business. And not the question you were about to ask."
"I wanted to ask you why you came to this place, of all places, if it, for you, so clearly defined the loss of culture. Or lack thereof."

There was nothing to dwell on, yet Joe took her time, finishing the burger, washing it down with a big sip of diet cola she preferred for the taste, not the purported absence of calories. Calories weren't a concept she concerned herself with.

"Go where it hurts. Don't lament anything without doing something against it. I like these places, always have. I won't allow anyone to push me out. Not by force. Not by being a pain in the ass."

"That's noble."

"No, it's not. Why did you come over?"

"Because my table was dirty."

"Scammer."

"Because I didn't want to drink my milkshake in solitude."

"Clumsy poet."

"Because I find you interesting."

"That's better. I'd have taken you for an honest person, had you chosen just one word differently in that sentence."

"Okay."

"Replace interesting with attractive, and we're talking."

It stopped him right there, thinking of something to say but pondering too long. Joe took over.

"Don't sweat it, it's only natural."

"Is it?"

"Young men chase older women."

"Any guess why?"

"It's their butting masculinity. Gives them a feeling of triumph, taking the females from other males. Like young gorillas, going after the throne of the silver back."

"Or young lions, toppling the king."

"I can tell you why it works."

"I always wondered about the female side of it. Apart from the obvious beauty of youth."

"Don't get cocky. It's because our eggs are getting old and dry and we have that deeply-rooted wish to reproduce. Successful pregnancy without defects is more likely at high sperm quality."

Hearing that, he couldn't help but laugh.

"That's funny."

"You're not gonna get any bullshit from me, that's for sure."

"That's for sure. But to a guy like me, it's kinda new hearing a woman talking the truth so blatantly."

"It's because you haven't dealt with women thus far."

"A real shame."

"What's your favorite night club?"

"Excuse me?"

"Your favorite night club. What's it called?"

"It's– " he said and considered some more, playing with the degrading paper straw in his milkshake. "It's the Hooting Owl."

"You're lying to me."

"How come you think that?"

"The Hooting Owl is boring. What about the Red Tiger?"

Another baffled stare. This time, he got the better of himself much quicker.

Trying to impress me, Joe thought.

"What if I know places like that?"

"Places like that?"

"Places called something like that. Just not exactly Red Tiger."

"The night's still young."

"It is. But I'm not into playing somebody else's game."

"Didn't mean no offense. I'm Joe."

Her hand looked so feminine when she stretched it out, hanging in the air like silk laundry for drying. The young man stared at it. Whatever he saw in Joe's hand elevated his feelings, stimulating his vivid imagination.

"I'm Finn."

"Finn? Sounds assumed."

"The blame is all on my parents."

When they shook, she made sure to maintain a firm grip on his hand, which was masculine only in the palm. The fingers were short and showed no signs of physical labor. Something that put Joe off.

"Let's go for a beer and talk, what do you say?" Joe suggested for reasons unknown even to herself.

"Sounds like I'd be a fool for taking a pass on that."

As they walked out together, the young folks wondered what utterly unlikely constellation had just evolved. Something they'd never seen before. It had all the guys staring and yearning in jealousy, for they were much too stupid to appreciate their girls. For a lack of anything else to do with it, they threw fries and bad words at each other, attempting to mimic what normalcy they knew.

Having a conversation with someone so far removed from her own life and experience turned out to challenge Joe. In her mind, it was better to make him do the talking instead of conveying too much personal information on herself. None of the things he said were of any particular interest to her, though. Not having been to college herself, she understood little of what it involved, and even less so would she regret not having made the same experiences. To her, it sounded like a rather boring episode, significant only insofar as being a stepping stone to adult life.

It was much too loud to have a proper conversation at the first pub they stumbled into, so their talking was reduced to the very typical gibberish and trash-talking that could only be uttered with a pint in hand. Finn could drink but was struggling to keep up with Joe.

"Where'd you learn that?" he asked when she finished her third pint, washing down half of it in one sip.

"Been around. I've had my share of the bad times."

"I'd be surprised if you hadn't been around."

"Where would you go if you wanted to have some fun? I mean, some serious fun. Not the kid's type of fun."

"There's several places."

"What's your favorite place?"

Finn downed his beer, buying some time.

"Okay then, let's go," he said and got up, pulling his wallet out. Joe wanted to protest, only to make up her mind. Let him have his way, she thought.

Some people looked at that odd couple, with the guys seemingly having a heightened interest in a guy this young parading the street of New Town by the side of a proper lady.

"Where are we headed to?" Joe asked to say something for a change. The silence between them felt like a parasite, coursing through her veins.

"The place you want to see."

"The Not-Exactly-Red-Tiger."

"Right," he said and they stopped in front of an inconspicuous residential building.

"That's not it, is it?"

"That's my place. I need to change clothes if you want to go to that special place."

"What about me?"

"You look fine. Maybe you just think of something to do with that gun on your belt."

"This here ain't Dodge City, pal," Joe uttered in her best American accent.

The building was a mixed bag, tenants from all over the world, all ages and professions. Students seemed an exception. Finn occupied a small flat under the roof. It was hot in summer and cold now in winter. Worse, he'd choked the radiators. Condensed water was running down the window panes.

"My apologies for the mess," he said walking straight for the kitchen, "I wasn't expecting anyone. You want a glass of water?"

"No, thanks."

The tap was running for some time. Someone needed to extinguish a fire. But Joe was fine. Some nights, the beer really got to her. Other nights, and that night was one of them, it never did anything.

When he returned, she'd taken a seat on the bed, which was the only piece of furniture apart from a worn and torn office chair in front of a tiny Ikea desk.

"Nice apartment," Joe said

"Thanks," he went and started unbuttoning his shirt. "It's not much but at least I got it for myself. Are you comfortable? I always wanted to get a sofa but I never came across anything that I liked."

"I'm good. If you find something more efficient for storing your books than piling them in a corner on the outside wall, where they will certainly get moist and wavy and moldy, maybe there's a chance you'll fit a sofa in here."

"That place we're going to isn't for walking in just like that. At least when you're a man."

The shirt landed on the floor carelessly, exposing a muscular torso with little extra meat on it. When he swung the door to the wardrobe open, he made sure to flex his triceps first, then his forearms, finishing off the pose with the biceps. It wasn't much to show, and hadn't he been lean, he would've been unimpressive altogether. But there sure was something about an athletic body with no fat on it.

"So it's different for the ladies," Joe said and kept him talking.

"Women look better than men, even in bad clothes. It's unfair but what can you do?"

"There's things to be done. It'd be perfectly-suitable to the zeitgeist, don't you think?"

"Oh, yeah," he answered, not really listening.

Now he removed his pants, exposing tight athletic underwear. The type you wear to the gym when your legs are too beefy.

"Skipped leg day?"

"My legs are much stronger than they look. I put one-hundred and fifty kgs on the leg press."

"I'm impressed."

"What's your max?"

"Two-hundred."

"Two-hundred?"

"Maybe a bit more."

"One rep max?"

"Ten reps."

That shushed him, yet it wouldn't change his intent.

"Can I see them?"

"See what?"

"Your legs. You've seen me in underwear. Now I'm naturally curious about those legs squeezing two-hundred kilos."

Joe got up unbuckling her belt, smiling at the stunned expression on Finn's face. The young man was holding his breath when she dropped her pants, exposing firm, muscular but certainly feminine legs. Her slip wouldn't leave much to the imagination.

"Oh, wow."

"Would you think those legs could press more weight than yours?"

"Those beautiful legs? I'd never suspected that."

"What's your bench press pr? One rep."

"It's– "

"How much?"

"It's eighty kgs. Or eighty-five."

"I can tell from that nice, wide chest. But guess what? I can match it."

"Think so?"

"I know for a fact. Wanna see the evidence?"

And without waiting, Joe swiftly unbuttoned her shirt, letting it fall to the floor like a silk scarf in a mild autumn breeze. Finn said nothing. As he crossed the room in few steps, Joe saw the excitement burning in his eyes. When he threw his arms around her, pressing his lips on hers, all civilization was eradicated. It was wild. Animal-like.

There was no containing himself. His hands moved effortlessly, closing firmly where they were supposed to. Joe would've been lying, had she tried telling herself it didn't arouse her.

"You're beautiful," he whispered in her ear, biting and sucking her earlobe. "Gosh, you're beautiful."

Instinctively, he noticed that Joe was holding back, her hands stationary at his shoulder blades. He grabbed her left hand and placed it where he needed it. Excitement was reaching a preliminary climax.

"I want you," he whispered in her other ear. "I want you bad."

Trying to remove her bra, he failed, with Joe taking responsibility. The view astounded him. It was much harder pulling down his underpants, but Joe's just slid to the floor with no resistance. Like ice gliding down her soft, smooth skin.

"You've ever been with an older woman?" she asked when they sat on the bed, seeing the sweat on his forehead, around his nipples, the rosy flesh in the groin.

"I–" he began when they both picked up the ringing of Joe's mobile phone.

"Hang on a second," she said and fished the phone from the pocket of her pants on the floor. As much as Finn wanted to protest, he said nothing. Not that he would've had anything appropriate to say.

The message was from Francis. It was short, too: Pig's blood, and another one.

"I gotta be going," Joe said and dressed herself even quicker and swifter than she'd undressed.

"No, you don't," Finn tried to appease her. But his attempts were vain.

"This has gone far enough."

"Not really, no."

"For me, certainly."

"What am I going to do about it? It's not fair."

"Don't give me that, college boy. You've had a much bigger share of the pie than you ever should have. Tell your friends whatever you like, it doesn't matter to me."

"I don't get this."

"Me neither," Joe said, readjusting her badge to the belt and straightening her hair.

"Why won't you stay? It won't take long."

"I'm sure it wouldn't."

"So?"

"So, I'm not staying because I'm a bloody fool. And you don't know jack about any tigers, yellow, orange or red."

With that, she left him to his own device, much in disbelief about what had happened, wondering forever what he could've said to close the deal instead of fumbling the ball just shy of the end zone.

8

Duke found her wandering up and down the main entrance hall without direction, coursing in straight lines and small turns. Much against the constant stream of visitors. School classes being too loud when they saw the gigantic whale bones. Lovers holding hands, kissing under the enormous glass and wrought iron roof. Old people you could tell were lonely. Maybe because their loved ones had passed. Maybe because they were still around. At first, he remained hidden from her view behind a pillar, curious how Rachel blended into this very average mix of average people. Not at all, he concluded.

"There you are, darling," he said when he approached her, giving himself away with nonchalance.

"Mr. Arrowsmith," she said and a thin smile appeared around her beautiful lips. Even when she was in a bad mood, it didn't reduce her beauty. Seeing it, Duke wondered if reducing her to tears would do the trick. A very sinister thought he had no way of telling where it was coming from.

"Did you get coffee for yourself?"

"No."

"Would you care for a cup?"

"Not right now. Look at you, Duke. You're so handsome today."

"It's what hard workouts do to me."

"Make you prettier?"

"Have you had trouble sleeping? I'm not saying you don't look gorgeous, because you certainly do."

"Do I look tired and lost in this world?"

"Tired, darling. Let's not get dramatic, it doesn't suit you."

"Where did you leave your car?"

"At the parking garage. They're charging an arm and a leg but it's convenient."

"That's true."

"Where did you leave yours?"

They started their tour, skipping Scotland's early history on display in the basement because they agreed it was more than a bore. Rachel told him about her day thus far. Self-evidently, she merely presented the version of actual events she found fit for sharing. Duke was the type of gentleman who could easily read between the lines. But there was no need for him weighing in on anything, other than short remarks confirming Rachel's unpleasant feelings as utterly conceivable.

"God," Rachel said when they were already on the second floor, "how time flies."

"A good conversation can do that. Easily."

"From the balconies, this building is even more beautiful."

"The view from street level would never do it justice."

"Certainly not."

"Are you open for a suggestion?"

"Any time."

"Let's go for coffee over there on the other side, look at business from our elevated view, then skip some chapters of history and wrap it up at the vantage point on the rooftop."

"I must say I was secretly hoping you'd suggest this. My feet are a bit sore from walking all forenoon and after."

Looking at the main hall from the café, with the glass roof towering over everything, felt like being at the mall on a shopping spree, not a museum. The Scottish National Museum was a treasure, for it oozed with personality and ingenuity, rather than waving the heavy stick of education to intimidate people. Down there was a kid, dragging her grandfather along by the hand, the old man somewhat crouched and trying to keep up pace with the little girl of four or five. With uncurtailed enthusiasm, she pulled her grandfather from one exhibit to the next, stunned at the details, the exotic pleasures experienced from her vantage point, asking questions at the cadence of an automatic gun.

"What was it like," Rachel wondered, "being that young and excitable about everything?"

She warmed her hands to the oversized cup of coffee. Duke had finished his cup already, never having been one to indulge too pleasantly in the easy temptations of life.

"I don't remember being young, really. But I know what it's like being excitable."

"It's not the same anymore."

"It all depends. You should see me standing in front of a car I like."

"Like your car."

"Exactly."

"Not anything like my car."

"No."

"You could've pleased a simpler mind here but I'm not fishing for compliments."

"What excites you?"

"Good food."

"You're taking the easy way out."

"Hammers. Sometimes, I go to the hardware store and pick them out from the shelf, one after the other, weighing them in my hand, the wooden handles, how the mass is distributed all across the length. I feel the girth, knowing that hammers were never meant for hands like mine. It gives me unprecedented pleasures."

"Hands like yours," Duke repeated, putting his hands in hers after she set the cup back on the saucer, now empty and cold.

"Let's get out of here," Rachel said, eyes closed, feeling the warmth of Duke's hands. Much stronger than from cheap china that had been warmed by stale coffee.

"Where would we go?"

"Burma."

"What's in Burma?"

"The Burmese."

"And what do we have in common with them?"

"That's a question to ponder upon. Or better answered by going and seeing for ourselves."

"Why not start with the rooftop? For today, at least?"

"It's as far as my legs will carry me."

For convenience, they took the elevator, with Duke remembering on the way that they might find themselves out of luck, if the rooftop was closed due to bad weather. Rachel found the weather to be not particularly bad and they simply climbed the stairs through an unlocked door to have one of the best views over Edinburgh.

"Always a nice feeling," Duke said instinctively shielding Rachel against the wind.

"Your arms around me is the best feeling I know."

"You're flattering me."

"There's something about you, Mr. Arrowsmith. But it's impossible to pin it down. At some time, they'll write books about you in places like that."

Rachel pointed at university down at The Meadows with her delicate index finger.

"What would a book like that be titled?"

Duke had a rather fitting suggestion in mind.

"They'd reference someone in the past, long gone, since that is all we're still capable of. Copying the past using electronic gizmos to make up for our personal shortcomings."

"I always admired your honesty."

She turned towards him, unable to help a smile when their eyes met, drowning. Again. And they kissed, with the wind pulling at their clothes, at Rachel's long, silky hair. It started as a soft, passionate kiss, then evolved quickly. Since they were alone up there, no social restraints demanded their hands being kept to themselves.

"I want you," Rachel said.

"I know."

"What would it take?"

"Think of your family."

"They don't need me."

"Don't be silly. They don't understand they need you. Or how to appreciate you."

"You do."

She led his hand to her cheek. The moment his palm touched her skin, Rachel closed her eyes, she exhaled, at ease. It was a powerful scene. Not that they hadn't had comparable occurrences between them before. The magnitude had shifted.

"Let's get you out of the cold," Duke said and instantly countered her disappointment: "There's a place nearby where I can warm you."

"Wonderful."

On the way back to the elevator, they passed a painting of steelworkers in Glasgow, casting smelted steel. Not that long ago, Scotland had been a beacon of the industrial world. But everything is prone to failure eventually, whether failure may strike sooner or later.

"You like that painting?" Rachel asked when she noticed him glancing at it.

"No."

"Why not?"

"It reminds me of the past."

While they were making out on the elevator, Duke wondered if they had surveillance cameras and waved at the ceiling just to be sure. Excitement was building like a tidal wave on their way to the parking garage, and once they arrived at red Lotus, sitting in a dark corner like a long-forgotten exhibit at the archives, it was hard to still contain it.

"Hurry up," Rachel said all she could manage, unbuckling while Duke unlocked the passenger's side door. The seat almost collapsed when he pulled the lever, making Rachel wonder for the briefest of moment if he'd modified it.

"Top or Bottom?" Duke asked.

"Bottom," she said stepping out of her pants and reclining on the seat.

The door clicked shut. It was dim inside the car. Hard to see more than the flicker in somebody's eyes. It didn't matter when Rachel felt his weight on her, his flexed biceps against her forearm. The smell of his cologne. The same her husband used, yet much more intense. Much more masculine. Rachel inhaled, holding her breath. They barely talked, if ever, their movements a choreography played out on a miniature stage. Duke had his pants down to his ankles, and Rachel moved her way down his six-pack – then she paused.

"What's that?" he asked.

Rachel said nothing, fearing someone was outside the car. Some bored warden, playing detective, seeking fifteen seconds of fame. With her heart pounding in her ears , it took her a second picking it up.

"It's my phone."

"Where is it?"

"Pocket of my pants."

The ringing wouldn't cease as Duke looked around. Suddenly, it dawned on both of them. The annoying ringtone got louder when Duke pushed the car's door open and fished Rachel's pants from the concrete floor.

"There you go," he said as he handed them to her. They were crumply and crinkly, making it harder getting the phone out. The ringing persisted relentlessly.

By the time Rachel got the phone out and answered the call, Duke had straightened his pants and shirt, buckled his belt, slipped into the driver's seat. Carefully, he pulled the door closed as not to give away his presence. It took him but one glance at Rachel, seeing the expression on her face, to know something had gone terribly wrong.

"I'll be there right away," she said surprisingly calm. "Just stay where you are, okay? No. No, don't do anything until I'm there. Yes. Fifteen minutes or so, okay? Just calm down and stay at the apartment, alright?"

The clicking when the line broke was much too loud for comfort against the silence inside their dark exile.

"Bad news?"

"Can you take me down to University campus?"

"University campus? "

"My daughter. I'm not going into detail."

"What's the– "

"I can't tell you, okay? Just take me down there. Please."

The engine roared to life, the headlights popping up, their glare reflected by the concrete walls, illuminating the scene while they climbed up the spiraling ramp, and Rachel slipped back into her beige pants. One leg down, she stopped.

"Duke, are you okay? You're sweating."

"I'm fine, Rachel. It's nothing. Sometimes, after a heavy workout, I get those bouts of sweating even after hours. I'll have you down there in no time, I promise."

Hands folded in her lap, back straight since they had both forgotten getting the seat upright again, Rachel just sat through the short ride, not saying a word. Whatever images were running through her head like a bad pulp movie were left all to herself, the worries numbing, deafening, defeating. When they were almost there, Duke wiped the sweat off his forehead, thinking of something to say. Nothing was what he came up with.

The sentence he began was cut off when campus grounds appeared right in front of them.

"She didn't wait inside, bloody hell. Stupid kid. I was hoping she wouldn't see us."

"Want me to pull over before she spots the car?"

"Screw this," Rachel said checking her features in the small mirror under the sunshade. "I'll tell her you're a childhood friend."

To this, Duke had nothing to answer. All he could do was steer the red Lotus towards the sidewalk, where Natalie was standing in waiting, shortest of skirts, no leggings and a heavy fur coat drawn over her shoulders. Simultaneously, they spotted the black eye she was trying to hide under her big sunglasses much better suited to the French Riviera. They couldn't have done anything to conceal her fat, swollen and split lips.

"Someone did her well," Duke said when he noticed Rachel's desperation.

"I'll kill the bastard. Whatever man did this to her will pay."

"What makes you sure it was a man?" Duke asked automatically, cursing internally. But she didn't hear. The tires squealed when he brought the car to a stop. Trying to hide, he knew, would've been to no avail. Both the car and the features of his face were tell-tale signs.

"Thanks for taking me, Duke," Rachel said popping the door open to get out. When she wanted to kiss him on the cheek, she made up her mind and left the car.

"Call if you need anything," Duke said.

She nodded, then threw the door shut much too hard. Rolling off, easy on the throttle, he could see them in the rearview mirror. Mother and daughter, embracing first, soon doing the inevitable talking. Duke knew he was at the center of their conversation.

"Damn," he said to himself, riding off.

9

Listening to a Texan rambling on about the magnificence of Faulkner's writing, and how he represented to the South what Hemingway, maybe Fitzgerald, had promised to the North but failed to deliver within their selfish European escapism, didn't do much in changing Emily's mind. Whatever Professor Briggs, or Neal, rather, saw in Faulkner's style and prose and character development was lost on her. Had Neal singled her out and challenged her disdain, she would've found subtle and affirmative and appreciative words to make herself clear. The blatant truth was, there was no sparks flying when she read Faulkner, so she couldn't be bothered. Truth was something she increasingly found exclusively in simplicity.

The simplicity of the matter at hand allowed her mind to wander. Even though the truth in her essay would have to differ from her personal truth, Emily knew how to find the right words. And pass. Hence her mind was free to wander, back to the day before, the night, the early morning. To the land of imagination, picturing that night's dinner with a man called Duke Arrowsmith.

As much as the thought had crossed her mind, she knew it was foolish to even suspect the name was assumed. What would a man of his qualities have to assume? And yet, she couldn't imagine even in the faintest what Duke was doing for a living. There was little room for people that were cultivated, honored integrity and, not to forget, looked good. Without feeling smug about it, she concluded that she knew for herself.

If studying, working too much at a café and crying over rejection slips coming back from newspapers, publishers and – God forbid – second-rate websites, was all the world had to offer to her, and Emily was struggling hard trying to figure out what choices she had, made it even harder imagining how Duke had gotten where he was.

"...don't you think?" Emily picked up from something someone had said to her left in a thick Hebridean accent she knew from one of her grandmother's best friends.

"Can you say that again?" she whispered while she turned, spotting a handsome but obviously cocky guy sitting one row behind her to the left.

"Did my accent get in the way again?" he asked with a smile on his face, making sure she saw his forearms flexing and bulging as he leaned forward and closer. "I said, I wish he'd stop waffling on about Pylon already and move to As I lay Dying, don't you think?"

"I know your accent, it's Hebridean and you're overemphasizing it."

"How would you know?"

"That's not the question you were asking."

"Okay, what about that?"

You could tell from the look on his face he was desperately longing to impress Emily. Which made her wonder if her first hit on the counter attack had been too soft.

"Pylon is a work of hope, whereas As I Lay Dying is hard to read. On many levels. Which sounds contradictory, given the fact it's got a chapter only one short paragraph long. Something I consider a cheap party trick, but anyway. If anything, we should ponder on hope much more than desperation."

"Well said. Pylon is still garbage."

With that, he got up to leave, another of his show effects. But Professor Briggs dismissed the class that moment, compelling them to read up on Sherwood Anderson, who never wrote anything that wasn't true, and dwell on the idea why that inspired so many contemporaries that rose to much bigger fame.

"Consider the irony in that," Briggs told them, leaning casually on the dais, "and the disparity between a student's fame and a teacher's despair. Who's more valuable when the chips are down?"

Sporting a leather briefcase instead of a plastic backpack, the Hebridean wasn't hard to spot in the crowd. It wasn't new to Emily being hit on in class, not since she'd turned fourteen first, then heads all of a sudden. But something about him sparked her curiosity.

"You're running a big mouth, hot shot," she said when she'd caught up with him.

"I can back it."

"Taming that accent now that I figured your trick out?"

"My trick's certainly not being exotic."

"If anyone would ever consider the Hebrides exotic in this day and age."

"Where're you from?"

"None of your business."

"Is that your catch phrase?"

Emily considered this.

"Maybe. I'm not overusing it, though. And it's not original anyway."

"Why say it, then?"

"Because I'm pretty and nobody really cares what I'm saying and why or would ever contradict me as long as there's still a chance at getting into my panties."

"I won't argue with that."

"Why not? You seem like a controversial guy to me."

Now he stopped, suddenly slapping her shoulder as if they were old friends from the cricket oval. It baffled Emily. The way it was supposed to.

"Simple. Because I figured the same and concluded I was better off doing the exact opposite from everyone else if I ever wanted a shot at getting into your panties. Come now, let's go for coffee. It's on me."

"I got a condition."

"Name it."

"I never drink coffee with anyone whose name I don't know. I'm Emily."

"Samuel. But they call me Sport."
"They."
"My friends."
"Seems like you don't have any friends."
"Isn't it a bit premature, and rude actually, saying that now?"
"You'll have your shot at convincing me otherwise."

They went for coffee on the other side of the street to the campus a bit down the road, as Sport considered student's cafés to be bourgie, and very much hated the prospect of pushing another dime down the throat of a big company keeping people like slaves. The place was very old and traditional, dim instead of cozy. The coffee tasted burned and sour, prompting Emily to pour condensed milk in it.

"Isn't that something," Sport said when he saw it, "a young, pretty girl pouring condensed milk into coffee as if it was nineteen-thirty-seven."

"You have an opinion on everything."

"Yes."

"That wasn't a question. And rub off that smug face of yours, it's boring and corny."

"You're running a big mouth, too."

"Only when you're asking for it. Which you clearly do. The coffee's very bad."

"Should've ordered tea like a good Scot."

"How would you establish what a good Scot does?"

"I wouldn't. It's one of those truths, deeply rooted in our society. Even though I tried, I couldn't really find out who defined them or how they came to develop a life of their own. Am I boring you?"

Emily took another sip off the coffee, wondering if she should order a beer since it was hard messing that up. But then she spotted the ugly tap, deciding against it.

"What bores me," she said diverting her attention back to Sport, still wondering what the nickname was all about, "is that you're so desperately trying to impress. Even when you're hitting a low key, you're trying to make it ring like a church bell."

"You say it as if I was doing that on purpose. As if I enjoyed being like that."

"Do you?"

"Not at all," he said leaning back, cup suspended from an arm supported on thick, dark brown leather. It was the first time Emily suspected he was more than just a clown.

"Tell me about your friends."

"I had two. One called me Samuel and said I was a fool for studying literature instead of anything useful."

"Like engineering. Or accounting."

"I lost all respect for him right there. And he for me. We went our separate ways. As it happened with the rest of the people you see come and go in your life."

"Who's the other one?"

"The best guy I ever knew. He called me Sport. I called him Brick. Because he was tough as nails. Once saved me from a pub brawl sending a guy sitting down weighing about three-hundred pounds with two blows. Broke his wrist punching him but we chanted Irish songs on the way home."

"Where is he now?"

"Some desert in Afghanistan. Sleeping the big sleep."

"Oh."

"Enlisted as paramedic. Never touched a gun. Said they were for mice, not men. Volunteered for the big show, trying to do the right thing. Six weeks after completing his training, he stepped on a bucket bomb. Blew him to little bits and pieces."

"I'm sorry."

"Why would you? You didn't know him."

He said that with no hostility.

"You can feel sorry for someone even though you don't directly know the feeling. It's called empathy."

"Empathy is a lie. If we ever feel anything that remotely resembles empathy, it's relief over not having to live through the same misery."

"That's cynical."

"Or down to earth. Make your pick."

"I can easily see why it's tough being friends with you."

"You're no shit-talker. I like that."

"Is there anyone you know in Edinburgh?"

Oddly enough, Sport considered this.

"Tough question."

"How would a simple question like that ever be tough? Unless you got something to hide."

"There's no need for throwing punches."

Again, he said it free of all emotion. The waitress watched from the bar, mumbling something to the line cook leaning out of the service window. They were suspicious of this odd couple. Which made Emily wonder. There shouldn't have been anything suspicious about them.

"I'm not throwing punches. I'm– "

"Having a conversation?" he finished for her.

"Not anymore, I'm afraid," Emily said and got up to leave, fishing for change in her coat's pocket.

"Please, let me take care of this."

"Thanks."

"I didn't mean to bug you. You're a very friendly person."

"I'm frankly not sure if I could say the same about you."

Whatever it was about him that rubbed her the wrong way, Emily could barely conceal it any longer. At first, she had felt sympathy for him. Not anymore. Somehow, she wondered if anything he ever said was true.

"Is there any way I could convince you otherwise? If you just sit down again and we talk. Or we go for a walk? I could use some fresh air."

"Thank you, Sport. But I gotta be going anyway."

"Seeing your boyfriend?"

"Yes."

"What type is he?"

"That's none of your business."

"Not like me, is he? I mean, it'd be funny. Since you're so clearly my type. In fact, you look exactly like the other girls I've been with."

"Take care," she said walking but felt his grip closing around her wrist, holding her back. Much harder than she would've anticipated a man of his build to be able to grip so nonchalantly.

"Just one more thing. If you ever feel like going out, painting the town, and you're bored with the familiar, mundane entertainment, maybe you should go where I go when I want to have a good time. A real good time, I mean."

The business card he held out to her was a dark red in color, some shade of burgundy. Emily couldn't see the printing on it at first, but then she understood. It was supposed to be subtle. Not every unsuspecting bystander was to make out what was embossed there. Sport smiled at her, sending a bad shiver down her spine. Emily took the business card with her free hand.

"Thanks," she said.

"Consider it. Might be for you."

"I sure will."

"We got a problem over there?" the line cook built like a brick shithouse hollered from behind the bar, sporting a pot belly but also strong arms and a barrel chest, certainly not fearing anyone weighing less than two-hundred and ten pounds.

Just as Emily was about to state the obvious, that no, there was no problem at all, the door flew open. In waltzed Professor Briggs, accompanied by a mid-aged woman. At first, she didn't seem familiar, but then Emily recognized her as one of the instructors she hadn't taken any classes of. With her striking appearance – attractive while still maturely feminine – she was the type of lady to be remembered.

"How is everyone this afternoon?" Professor Briggs asked the waitress and the line cook.

"I'll get you the same as always, Neal," the waitress said.

"Good call."

"And for the lady?"

"Pale ale and a cucumber sandwich."

"Take any seats you like," she said and went to work on the tap. The line cook retreated to the kitchen, throwing one last condescending glance at Sport making sure he'd received the news alright.

"What about over there?" Briggs said and pointed at the only occupied table. "Now, isn't that something. Two of my students on their best behavior, doing some serious day-drinking."

Sport hadn't let go of Emily's wrist but she could feel his grip softening.

"Good afternoon, Professor," Emily said and smiled for good measure.

"Hi, Emily. Please, make that Neal. Now, who's that fellow you're with? I recognize you from the lecture but I'm afraid we haven't been introduced."

He extended a hand, prompting Sport to let go of Emily's wrist.

"This is Samuel," Emily took over. "They call him Sport."

"They?" the instructor said with a smile.

"Everyone may call me Sport," he said for himself. "I hope you don't mind?"

"We'll see," she said pointing a slender finger at the table. "You two mind if we sit with you?"

Neal laughed at that while shaking with Sport, almost crushing his hand.

"Never mind Fiona," he said. "They call her Your Straightforwardness. Fio, say, did either of the two attend your class on Richard Yates?"

"I'm afraid not."

"And you're sure you didn't miss them in the crowd?"

"Oh, screw you."

"It's so interesting when a mid-aged woman is defending a misogynistic boozehound that loathed Old Dixie like the black plague and ironically went there to die, alternately taking hits from his cigarettes and oxygen tank."

"Here we go again, another boner for Faulkner. Hooray!"

"I was about to leave," Emily threw in.

"Seeing your boyfriend?" Neal asked, then added: "Just kiddin'. Please, stay for another drink. I'm buying."

"I wish we could eradicate the Texan in you already," Fiona said taking the seat that was still warm with Emily's radiated body heat. Neal hollered for a round of lagers before pushing Sport in and having a seat too. They quickly engaged in their talking, leaving Emily stranded at the corner of the table. Awkwardly, not moving, trying to think of some way of getting out of the situation, but failing miserably. When the waitress brought the beer and the cucumber sandwich, she was still standing around like a cheap piece of plasticky decoration.

"Thanks, honey," Neal said to the waitress, who rolled her eyes when she stomped away. "Emily, you remind me of my days making money on the side as a type clerk."

"Why's that?"

"At the end of the day, I was so tired of sitting in front of a keyboard I got drunk standing as well."

Knowing she'd let her chance to get away pass, Emily sat down, listening for a while as they talked without weighing in on the discussion. It was all about wokeism and equality and sexists and feminists and rights. Everything seemed to be about rights these days. As much as Emily felt the need to consider social changes, her status as a woman and all the ramifications of human existence, sitting there sipping beer, she found she'd rather have been another place.

"You're disregarding the gender pay gap," Fiona said, having Neal roll his eyes after they'd moved on from Hemingway and why Yates was different – The Easter Parade serving as undisputable evidence – drifting yet again to the battlefield they called gender. It seemed the primed topic at universities all around the globe. Something that could by no means ever be exhausted.

"How much do you make, Fiona?" Neal asked, then finished his beer.

"Screw you."

"Seriously, how much?"

"Less than you."

"How would you know?"

"How would I know? How would I know if the skies are blue? Look at them? Duh."

"Weak defense."

"At least I work for the money I make when you're pretending to do so flirting with teenage girls, getting giggles because they're too young to figure out your antics."

"Getting personal, huh?"

"Why wouldn't I?"

"Do you think," Sport suddenly took over, "that Richard Yates would've approved of gender equality?"

"I could tell you that Hemingway– "

"Cut that out," Neal interrupted. "You're not evading the question. What about good old Dick?"

"If we look at A Good School and social patterns– "

"Stop it," Emily burst out. "Would you please, please stop it already? How would you know what somebody else was felling? Why'd you even care if you never respect anyone? You think you have the right to put words into somebody's mouth after they're dead and have no chance to ever oppose you? It's presumptuous. You're literary scholars and that's all you got to offer? Looking at people and putting words in their mouths instead of reading fiction and having it speak for itself? The author's still dead. And I've had plenty of woke gibberish for one day."

Fiona and Sport were shushed. Neal nodded, approvingly.

"You're right," was all he said.

That stirred another fight, prompting Emily to get up and walk out as quickly as she could. It was dark already, the black night sky and the coldness smacking her right in the face. Turning towards downtown, she felt a hand closing its grip around her wrist yet again.

"Emily," Sport said, "please wait."

"Let go of my wrist."

He did. Reluctantly, but he did.

"You want to go out tonight?"

"You got some nerve."

"What did I do wrong?"

"Everything."

"Everything?"

"Everything. Everything about you is wrong. Not in the quirky way. And not just about you. It's like the world is trying to hijack my brain and body and do whatever they please."

"Okay. What do you mean?"

"I want to be taken into the arms of a man."

"Any time," he said spreading his arms. But he wouldn't react quick enough to evade Emily's palm when she slapped him right across the cheek and mouth, leaving him there.

"Have a nice evening, Emily," he hollered after her.

10

It was easy to spot her over half a mile as she walked down Princes Street. The elegance in her strides. The dark blonde hair, falling like waves breaking on a reef. The perfection of her proportions. To those who had an eye for finesse and an understanding of arts at heart, she stood out of the crowd as much as a nail out of an ancient beam. When he saw her, conceiving that comparison, Duke felt that it was just as easy getting caught and rip a deep wound on her as on the nail.

Emily heard the engine first, then saw the beams of the headlights illuminating her on the sidewalk. As if all the world was a stage and she in the lead, in the spotlight, if only for the glimpse of a moment. Against the light, she couldn't see inside the cockpit. But the red Lotus was a tell-tale sign. As she opened the door and sat down riding shotgun, Emily wanted to say something. Something funny. Just to pretend there was nothing to worry about. To pretend that everything was alright. Something nice about the engine. Or how much she loved his cologne, if only on him, for his skin made it smell heavenly, not mundane, like everyone else's. She kept her mouth shut, though.

"Where to?" Duke asked.

"Anywhere."

"Anywhere?"

"Away from here. That's plenty."

He nodded, then put the car in gear and dashed into traffic, tires squealing. Someone blew the horn. It sounded faint. Distant. Simply irrelevant. On the passenger's side seat, Emily rolled up, resting her head against the door, falling sound asleep soon. Even when Duke forced the car around a turn in a slide she wouldn't wake up.

The Lotus was giving him direction, telling him where to go, when to turn, when to put the pedal back down. The roads beneath Carlton Hill were deserted, free of traffic and a joy to drive. The nagging in the back got softer, losing its touch. Soon they were crossing city limits, the Excel finding its natural environment. With the evening cold rolling in from the ocean, the car was a bit loose on the tarmac freezing over with a thin layer of ice. But it was still far from reaching its limitations.

"It'll be alright," Duke said stroking Emily's cheek, holding a drift one-handed.

When she woke up, all the windows were fogged, the heater spitting out the last of the engine's heat. It hadn't been much more than half an hour. But it had done her a world of good.

"Where are we?" she asked rubbing her eyes, straightening her hair.

"Anywhere. Or somewhere else, rather."

"You're funny," she said and kissed him on the cheek.

"Outside of Musselburgh."

"The Lagoons."

"Close. It's a place I used to go to but haven't been to in a long time."

"How long?"

"Years."

"Why didn't you go?"

"I never established that for myself. I felt that I wouldn't belong here, so I stayed away. Never went to see the ocean at all."

"I'm not sure if I understand."

"Me neither."

"You're a very sensitive person, I feel. And I don't mean that in any disrespectful way. Sensitive in the most positive way."

"I wouldn't ever take any offense in anything you said, Emily."

"Don't jump at conclusions prematurely. It doesn't feel like it, but we barely know each other."

"So far, I frowned upon asking any basic questions. It turns everything so goddamn mundane, all of a sudden."

"Mundane life always strikes at some point."

"I'd like to delay that. But I know it's not fair."

"How's that?"

"If we never move ahead, take that step towards mundanity and normalcy because we want to preserve a fairytale, it's exploitation. We're only taking what we want and leave the rest to rot."

"No man has ever said that to me. Not anything quite like it."

"Maybe they weren't men to begin with."

"I've never felt so secure with anyone."

And she put her head to his shoulder, and they sat there, saying neither good nor bad things for a while. It was slowly getting cold inside the car but they wouldn't mind. Once the front window was fully fogged over, Duke wiped it clean. In the darkness ahead, you could barely see the ocean, only the shadows and silhouettes of waves rolling in. Farther ahead were the signal lights of a ship, flashing through the night sky. But there was no way of telling its size. It could've been a speed boat as much as a massive oil tanker.

"Are you cold?" Duke asked her.

"No," she said snuggling a little closer.

"Want me to drive you home?"

"There is no home you could take me. Not tonight."

"Okay."

Duke started the engine, then backed the car slowly off the grass, to the small gravel road that led to this vantage point outside of Musselburgh. It was a private road, closed to general traffic, but the owner wouldn't mind as long as you didn't throw gravel and kept everything tidy.

The country roads were clear. It was the middle of the night and people wouldn't get up for work until some hours later. But Duke took a pass at making the roads his own. They cruised through the night at a relaxed pace, with Emily falling asleep again quite soon. This time, he left the car inside the garage, closing the gate, locking it.

Emily was still asleep, both beautifully and peacefully. Not wanting to wake her up, Duke carried her to bed, stripping her pants off, folding the nice but unusual corduroy shirt she was wearing without waking her up.

"Sleep well," he said putting a kiss on her forehead, covering her with a quilted blanket he'd brought from back home before retreating to the sofa, struggling to fall asleep.

The next morning, she found him at his garage workshop, cutting leather. It was something she'd never seen done before.

"How did you sleep?" Duke asked her, finishing a cut swiftly.

"Like a rock. What about you?"

"Fine."

"You don't look fine. I mean, you do. But you look tired. And worried."

"Just a mild case of mid-month crisis."

"What're you building this time?"

"A sheath for a hunting knife I made myself some time back."

"Beautiful knife," Emily said picking it up, inspecting the edge, astounded by the accuracy of the bevels, the nice finishing touches.

"It's inspired by the K-bar, the standard-issue knife of the US Marine Corps. I always loved that knife. But the handle isn't stacked leather like the original. I used black walnut. Looks similar but I like the feel better."

"Why don't you do that for a living?"

"Making knives?"

"Making anything, really. To me, it looks like you're awfully talented in many ways. Hard to believe you couldn't cash in on that somehow."

"It's not that simple."

"Obviously. But it's possible, isn't it?"

"Anything's possible. Both good and bad things."

"Doesn't look like you're happy with your current line of work."

"You forget to add: Whatever that is."

"I'm not trying to bug you."

"I know."

"It was just an idea that popped into my head."

With that, she left him at the workbench, wandering around the shop, to the weights, trying to pick up a dumbbell that looked like it was over a hundred years old.

"Careful, it's heavy."

"Why's the bar so thick?"

"Makes it harder to lift."

"It's not moving an inch. Uff."

"It's hard to lift. That's the point."

"Can you lift it?"

"Yes."

"Overhead press?"

"Yes."

"Fluke?"

"No."

For good fun, Duke crossed over, took a deep breath, then lifted and pressed the dumbbell over his head.

"Astonishing. How heavy is it?"

"I never had it weighed," he said and put it back down as carefully as he possibly could. Which was still hard enough to send a shockwave through the garage floor.

"Where'd you get it?"

"From a small island village off the coast. They had it there for no one really knew how long. Was used in an annual strongman competition."

"Why did they sell it to you if it's a piece of local history?"

"The old shepherd that had it in his shed told me the young men and women were all moving away. To the cities. To other countries. Said there was no point trying to cling on to the irretrievably lost."

"Wow."

"He told me he'd rather see it go than put it on display somewhere, for the village and island he was born in, grew up in, spent his whole life in, was no museum."

"Did he lift it? As a young man?"

"Before I left, he told me he'd done it when he was eighteen, weighing around one-hundred and sixty pounds. And then he cleared the lift one final time."

"How old was he?"

"In his seventies."

"Amazing. A girl like me could never clear that lift."

"Don't say that. I've seen the tiniest women do the most impressive lifts. Some of which men even heavier than me couldn't accomplish."

"One day," she said putting her left hand around the enormous bar, struggling for grip, "I'll lift this dumbbell."

But it wasn't that day. As much as she tried, giving her all, the dumbbell wouldn't move.

"You want to stay here?" Duke asked. "For the time being?"

"Yes."

"There's a bus connection to town. You'd have to walk down the block to the stop."

"And I was hoping you'd let me drive the Lotus."

"I'm sorry, you can't have it."

"I was joking."

"It's not that I wouldn't let you drive it. Heard a knock on the way back home yesterday. Don't know what it is. The engine shouldn't be run until I figured it out."

"Didn't hear a thing."

"You'll learn," he said and kissed her on the forehead, forcing a smile.

"How come you look good even in those carpenter's pants and the washed-out t-shirt?"

"That's for smarter people than me to establish. Let's have some tea."

They talked for an hour, drinking tea and laughing and smiling and arguing without fighting, learning from each other. It was with awe that Emily realized she would have to at least go hit her shift at the café now that she'd skipped classes all day, something Duke encouraged. When he explained how to get to the bus stop, it was matter-of-factly. You could sense a change of ambience. The room got a bit colder.

"Think my clothes will still do?" Emily asked. "I got a change sweater and apron at my locker."

"It'll do."

"What're you going to do?"

"I don't have any appointments, so I'll just take it from there, see where I get."

"Wish I could have a full day off in the middle of the week."

"If you care about bringing some clothes over from your place, I can meet you there tonight and help you."

"There's not much I need. You got a washing machine, don't you?"

"Yes."

"I'll manage, no problem."

He wanted to ask her what she wanted for dinner, but then he remembered she would be late anyway. And a surprise was always pleasant, at least in his mind. With the spare key he sent her on her way, standing in the door watching her until she turned the corner. Duke sighed, glancing at the garage in the corner of his eye. Fred, the old-timer living on the other side of the street, waved at him when he took the trash out. Duke returned the regards before retreating back inside.

At the kitchen table, he checked his phone. Several messages and mails but he didn't have the heart checking them. It wasn't the right time. For a moment, which felt like the longest of time, he just sat there. Like a stranded fish. Yet there was no point in despair. Nothing good had ever come from it. The phone still felt like a brick in his hand.

Looking at himself in the mirror, he remembered Emily's words. It was true. He looked good in work clothes. For what it was worth, it lit a small fire underneath him. On his way out, Duke put on the heaviest jacket he had, something oil riggers wore, then added his New York Mets baseball cap to the attire. A relic, some old piece from a time past and gone. The brim had a ring of white, salty sweat mark on it.

11

Night clubs had always been a mystery to Joe. The concept was quite conceivable, if only once she'd broken it down to its core. People felt a desperate need for other people. Certain desires sure needed to be fulfilled. Even if it was all delusional to most, and a genuine pleasure only to few, the night club was a much a societal convention as the pub. Running several theories through her head, while looking at young and old and pretty and ugly and even embarrassing people alike, Joe told herself to screw it and take it for face value.

Three nights in a row had been a stretch on her mind. And nothing serious had materialized. It was all a bit ugly, skewed, absurd. But it was legal. If she had to make a guess, it was simple. Whatever it was she was looking for, she wouldn't be finding it on the surface. She had to dig deeper. The gun and badge on her belt wouldn't help.

"Look at you, gorgeous," some track suit hollered at her, his breath reeking of vodka even over a couple of feet's distance.

"Look at you, athlete," Joe hollered back. His friends broke out laughing.

"In for a party?" he inquired.

"I've had plenty for one night."

"That so? Got some more in store."

"Like what?"

"Like what would you like?"

Joe stepped closer. It wasn't hard to establish he had no clue what he was getting himself into. If she had to profile him, she'd assume he was in his late twenties, working a common day job, taking some, if not great care of his body, living all for the nights out and scoring another unsuspecting female body. It was fair enough. Only the appeal of such existence was beyond her.

"Like getting it rough," she said moving closer.

"Uh-huh."

"Like using those nice muscles of yours," she said standing right in front of him.

"Strong arms, holding you."

"Why stop there? What could those arms do?"

"Whatever you want."

"What about showing me my place?"

"I can get real physical."

"For sure."

"Show you what it feels like, being a woman."

"Mm, I'd love that."
And then she leaned over his shoulder, whispering in his ear.
"I'd love it even more if you poured something over me."
"Uh-huh."
"No champagne, that bores me."
"Champagne's for drinking."
"We'll have the whole bottle."
"That's right."
"And then you get a bucket of what I want. Take it out the fridge so it'll warm. Just a bit. I get stiff when it's too cold."
"We'll do that with ice cubes."
"Mm."
"So, what is it? What would you want me to pour over you?"
"Pig's blood."
"Pig's blood?"
"Now, what about that?"
He took a step back. The expression on his face had changed.
"Screw that, I say."
With that, he and his entourage took off, wondering. It didn't phase Joe. It had been worth the try, even though she felt it had been a shot at the dark to begin with.

Their show hadn't drawn much attention, but when she'd started whispering into the guy's ear, she'd noticed someone in the corner of her left eye. The guy was retreating to the restrooms, but Joe knew there was a fire escape in the back where people used to step out and have a smoke. Checking the escape routes was essential.

People were standing in line in front of the restrooms, some queuing for the women's room, other chatting or making out in the black and purple light. The smell was intense if you weren't drunk, which Joe wasn't, despite the fact she'd downed five beers that night. Working her way through the crowd with authority, she divided most of the lines like the Red Sea.

"Excuse me!" some girl that looked like a climate protester complained when Joe forced her way through.

"Step out of the way," Joe snapped at her, shutting her up with no bad feelings to be had on her part.

Turning the corner, she saw the steel fire door swinging shut in front of her. She caught it before it locked. It led out to a narrow alley next to the dumpsters. In the summer, the smell must've been bad. Not that people smoking at night clubs would care much about such inconveniences.

Few people were standing around outside, and you could hear the street noise over their talking. There was the guy, leaning against a brick wall, fishing for his pack of cigarettes. Joe went right at him, forcing a smile she knew looked false.

"Got a cigarette to spare?" she asked.
"Uh-huh," he went, offering the pack.
"Been a while since I've seen a soft pack. Cheers."
"Everything stylish is going out of style," he said popping one in his mouth, flicking a match, holding it out for Joe.

"Thanks."
"Never mind."
"Oh, they're strong."
"Never saw any point in smoking sissy cigarettes."
"More bang for the buck, right?"
"Well said. Just like Eisenhower."
"Did he coin the phrase?"
"Yup. He was talking about atomic bombs."
"It figures."
"How do you like it here?"
"It's lame."
"What would you expect with that six-shooter on you, cowgirl?"
"I got hit on, mind you."
"And how did it go?"
"Guess you know," she said exhaling a jet of smoke, liking it more than she appreciated. "You been watching."
"Maybe I did. Or maybe I just know what I make from it."
"Plausible deniability. To stick with American proverbs."
"Very good."

Nothing about him struck Joe as exceptional. If anything, she could tell he was perfectly disguised in his apparent mundane looks.

"Former SAS?"
"What's it to you?"
"I like knowing who I'm dealing with."
"Foreign Legion."
"I'll think twice before messing with you."
"Same here. Always been with the rozzers?"
"Yes."
"You should've left a while ago. There's places better suited to someone like you."
"Shove that right up where the sun don't shine, if you pardon my French."
"Once I'm home. With joy."
"You're looking for someone."
"Who's not. And that's not the police's business. Who I'm looking for."
"I make it mine, not the police's. You're a private eye."
"I prefer private dick."
"As you wish, Dickie. I'm positive we're looking for the same suspect out here."
"What makes you think so?"
"Don't you play me like a cheap fiddle. This is Edinburgh, not Los Angeles."
"Okay."
"You know what's been going down."
"Maybe. What's it to you? Personally, I mean. You're sporting the brass and police issue but you're here all on your own accord. I can tell."
"Let's say I don't appreciate it when some lunatic is running around my town, molesting people."
"Why was information on the second case sparse then?"
"Ask my boss."

"If you give me his phone number."

The second case was like an open wound rubbed in salt. It matched their first case perfectly, save for the purported victim. Joe took another deep drag off the cigarette. This was a gamble, right in front of her. Information was confidential. But if she managed to extend her network, chances were she would eventually get to the bottom of this.

"What's your name?" she asked. "And don't you give me any assumed alias or something."

"Roman Sykes. From Aberdeen, originally."

"I knew that."

"What gives me away?"

"I'm Joe."

"Simply Joe?"

"Josephine Martin."

"Hm."

"Disappointed?"

"Just a tad. I was hoping for a flashier name, sorry."

"I suggest we cooperate on this, Roman. A little bazar of information. At the end of the day, we all want our streets safe."

"You know there's some money to be made on my part if I beat the brass to it?"

"Your call."

"One condition. Quite obviously."

"What's not in the papers."

"Exactly."

"I could lose my job."

"Your call."

Joe took a last drag, then stabbed the cigarette out on the brick wall.

"Not here."

"My office isn't far."

"Let's grab something to eat along the way."

Roman wanted takeout burgers but Joe insisted on having them at the restaurant. It was the same scene as always, as interchangeable as the nights before. This gave Roman some sense of unease, and he was struggling not to say anything. The open anarchy and subconscious left-leaning ideologies at display certainly prompted him to take action. To him, it was a call of duty. But he remained quiet.

If Joe expected the office of a private eye from a movie or cartoon, she was disappointed. The place was small but tidy. It spoke volumes of Roman and his training. Even though he seemed like a conservative person, there were few folders. This private eye had adopted the digital world, love it or hate it.

"Want a drink?" he asked pointing at the chair in front of his desk. Mid-century pieces, and even Joe could tell they weren't reproductions.

"Why not. Scotch?"

"You got it."

In a cabinet, Roman kept a bottle of Scotch from the Isle of Skye that hadn't been produced under law. Clear bottle, hand-written label. But the distiller had had plenty of confidence, putting his signature on. He poured two big and plain glasses full of whiskey. Enough to put an inexperienced drinker out of commission.

"Can I make a guess on who your client is?" Joe asked.

"You very well may. Just don't expect me to answer. Here you go."

"Thank you."

They touched glasses for cheers, and both downed a good portion of the whiskey.

"Revitalizing," Roman said.

"Strong but tasty. I like fire in whiskey."

"The Irish are good at that."

"I'm assuming your client is some concerned parent, not pleased at all with something that happened to their child."

"Why child?" Roman asked, taking his seat behind the desk with some authority. "Why not daughter?"

"What you didn't read in the papers is that the second victim was not a young woman."

"A man?"

"As far as his ID goes. You know how it is today. When we questioned the concerned citizens knowing him, they were somewhat aggressive when we referred to him as he and as a man."

"That gender and pronoun crap."

"Wish it was beside the point but who knows."

"Lots of blood again and not his?"

"Similar crime scene. Lots of pig's blood."

"New fresco on the wall."

"There's a catch. One of the forensics team members was very meticulous. Turned out there was a whole bunch of human blood in the mix, too."

"Whoever did this got a bit carried away this time."

"That's what we think."

"Because the victim was a boy."

The moment he said it, Joe wondered if that was conceivable. After all, and after the fuss they'd been through with the witnesses over using the wrong pronouns, she couldn't really put it all together.

"Even if we assumed that, what would it change?"

"Everything. Nothing. Whatever you make of it. We live in Fantasyland, anyway."

"None of the leads got us anywhere. We traced his steps back until he disappeared. There wasn't really anything that stood out as exceptional. Average person, molested in his own bed, disappeared without a trace.

"There's a mole infiltrating that campus. Who knows what's smoldering under the surface once we dig deep enough."

"That's what has me worried," Joe replied and downed some more of the whiskey, helping her, making her dizzy enough to get through the night.

"Whatever it is we're dealing with, there's the obvious problem. If these victims consented and won't press any charges later, there's nothing there for the prosecution even if we crack this case."

"Which brings me to your client."

This time, it was Roman, contemplating his words. If there was anything about being a private eye he valued, it was the confidentiality between himself and the client. Whoever hired him would never blow the whistle on him. They were both much too vulnerable for that.

"Okay, then. You've been stand-up and honest with me. I'll return the courtesy."

"Roman?"

"Hm?"

"If you feed me chickenshit, I'll know. And I'll get away with claiming self-defense."

"Understood."

"One last toast," Joe said raising her glass. "To fighting the good fight and keeping the world safe and sane."

"Hear ye. Cheers."

"Cheers."

Both finished their whiskey before Roman recounted the string of events that had led him into this wicked game.

12

The knocking at the door had woken Roman Sykes, private dick, out of a shallow afternoon nap. Napping had never come naturally to him, but during his military training in the South American jungle he'd really taken to it. If being alert and on time with senses working perfectly was essential to survival, there was no room for personal preference.

Coming to his senses quickly, Roman pushed himself out of the chair, noticing the pounds he'd gained since finding himself in a civilian career. Ten to fifteen pounds. They made all the difference.

"I'll be right there," he said answering another knocking.

And then he was stunned when he opened the door. A lady in her mid-forties, most beautiful features, perfectly-shaped body, perfectly-maintained too, her dark blonde hair like silk. Expensive designer clothes chosen with taste, not vulgarity. Even the scent of her perfume complemented her.

"Good afternoon," she said. "I've been referred to you, Mr. Sykes."

"By whom, if you don't mind my asking. Mrs.?"

"Mrs. Townshend. Mr. Henry Pike is an old friend of mine. He said, quote, you're the right man for the ob."

"Please, come inside," he said moving out of the way, unable to keep himself from gazing down on her back and legs when she entered.

"A very nice office," she said taking a look around, removing the calf-leather gloves but keeping the coat on.

"Thank you very much, Mrs. Townshend."

"Frankly, I didn't expect a private investigator to operate from such a tidy place. And please, make that Rachel. You calling me Mrs. Townshend makes me feel like I'm attending one of my husband's banquets, where all I'm expected to do is look presentable next to him."

"I should think you would be hard-pressed to merely look presentable, Rachel. Call me Roman, please."

"Would you mind brewing some Earl Grey tea, Roman? I need something to calm my nerves."

"Certainly," he said not mentioning seeing her hands shaking now that she'd tucked away the gloves like a coachman.

The tea pot was puffing in a minute and Roman returned with two steaming cups of tea, finding Rachel sitting at his desk in waiting, hands folded, looking as beautiful as she looked worried. Roman knew the state of mind. There was nothing else she could do, apart from holding herself together. No browsing, no chatting, nothing. It was still a mystery to him why it was so hard on men to act rational around beautiful women. All he could say for himself was that anyone assuming masculinity was a social construct clearly either had no significant testosterone levels or was simply a fool.

"Mr. Pike was a real gentleman," Roman said putting the cups on the desk. "Once the assignment was met to his satisfaction, he shook my hand, gave me a slap on the shoulder like a cricketeer and handed me an envelope containing exactly the sum we'd agreed upon. Added a bonus. I was impressed by that."

"Henry is a gentleman. And while my assignment to you is of a very different nature, Henry felt sure you would be the man to handle it right. Handle it the way it is supposed to be handled. Mm, that tea is delicious."

"Let's talk turkey, then," Roman almost interrupted, trying not to follow the fallacy that all good-looking women should be treated like queens, for they certainly wouldn't deserve it.

"Talk turkey?"

"Say it as it is. Why did you come to me?"

The words wouldn't come right away, even though she'd rehearsed them, over and over again. It sounded outlandish. It sounded like something that happened in the movies. Or to other people. But not to her. Clearly, not to her. Not in her life.

"I have to contemplate my words."

"Nothing you'll ever say to me will be held against you. I prefer hearing a straight story, that's all. Don't concern yourself with your choice of words."

"Did you follow the news?"

"I have to."

"There's been two cases of young women first being molested, if not worse, before they disappeared."

"Yes."

"I know who did it."

"Do you?"

"Yes."

"Why wouldn't you tell the police?"

"It's not that simple. My daughter, she– "

"She what?"

"She got assaulted by the man."

"When?"

"Two days ago."

"How?"

"At her apartment, down at The Meadows."

"That's where, not how. What did he do?"

"Forced himself upon her. Asked her to be quiet, do whatever he said. Even brought a plastic bag full of pig's blood."

"Hang on," Roman said starting to take notes. "Let's start at the beginning. How did she meet him? She invited him over to her apartment, didn't she?"

"Yes, she did. After they met at a night club. Not one of those regular night clubs."

"Remember the name?"

"Something like Orange Leopard."

"Or Red Tiger?"

"Maybe."

"She'll know."

"You're not going to question her. And I'm not going to bring it up ever again. All I said to her is that mummy would take care of it so she'd soon believe it was all but a bad dream."

The words made her emotional. Roman knew there was no point trying to weasel himself into talking to the girl. At least not right away.

"It's alright. So, she met him at a night club. Your daughter was unsuspecting."

"Yes."

"She invited him over to the apartment."

"About a week after they first met. They talked on the phone before. She's a good kid. She wanted to make sure she knew who she was dealing with."

"He acted normal, then started harassing her."

"Yes."

"What did he do?"

Rachel Townshend sighed, feeling the weight of the situation on her shoulders. What she also felt, and weighing much heavier, was the obligation to do the right thing. As tough as it was, she pulled herself together, telling herself it would soon all be over.

"All types of perversions," she said.

"Spanking?"

"He socked her in the right eye."

"Whipping her?"

"When she wouldn't do what he said, he split her lip."

"Choking her."

"He presented the bag with the pig's blood. Told her, I'll mix your blood with this, you little bitch. You'll take it and you'll like it. Or something along those lines."

"Is he strong?"

"Very strong. You wouldn't expect from his looks. But his muscles are like iron cords."

"How did your daughter defend herself?"

"Her father gave her a Japanese sword for her sixteenth birthday he'd bought on a business trip."

"A katana?"

"I think that's the correct term. It's about four-hundred years old. Technically, it's illegal to be had."

There were trading restrictions on cultural heritage like genuine katanas, Roman knew. The blade was also much too long and dangerous for a common citizen to be wielded.

"And she pulled it out?"

"Scared him off."

"Did she get him? Any physical evidence that would link him to the crime scene?"

"She got him in the shoulder, not a deep cut. And she shattered a vase."

"What about the blood?"

With shaky hands, she produced a stack of polaroids from her purse. They showed the apartment. Shattered Ming vase, a katana on the floor. Bathroom full of blood. Several angles, all of them like a cheap horror movie.

"This has to be stopped," she said while Roman was flicking through the pictures.

"That's something we agree upon," he said and put the pictures in the middle of the desk. "But my instincts are telling me we won't be agreeing upon the methods."

"Pardon?"

"Hand this over to the police. Even if the katana was illegally imported, the police is not going to press any charges. You have a clear description of the suspect. A crime was committed. I'm sure you also have his name and phone number."

"I'm not going to let this out to the police. Or the media."

"What am I supposed to do about the guy without evidence. If I find him?"

"Accidents happen."

"Accidents happen, yes," Roman replied without even twitching.

"I knew you'd be understanding of the situation, Mr. Sykes. Have you memorized the pictures?"

"Yes."

"Mind if I use your waste bucket?"

"Go ahead."

She shoved the stack of polaroids into the metal bucket, then produced a small can of lighter fluid, squeezed some over it and dropped a match into the mix. Flames licked out of the bucket when the images turned from celluloid to smoke.

"What are you charging? Your usual rate?"

"Aye. I'm asking fifteen percent extra, plus a bonus upon completion."

"As you wish. Here's your advance. I presumed the same amount you charged Mr. Pike would do?"

"It will."

The envelope had a familiar thickness and weight to it. Roman saw no need for counting the money.

"Here is my contact information. Please, do not call me but text first and I'll get back to you."

"You really have the guy's phone number and name?"

"Yes."

They were written on a small slip of paper that had been folded along the center line.

"I assume he hightailed out of town after that showing two nights ago."

"If he's in his right mind. Which he doubtlessly isn't. But you'll find him. Thank you for your time, Mr. Sykes."

"Thank you, Mrs. Townshend. I'll see you out."

Putting the calf leather gloves on first, she also added a fur hood and sunglasses to her daytime disguise. The door clicked shut, leaving Roman wondering. None of this seemed to make much sense to him. For whatever reason, he felt like having a drink but restrained himself. Instead, he picked up that slip of paper and unfolded it. The phone number was right there. And a name.

"Guy's a fan of classic rock," Roman said to himself.

13

Waverley Station was busier than normal, but still not one of those buzzing beehives they had for train stations in bigger towns and the metropolises of this world. Wearing his woodworking clothes and the Mets cap, Duke didn't stand out when he mingled with the crowd, people coming to and from, minding their own business. It was cold inside but the light shining in from the ramps leading out on Waverley Bridge was beautiful. For a moment, he just stood there, looking at the cold winter day, framed wonderfully by the old iron works and ornaments that made this station homely, not one of those postmodern pieces of glass and fake luxury self-indulgence.

But then he remembered things needed to be attended. A man in a Scottish Railway jacket asked him if he was putting in the trimming, something Duke decidedly declined, even though he felt up to the job. The man smiled, apologized and took off.

The lockers were a line of doors that inspired the imaginative side of Duke's personality. Enough to make him envision them as portals. What if every locker door was a portal leading to a different time or dimension or whatever it was that you imagined that very moment? The thought was as comforting as it was foolish.

In a far, dark corner, Duke checked around, ignorant of what he was looking for. Or of what he was expecting in the first place. Then he just pulled the key out and opened the locker. 1408. It hadn't been touched in his absence. Another great comfort. The folders weren't what he'd come for. First, he pulled out the wallet, that looked exactly like the wallet he carried. Only the stitching was a bit off, the threading a paler shade of brown for whatever reason only the manufacturer knew. Checking its contents, finding them still complete, Duke replaced the wallet he carried in the locker, pocketing the one with the paler stitching.

The phone was next. Same model. Duke made sure it booted before he swapped it out with the phone he carried on himself, leaving it on standby and connecting a power bank to keep it running for a while.

Locking the door left him with a sour feeling. Like unattended business. But for the time being, he felt he had no choice but to go along with it. Worse than knowing the phone and the wallet would remain at the locker was doubtlessly lingering there for too long. There was only a tourist couple in his vicinity but he didn't feel like stretching his luck. Not that day.

The next stop was as far a walk as it was a bus ride, close to the Scottish

Parliament. But Duke didn't feel like walking. Uncharacteristic of himself, the cold was creeping up on him. It had been a while since he'd been on a bus and the lopping around still gave him nausea. Even ships sailing in storms were better on his stomach.

A girl of about five asked her mother about his cap because she liked the orange logo on gray. Duke pretended he hadn't heard, playing with his phone but not really doing anything. Since he already had it in hand, he felt like giving his friend a warning. But it had been years and writing felt cheap. Some guy in his thirties was talking to himself, uttering strange and incomprehensible phrases as if rapping. It was something Duke didn't know how to deal with, deciding only to intervene if the guy started bothering anyone. He was glad when he got off the bus, wondering if the world had gone nuts or if he'd gotten out of touch with it.

It was very quiet down at the Parliament. That close to Holyrood Park it was also colder. A strange atmosphere that left Duke wondering. If there was anything he wanted to steer clear off by any means, it was politics. Nothing about the exteriors gave away the ugliness of the profession. Like a pretty apple, rotting from the inside out, eaten by worms.

The office was in the back of the representational facades facing out to the streets, very modest and unbecoming. The doorbells had been labelled with hand-written strips of office paper, glued on with translucent adhesive tape.

"Hello?" a female voice asked over the intercom.

"Hi, I'm here to see Mr. Jamal Owens."

Waiting for subsequent questions, Duke wondered what to say. The buzzing door gave him a clear answer.

"Hi," the young woman working the front desk said again when he entered.

"Hi," he repeated himself, knowing she hadn't taken a second glance at him, taking no notice.

"Mr. Owens' office is down the hall, second to last door to the right."

"Thanks," Duke said when she instantly minded her own business again, and started down the carpeted hallway.

All the office doors stood wide-open, something he understood but disliked. There was something about privacy, even in the work space, that he appreciated. A man in his fifties in cyclist's sandals and a crooked-looking beard that was reminiscent of a bird's nest uttered a good morning as he passed. This reminded Duke of the fact that he didn't look like his usual self.

For some inexplicable reason, his heart started racing along the way. It made him feel like a schoolboy, like that one instance when he was ordered to the dean's office, assuming he'd find himself on the receiving end of some serious retribution for a recent offense he'd committed. Some schoolboy prank. But it had turned out the dean merely asked his opinion about a cricketeer's talent.

The door was wide-open and Jamal was sitting at his desk, studying a book with great intensity. Duke knocked, breaking Jamal's concentration. The second he saw him Jamal beamed from ear to ear.

"Now, if that's not Big D! My man, how are you doing?"

"Hi, Jamal. Mind if I come inside?"

"Please."

Duke closed the door while Jamal crossed over. It made him suspicious already.

"You look good, gained some muscle?" Duke asked and they hugged like men.

"That's right, homeboy's been lifting. Lots of deadlifts, some squats, bench press."

"Foundational work. But you're hiding something. Just look at you."

"Got me. Did some strongman stuff too."

"Like lifting the Blarney stones or what?"

"Like exactly that. Trained for it, did it. Or as Caesar would've said: I came, I saw, I triumphed."

"Good stuff."

"You're not too bad, either. Really, it's good to see you."

"I wanted to call. But it felt kind of cheap, Jamal."

He waved it off as if it was nothing, which it clearly wasn't.

"Your life changed. And that's something. It's good. Sometimes, everything changes along with the tide. It don't mean jack."

They talked for a while, making Duke forget why he'd come to his old friend for help in the first place.

"That was so much fun," Duke said closing a story. "Wish you'd been there."

"Yeah, so do I. But that's not what you've come for, is it?"

"No."

"Spill your heart out, then. You smell of cigarettes, which means either of two things. Either you've been around and didn't get to shower, which you're not dressed up for. Or my man's nervous about something. You promised not to touch those camel shit sticks anymore and you're not one to break a promise easily."

"I believe there's no need telling you what I've gotten myself into with my life. Because you know."

"I advised you to become a carpenter or mechanic but you didn't."

"You also know there's people you get in contact with when you do what I do. Powerful people. Rich people."

"Barely any decent people."

"There's something cooking. You've been following the news?"

"Heard a lot of bad stuff. Around here, you hear the truth about the scum. Every little dirty detail."

"I'm sure there's a hint you could drop me."

"Hm. Of course. But what's it got to do with you? The police aren't looking for you. Not that I know of."

"There's no suspects. So far."

"Is someone trying to frame you, Big D?"

"I have the feeling."

"How'd you make yourself so vulnerable?"

"I was messing around. Stupid. Got myself in a jam that's hard to get out of."

"Why not tell the cops?"

"Oh, they'd love hearing my story. And how I'm making the money I launder before spending."

"Still better than being locked up at the looney bin. And if they push that crap on you, they'll lock you up with the nutcases and throw away the key. God knows what they're going to do to you once you're in."

"I can't say a word."

"Now I see. You want to crack this yourself. Throw the evidence at the cops like chunks of meat to the dogs."

"Grasping for straws."

"Let's go for a walk, Big D. If you don't mind stepping outside. I've had plenty of this office for one day."

A colleague by the name Andrea took over Jamal's duties, much to a young woman's dismay. Being counselled by Jamal was the only thing in the week she was looking forward to, and the fact that he wouldn't be there for her caused him some pain.

"You sure you don't want to go back?" Duke asked him as they walked in Holyrood Park, which lay so peacefully, the meadows and hilltops and Arthur's Seat covered in a thin blanket of snow.

"She'll have to learn to trust someone else at some point anyway."

"But it's tough on you."

"So is your situation. I have a fair idea what they're trying to frame you with."

"Disgusting stuff. I never did anything of the kind. Never."

"But you did some sideways stuff."

"I was stupid."

"I wasn't getting at that. All I'm saying for the protocol is, you're a conceivable suspect. If the cops ever catch you, do some digging, they'll find dirt. Not saying it's all true but people do talk, Big D."

"I know."

"There's a lot about you I heard through the grapevine. Ugly stuff."

"You asked me about it once. I told you it wasn't characteristic of me doing things like that."

"I decided to believe you."

"You still believe me now?"

Jamal stopped. A flock of swans was skating over the lake. People stood watching them, snapping photos. Nobody would've anticipated the worries these two people had to figure out.

"When I read the papers, I didn't know what to make of it. Couldn't imagine who'd do something like that. I was wondering if it was a cult or anything. What I know for certain is, I wasn't picturing you. Neither do I now. Whatever you did since we've seen last time is none of my business."

"Good to know," Duke said fumbling a cigarette out of the soft pack he carried in his chest pocket ever since he bought it at a news stand down at Waverley Station. The idea of smoking disgusted him. The feeling worsened when he put the cigarette between his lips, biting the filter, trying to light it with shaky hands.

"Let me help you out," Jamal went. But instead of taking the lighter, he pulled the cigarette out of Duke's mouth, crumbling it. "That's not you."

"I can't shake it off, Jamal."

"It's a hound dog and it'll always be with you. But it'll get easier down the road. The farther you get from the crossroads."

It took Duke a moment to recompose himself. The smell of fresh and unburned tobacco from his shirt's pocket made him sick, so he crushed the pack and slung it away carelessly. An old lady called him names.

"Jamal, you heard something. I know you did. I'm not asking anything from you, other than a push in the right direction. I could never ask you to go any further than that. This is my business and I got to get myself out of it, now that I've gotten myself in way in over my head."

"The air is wonderful today. Cold. But wonderful."

"Yes."

"You're not seeing the forest for the trees, do you?"

"No."

"I know it's tough."

"Break it to me."

"Go talk to the bitch that did all this to you, all these years back. Should you need my back, give me a distress call, Big D. Changed ID and phones?"

"Yes."

"Been praying for that for years. When I see an unknown caller, I'll know it'll be you."

A slap on the shoulder, then Jamal started back to the office. Walking swiftly, he never turned around.

All he'd said had rung true to Duke. Knowing that was something. To acknowledge it, embracing it, and taking the right steps forward, was something else. For the time being, he enjoyed the anonymity of Holyrood Park, a place he'd rarely come to but had grown fond of anyway, despite of events weighing down on his shoulders.

Seeing the bitch Jamal had called out was something but Duke didn't have the heart, not right away. With no work to be done, and Emily not being back to his place until the evening, there was little Duke could do about himself. When he looked up at Arthur's Seat, there was a queue of people like a rainbow-colored snake on its way to the summit.

"What the hell," he told himself, walking across the frozen meadows to start the ascent.

The Carhartt boots were very comfortable, soles gripping nicely on the slippery, frozen rock. Climbing Arthur's Seat was more of a hike than actual climbing. A group of French tourists greeted Duke on their descent, surprising him. These days, polite people were a minority. During vacation, people tended to show their most friendly self. It made him question how they would behave once they were back home, in Paris or Toulouse or Lyon, smoking French cigarettes and drinking Côtes du Rhône whenever the occasional allowed, which was always, turning their noses up on the rest of Europe. Not the world, mind you. The rest of the world was too far beneath them to ever be in the vicinity of their noses.

As he climbed higher, breath still solid, heart rate the equivalent of a mild workout, Duke couldn't understand where that universal disdain was coming from. It wasn't like him, seeing only the bad in everyone. If it turned out to be his new self then he'd have to make amends.

"Good afternoon," another pair of hikers said in unison in a very Germanic accent. Fighting the instinctive feeling, Duke considered first.

"Good afternoon," he said. "Mind your step over there, it's particularly icy underneath the thin layer of snow."

"Thank you!"

And they both smiled at him. For whatever reason, that made him feel better to some degree. It didn't matter how people were back home when they were working stupid day jobs, running errands and paying their bills. What mattered was the here and then and the now. Nothing mattered more than the now, the moment right ahead. It dawned on Duke that, if he lost the ability to cherish the moment, he'd end up bitter and sad and he'd see himself reduced to a shadow of his former self. Even in light of recent events, there was no way he could allow that. Thinking of Emily solidified the notion.

When he turned around to the city from halfway up to the summit, he could already enjoy a splendid view of Edinburgh. From Arthur's Seat, it looked much different than from Carlton Hill. Edinburgh looked like a purer version of itself. It was almost like looking through time. To the days that – purportedly – were easier. This gave Duke peace of mind. Enough strength to climb to the top.

Snow crunched underneath his soles. The boots held him on track. The physical strain only occurred to him when he unzipped his jacket and a cloud of vapor escaped. The ascent had taken more out of him than he'd anticipated. Something else he had to keep in mind. There was always more to be had, even if you didn't feel quite like it. On that attitude, the rest of the climb felt like a breeze and was done in no time.

There were strong winds up at the summit but they carried the freshest of air, making up for the coldness. People were snapping pictures, posing for their social media and family photobooks, none of which Duke had any interest in. Even if there was no solitude to be had on Arthur's Seat, he enjoyed the moment.

"Could you please take a picture of me and my boyfriend?" a very Swedish woman asked.

"With pleasure," Duke replied with a smile, making sure that all of Edinburgh Castle was in frame when he snapped the picture. Just to be on the safe side.

"Thank you so much," the not-so-Swedish-looking guy said, tall and slender and no trace of blonde hair or blue eyes. "Can I ask you something?"

"Shoot."

That confused him but he nevertheless continued on the assumption that Duke had said something appropriate.

"Is there anything we should 100 percent do during our visit to Edinburgh?"

"Sure. Have haggis at Edinburgh Castle. You're not going to regret that."

They laughed, apparently thinking it was a joke. Duke didn't intent on making himself clearer than he already had.

At the edge of the summit, you could look out over the ocean, drown out the voices around you, be for yourself in the midst of an abundance of people. Jamal's words came back to him. Eventually, he'd have to go there. Go see the bitch. If she knew something, or worse, if she was trying to set him up, they'd have to sit down and talk.

14

It was funny how people could pretend to be dumb, or dumber, rather, than they actually were, in the face of facts or pressure. Dialing the number had been much too easy, and Roman knew whoever he was chasing had the basic intelligence to record incoming calls. Asking for a man by his name sounded equally easy. Only it wasn't when people were trying to play him like a fool.

Two days and nights, looking for the man, assuming that someone must've known the name. But no, nothing there. Maybe he was on another alias now, depending on the circles he usually moved in. Maybe Roman was wrong and a man of that caliber wouldn't crawl any night clubs at all.

"Looking for prey elsewhere," he said to himself, needing to hear words uttered by an intelligent person for a change.

"What was that?" the girl in her early twenties spending her father's money asked.

Putting the screws on those overgrown children hadn't worked. If there was no character or integrity to be crushed, there was no point trying in the first place. Being nice would have to yield better results.

"You know the guy, don't you?" Roman asked her back. At least she'd had the basic decency of taking care of her physique.

"What's he to you?" she asked, still dancing. It was hilarious. Several guys were trying to dance up on her but Roman blocked the way quite effectively, looking like a picture hung from a nine-inch nail.

"Everything. He owes me money."

"You break my heart."

"I want to give this back to him in return for the payment," Roman said and pulled out an old Swiss wristwatch. "It's his father's. Gave it to me as security. His old man just died. I'm sure he'll want it back."

None of this evoked any feelings in her. One of the young guns tapped Roman's shoulder, trying to persuade him to leave but finding himself dissuaded.

"That guy was cute," she then complained to Roman. "Would you please stop freaking everybody out?"

Roman pocketed the watch.

"As you wish. Tell me where I can find him."

For whatever reason exclusively her own, she considered what to do. And then she felt, what the hell, deciding to give something to Roman to get rid of him.

"Okay," she said and stopped dancing. "If you're looking for a guy like that, why don't you go talk to Rayne? She's in tonight."

"Where?"

She pointed at the VIP-section, guarded by watchdogs and baboons.

"Over there. Ask for her. And please, get the hell out of my way."

The second she started dancing again, picking up the vibe as if nothing had ever happened, as if there was nothing to worry about in the world for anyone, the knights of a new generation pushed their way past Roman. This time, he let them, leaving without saying anything else this young, spoiled brat wasn't deserving of.

Rayne. Not a new name to him. More like a legend. A myth. None of the things Roman had heard seemed to suggest a very becoming set of qualities. With authority, he marched right at the VIP-section, tainted in purple and blue light. The baboons found themselves almost tricked when Roman went past them without saying a word.

"Hold it right there, sucker," one of them wearing a poorly-fitting Armani suit uttered, grabbing Roman by the collar. He stopped.

"Let go," Roman told him.

"Where do you think you're going?"

"Let go."

They laughed at that.

"Last chance. Where do you think you're going?"

"See Rayne."

"You're crazy."

"No, you are. Last warning."

"Drake, can you believe this– "

The wrist broke with a snap loud enough to ring over the blasting acid techno music like a sound effect. Baboon #1 now had other fish to fry, with no right hand in service. Baboon #2 took a swing that caught nothing but air, then got two jabs in the kidneys, serving him well. The blows knocked the wind out of him. Roman caught him.

"It's nothing personal, buddy. I'm not doing anything to her. Just talk."

A pat on the shoulder, and Roman helped him sit down at a wrap-around couch on a table with the most beautiful girls pretending to be some rich guy's girlfriends, snoring at him and telling him to get lost.

Nobody else dared stepping in Roman's way as he crossed the VIP-section. In the far back, she sat with her arms around two slender boys that were girlishly pretty but seemed not to be much older than eighteen, if at all. Even in the stark contrast of age, she looked very attractive. But you could tell she was almost three-times as old as her company and not as young as she so actively tried to appear.

"What a show," Rayne said when Roman stopped in front of her table, folding his hands behind his back.

"My apologies for the mess," he said. "His wrist will heal up just fine in a matter of six weeks if set correctly."

"I'll let somebody else concern themselves with that. He'll receive his last paycheck tonight."

"No room for failure?"

"No room for failure."

"Seems like that principle is working out for you."

"I could say the same about you, Roman."

"If you think that's going to shock me, think again. I've had my work cut out for me. Made a name for myself. Count to two and you'll see who I really am."

"Touché."

This seemed to have lightened her attitude towards him, at least some. Rayne took another sip off her Cosmopolitan before leaning forward, smiling.

"I'm looking for someone," Roman continued.

"The guy that butchered those two girls."

"Trying to trick me again."

"Maybe I know a bit more about it than the papers said."

"Conceivable."

"Maybe I also know a guy that's got a taste for young girls and even more so when they're green and blue from beating."

This time, Roman smiled.

"Seriously, do we have to go through this?"

"If you don't want my help, fine. I could think of better things to waste my time on other than yelling at you over this music."

"Like dancing."

"Or having a drink."

"Or hustling teenage boys."

"Better watch your tongue now. Should you prefer to keep it."

"I sure will. Now that I've got your attention."

"Okay, then," she said and finished her drink in one gulp. "Let's boogie, Mr. Sykes."

"That wife beater who's got nothing to say at home is none of my business. I'm looking for someone you might know."

"Ah, you're hired muscle. Let me guess, some rich daddy didn't like his innocent little angel whoring around New Town and ending up with a guy that'll only get it up when he's pouring blood over her."

"Bingo."

"What's my prize?"

"The ease of mind that our community will always be grateful."

"Buh. I'm not the rozzers. Or the Salvation Army."

"But you know guys with, let's say, strikingly similar CVs."

"What're you trying to get at?"

"I'll make it easy. Where's Duke Arrowsmith."

Hearing the name hit her, but it was all a front. A nice act she put up in disguise. All this was a theater performance. It disgusted Roman a great deal. In retrospect, starving with sixty pounds of baggage on his shoulders and getting eaten by bugs in the jungle didn't seem like a bad deal anymore.

"Duke..."

"Duke. Yeah."

"Such a pretty boy."

"I wouldn't contest that."

"Talented, too."

"Otherwise, he'd have found a different occupation past 30."

"If there's anyone I always favored in my heart, it's Duke Arrowsmith. Please, sit down and have a drink with me, Roman."

The young man to her left was waved off. Roman took a seat. Two Cosmos were served right away. Nobody had asked Roman what he wanted to drink. Reluctantly, he lifted the glass, thinking it for a rather girlish drink.

"To him," Roman said, toasting.

"To Duke. Cheers."

"Interesting."

"You like it?"

"No. And as much as I love listening to you reminiscing of the good old times, I've had it with horsing around for one night."

"I don't know where he is," Rayne said setting down the glass. The boy to her right was getting increasingly uneasy.

"You're not talking on the phone on a weekly basis?"

"He cut all ties with me."

"The ungrateful, lost son."

"That's what he is. Forgot where he came from, hanging around in the streets, down in Leith where he was another nothing like the rest of them."

"You picked him up, offered him an alternative."

"I taught him everything he knows!" she suddenly burst out. "And the moment he thinks he's big enough to stand by himself and steal my customers, he walks. No thank you. No goodbye. Gone with the wind."

"Not quite. He's still in town."

"Old Town. New Town. University, from what I hear."

"Oh, you hear about him?"

Something about that made her reconsider. Maybe it was the realization that talking emotionally on a whim wasn't the best agenda.

"People talk."

"Where was he? Last time people talked?"

"National Museum. Someone saw him."

"When?"

"Two or three days ago. Maybe a week, I don't really remember."

"Who was he with?"

"Some prime beef."

"You're funny."

"Classy lady. Major League."

"Good for him."

"Bad for you?"

"Uh-huh."

"Keiran, why won't you go to bed, you're cold to the touch. I'll be right there."

Keiran, the young man way in over his head, got up from the table without a word, working his way through the people, mingling with the crowd, soon to be gone.

"Nice fella," Roman said. "He's got a bright future ahead of himself."

"Come over here, Mr. Sykes. I got something to say not meant for anyone else's ears."

Wondering who'd ever eavesdrop on them in that location, Roman did as asked. Sliding up close, he wasn't surprised when Rayne put a hand on his neck first, then forced her lips on his. It was the most professional and skilled kiss Roman ever received. It was also the most lifeless kiss, too.

"Nice tongue work," he said when she released him, signaling the end of another act.

"If you're looking for Duke, you should be looking for the red Lotus. You'll hear that rattling and humming darn thing coming for a mile."

"My pleasure, Rayne. Thanks for the Cosmo."

Roman got up on his own accord, planted a kiss on her cheek and left. Blue and purple light was dancing over his face, acid techno music blaring, messing with his senses.

15

The first thing Kate asked Emily when she walked in on time, but cutting it close, was if she'd seen the stud hitting on her. Emily swiftly informed her it was none of her business, adding she should go buy a tabloid if she cared for gossip, wondering about her uncharacteristically short fuze.

"Relax," Kate answered, disgruntled. "I didn't ask if he was hung or anything."

"Fine," Emily replied. To end it. Even though she'd had other things to say to Kate, the go-easy, easy to have halfwit that looked good at 23 but already showed signs of future decay, and would clearly have to marry some unsuspecting slob before 30 to avoid being sidelined.

The café was busy, and as Emily smelled her spare t-shirt, noticing the odor of manual labor, she decided it wouldn't matter. On her looks, nobody really cared. It was a typical day at a typical café, serving very typical coffee. Even if she'd praised the Angel Stain to Duke, Emily knew about its mediocrity. It was nothing special, and it never could be, since the beans weren't special, the espresso machine wasn't special, and the girls drawing it even less so.

"Enjoy your cheesecake," she said with a smile to an elderly lady, dressed elegantly to disguise her loneliness.

"I will," the lady replied. "It's the best in town."

"Oh, thank you so much for saying that."

"Kudos to the pâtissier."

"I'll give them your regards," Emily said and walked off, back past the counter before anyone else could place an order. As much as she depended on tips, this just wasn't the day to cash in on the simple facts of life, like people finding her attractive and sympathetic. Two very arbitrary qualities usually associated for no rational reason at all.

"What did she say?" Kate asked, looking for a conversation at gunpoint.

"That the cheesecake tastes like cat shit."

"Screw you. You know that my brother is making the cakes?"

"Then maybe she should apologize to him. Or he starts making better cake."

"Bitch."

"Love you too, Kate."

Emily blew her a kiss. To make matters worse. Kate stomped off, banging a plate of hash browns down on the table in front of a man sunk deep into his phone, noticing nothing.

At first it was beyond her why she couldn't help being rude to Kate, the rest of the staff and even some customers. And then it dawned on her. Admitting to her feelings and emotions had always been tough on Emily. But this time, she knew there was no way out. Somehow, she knew Duke was in a pinch. No matter what, she'd help him out of it. At all cost.

"Another Angel Stain for table 5!" Kate snapped at her.

"In a minute," Emily replied taking her phone out.

When she hoped for news from Duke, a short text, a workshop picture, even a Gif he found funny, Emily was disappointed. Over a dozen unread messages, plus some alerts from the dating apps she'd engaged in for a while but found nobody interesting on. But nothing from Duke. It boiled down to that. Emily sighed.

"Chai Latte for table 3!" Kate snapped at her.

"In a minute," Emily replied, starting to text.

Whatever she was conjuring sounded adequate at first, then dull, then silly and inappropriate. It took her four attempts until she arrived at something: All a grind at the café, looking forward to spending the evening with you. Of course, it was foolish expecting an answer right back but as much as she knew, it still affected her. From then on, the day was a much harder grind, with the ugly Scandinavian faux-mid-century clock on the wall seemingly turning backward.

The best Emily could do was plan what to take and what to leave when she went to her room after work and manage dealing with the customers, regardless of how uninterested she felt in their needs. Kate wouldn't talk, or even as much as look at her for the remained of their shift. Something at last Emily condoned.

"Can you put in other hour?" Sarah, the shop manager asked when Emily removed her apron on time. It was a phrase she beat to death repeatedly. Emily knew that, would she agree, the arrangement was more of an open ending rather than a favor for a given amount of time.

"Can't. Gotta catch a seminar back at U."

"This late in the afternoon?"

"I'll be back for my shift in two days."

"Can't you stay? We really need you."

"You don't need me, you need anyone doing this shit job, Sarah. So please, stop this BS already."

The customers started looking at them at the counter, which made Sarah a whole lot more uncomfortable than Emily. For Emily, this didn't mean anything. That moment, she understood how much she'd disliked this gig from the get go, and how being strapped for money had kept her from doing things more productive, and much more conducive to her future life.

"Emily," Sarah said almost in a whisper, "how dare you talking to me like that in front of the customers?"

"How dare you asking me to stay because you couldn't adhere to the simplest of agreements? I'm out of here."

"If you walk now, you might as well stay gone."

"I'll grab my gear and wait for my last payment."

When she realized she meant it, Sarah followed Emily to the makeshift locker and change room in the hallway connecting the café with the kitchen. But Emily wouldn't have any of her pleading and babbling, asking her to cut it out already when she changed back into her t-shirt and put on a heavy sweater to protect her from the drizzle and cold outside. Then she stuffed the few belongings she'd stashed at the locker into her backpack and slammed the metal door shut, breaking the already flimsy hinge hanging on by a threat.

Walking out the back door, Emily didn't feel like she'd lost anything, or even pushed her luck. It never occurred to her that losing that job might present her with any trouble in the foreseeable future. By contrast, she smiled when she zipped her coat up right to the neck. Cold air filled her lungs, refreshing her.

It was a short walk to Fountainbridge, where she shared a subterranean flat with two girls she'd never really cared for. They were agreeably tidy, if not clean. And they barely ever ate any of her food from the fridge. Asking any more would've been delusional. Trying not to slip on the stairs leading down some eight feet below street level, maybe nine, Emily wondered why it didn't feel like coming home after a hard day's work. The flat was cold and the wind was piping through openings in the window frames. It smelled old and the ancient wood popped and creaked, sometimes waking her at night. The city of Edinburgh hadn't changed much since the 19th century. A fact you could either cherish or abhor. When you were cold and lonely, unaware of how much money exactly was left in the bank, feeling like a Victorian Age hooker wasn't much to write home about.

"Who's that?" Christie asked from the kitchen the second she heard the lock jingling.

"It's Emily."

"Hi there. Ate your papaya, awfully sorry. I'll buy a fresh one."

"Don't bother," Emily said, thinking the papaya cost about five pounds and hating her for eating it as if it was nothing. All Emily wanted was a moment for herself, minutes she wouldn't have to consider anything. The second she fell into her unmade bed and closed her eyes, Christie poked her head in the door, beaming.

"Didn't see you in a while. Got around?"

"Sort of."

"It's a fun time to be alive, really. Lots of parties around town."

"Some red-themed specials, too."

"I was wondering if we should get something going around the apartment. Rub shoulders with some friendly people, see?"

"Uh-huh."

"Alex isn't in town so I just wanted to know what your plans were for Friday night and if you'd help me go buy some drinks and some snacks, nothing fancy, just the ordinary. And– "

"Christie?"

"Yeah."

"I won't be here on Friday. And frankly, I'm not sure if I'm ever coming back. So please, do whatever the freakin' hell you want. But get the hell out of my face, won't you? You spoiled, stupid goose."

The last sentence had been added without any attention at all. Yet Emily had said it anyway, putting Christie off much more than she'd expected from someone so shallow-minded. Whatever it was she said and threw at Emily, it was beyond her. An eternity had elapsed when Christie finally left. But the peace was gone. Even if she tried, Emily knew there was no appeal to relaxation anymore.

The room was small and very impersonal, she noticed that only then, scanning for what was worth being taken. It finally dawned on her how she'd been spending her time after entering college. Or rather, how she'd been wasting the precious time, working a tedious, menial job, partying and dating guys not worth a dime, least so their weight in gold. Everything she saw filled her with anxiety, pushed a void farther into her. It was tough snapping out of it.

"Don't bother," she told herself, getting to work at the built-in wardrobe, putting her crinkly but at least clean clothes on the still unmade bed in some kind of order. On the top shelf, she spotted a gigantic backpack, once bought for a trip to the Highlands or the Lofoten or wherever, which never materialized. In part because Emily had never taken the time, but primarily because she hated everything about hiking and camping and rolling around in a rusted-out Volkswagen van.

The only upside about that abomination of a backpack was that all the clothes she cared for fit inside it. Once that was done, she stuffed her laptop in the backpack as well. Then she took another look around, understanding there was virtually nothing else inside the room. The carpet hadn't been cleaned in a while, not vacuumed either, and only then she saw the many stains, feeling comfortable about only being responsible for a few of them. All her life in Edinburgh fit in one backpack she hated with passion, noticing with disdain the very strong and artificial plasticky smell it still omitted.

But that life in Edinburgh was all she had, since she'd left that other life behind, burning as many bridges as she'd felt fit at that time. Too many to be proud of, knowing the damage had been done but then again, understanding that nothing was irreversible. Retroactive amends presented yet another problem for another day.

Ready to go, Emily did what she always did for a last step when she was checking out of a hotel room. The idea of leaving something behind, even the smallest and trivial thing such as a toothbrush or a stained, crumbled sock, strangely filled her with unease. The room was quickly scanned, with nothing left unintentionally. Checking underneath the bed was saved for last, and when Emily kneeled down and lifted the blanket, she was surprised to spot something. It didn't feel like seeing an old friend in an unsuspecting crowd, poking out of the masses of a strange and alien city like a nail out of a coffin. It should've felt that way, and when Emily realized, she felt tears dripping down her cheeks, warm and salty, almost like vinegar to her skin.

The small bag had a leather strap and she pulled at it, retrieving it from underneath the bed. Sitting down, she wiped the tears only for new salty drops to well. Then she unzipped the bag, finding what she now expected. It was a Japanese camera with three lenses, the one her late grandfather bought maybe two years before his passing. A jet black housing, free of scratches or blemishes. It looked like new. That was characteristic of her grandpa, a man who had always taken great care of everything. Or rather, the few things in his possession he cared about.

Emily took it out, traced its lines with her fingers, taking in its scent. A scent she couldn't place but reminded her of her grandpa. Sean, a name she never used for him, that had been replaced even long before she was born. The lens hooked to the camera was of medium size. 35 mm was printed on it, somewhat embossed.

Back when Emily was a young girl, Grandpa had taken her sometimes, out to the lake or the woods or a small coastal town of his choosing, anywhere really where they could spend a relaxed day in fall, when the weather was still nice during the day. Much nicer than in summer, for the air smelled fresh and of fallen leaves, and you knew any warmth would have to be cherished, since it would get cold in the evenings. Cold enough for your breath to condense and form clouds of vapor when they walked back to the car in falling darkness.

It had never really occurred to her there was anything special about Grandpa taking his camera and snapping pictures of anything he found pretty enough to preserve on film. Film had been his choice for much of his life, the pictures hidden inside a black box until he brought them to existence at his basement studio, with the red light bulb in the corner and all the liquids it took for the process, an unpleasant smell to it Emily had never minded when she'd stood at his side. The smell came right back to her first, then the scent of her grandpa's hands, stronger and much more pleasant, when he'd taken her into his arms every time he'd spotted the gem out of the bunch. The one photograph that had made it all worth the while.

The digital world had never been for him, but during his final years he'd softened up, realizing his detachment with his children and many grandchildren. Not that he'd gotten himself a computer. The old Olivetti typewriter had sufficed him until the end of his life. But this camera had been the last bridge he'd built. Nobody had claimed it when they had cleared out the small house and when Emily's father had found it, he'd given it to her.

"Take good care of it," he'd said. "Grandpa would've wanted you to have it."

The words rang back and forth in her ears, as if her father was standing right next to her, saying them again. Emily turned the camera around in her hands, not fighting the tears anymore, only making sure they wouldn't drip on the only thing she'd still left of her beloved Grandpa. Take good care of it, she suddenly thought and felt ashamed of herself. What great care she'd taken of it, throwing it underneath the bed to get it out of the way and forget about it. It took her a moment to come to terms with it.

And when she'd forgiven herself enough to go on, she tried switching it on, not at all surprised it wouldn't start. The camera had been sitting there for a while and certainly, the battery was dead. Emily popped it out, fished for the charger inside the bag, then plugged it in. A green light started flashing, indicating the battery wasn't broken. But what if the camera is, she asked herself. What if it won't start on a fresh charge. The idea concerned her, even when she went to the bathroom collecting her toiletries and appliances. Christie spotted her from the kitchen but looked away quickly.

There wasn't much else to take, Emily realized. Most of the inventory was second-hand or handed-down crap they'd scored somewhere, nothing anyone would ever care about. Back at her room, Emily stuffed the rest of her belongings in a plastic shopping bag first, then into the backpack. It still had some room to spare but there was nothing else she would take.

The camera's charger was still flashing green, and the battery wasn't on a full charge when she yanked it off and popped it back into the compartment. This time, the camera started right up. Emily sighed in relief.

"Thank God," she said to herself.

Two more lenses were stored inside the bag, one big and clunky, with 50-230 mm printed where the one hooked to the camera had 35 mm. The other one read 15-45 mm and was of comparable size. None of this meant anything to Emily. With the camera replaced in its bag, she first slung the backpack over her shoulders, then the camera. The last thing she did was check her phone. Some more messages, none from Duke. Emily sighed again, turned off the lights and left the apartment without saying goodbye to Christie. Christie, who was blasting R&B music over a Bluetooth speaker in the kitchen, yet another shadow soon blurred in Emily's memory.

Stockbridge was cold and gray and Emily almost slipped on the stairs on her way up, cursing because she would've hated breaking the camera. Traffic was scarce. Somewhere up in the clouds it looked like it would clear up. Only when she'd walked down to the corner did she wonder where she was going. The way back to Duke's place on the outskirts of town was clear inside her head, and still she had to pause and reconsider.

Whatever she came up with seemed like an incoherent thought. Nothing made much sense. Then she remembered there was a class in university but quickly abandoned the idea actually attending it. It seemed even more foolish than ever before. Then she asked herself what she would do without a degree to her name in this world, wondering who would hire her and why, and her heart started racing. Still, just going there and attending class was impossible. And that was the end of it.

With no other thought on her mind, she checked her phone again as she waited on the bus, a bunch of young guns chatting about her on the other side of the road, where they were standing in front of a kebab place that looked both fishy and sketchy. When the bus rolled to the stop, Emily was glad she didn't have to deal with those clowns, not like other times when she had to fend them off. Vigorously, sometimes.

The people on the bus were a cross-section through society. Whatever that implied. It was unusual for Emily feeling odd and out of place in public spaces. To give herself something to do and occupy her hands, she produced the camera and started exploring it. Cameras were terra incognita for her, and even when she leafed through the many menus she hadn't expected to find, she wasn't making much progress.

"Nice Fuji," a guy sitting across from her said.

He was in his thirties and showing signs of utter neglect. Only faintly could one have imagined him handsome in his teens or his early twenties. The days when a healthy and fair-looking body was more or less free.

"Thanks," she said automatically instead of pretending she hadn't heard him. It instantly dawned on her it was an invitation for a talk or flirting.

"I'm a Sony guy myself," he continued. "Always been. Maybe it's because I loved the first Playstation when it came out."

"Oh," Emily replied without looking up from the camera.

"You see, anyone can take pictures these days with their phones but they quickly fall apart when you know what you're talking about."

"That's true."

"It's been a while since I've been out with my Sony. Expensive thing I wanted and got for Christmas some years back but barely ever used it."

"Uh-huh."

"Are you a local or are you visiting Edinburgh."

"That's my stop," Emily said when the bus slowed on Princes Street, getting up and forcing a smile as not to put him off, making her way to the mechanical doors at the front, walking as if she were aboard a ship in a heavy storm.

The guy said nothing, and when Emily checked on him in the bus driver's rearview mirror, she noted he was looking at the people on the sidewalk.

Princes Street hadn't been in her plans but once the bus had gotten to a stop she almost jumped out and started walking. Suddenly, the crowd around her felt a lot more comfortable and safe.

Some homeless people were sitting in front of the hotel at the station, out in the cold as always. On the other side of the road was Waverley Hotel, catching Emily's attention. It seemed worth a try, so she lifted the camera, checking the viewfinder, finding it black. That wouldn't change when she pulled off the lens cap. The image appeared on screen but she knew it was impossible getting a good shot like that. Like that, you'd leave it to luck entirely, Grandpa used to say.

There was a small button next to the viewfinder. Out of curiosity, she pressed it, checked again and there it was. Somehow, the camera was set to show her info on screen she couldn't process, so Emily just snapped a picture and checked it on the bigger screen.

It looked decent. The skies above Edinburgh had been captured nicely, if not accurately. With more skill, this could've been helped. Skills she didn't have. What she could amend was framing the hotel right. For that, Emily had to cross the street and almost got run over by a speeding car. The driver lay on the horn, giving her the finger.

"Same to you!" she called out as he sped off, window rolled down and cursing at her.

While trying to get the right frame Emily remembered bits and pieces Grandpa had always shared with her. How to offset framed objects and using angles to give more depth to the scene. Within a couple of shots, she improved her results drastically.

The last shot she took seemed nice, and for the first time that day, she had a smile on her face. Something to be satisfied with. Even if it wasn't much.

But when she lowered the camera, she almost froze. The guy from the bus was giving some change to a homeless man in front of the station. It's not him, she tried convincing herself right away. Hands shaky all of a sudden, she lifted the camera again but couldn't focus on anything. In the corner of her left eye, she saw him when he turned for the briefest of moments. It was him, alright.

The day quickly faded back to a much darker shade of gray, even darker than it was before. Wondering if confronting him would solve anything, Emily decided against it. As she walked, starting down towards Carlton Hill, she told herself it was nothing but coincidence.

The world around her appeared normal, people walking and talking, minding their own business. Nobody seemed to take notice of Emily. Less so of anyone walking behind her.

The pathway up the hill was iced over, and there were fewer and fewer people. For a while, Emily didn't dare looking over her shoulder, clinging on to the camera, feeling the weight of the backpack dragging her down. Taking her breath. It was steep and every time her shoes lost grip on the ice, gaining back her balance cost her some more energy. Halfway up, she had to pause, looking down.

There he was. Standing some thirty yards away from her, looking right up at her. As if he had all the right in the world chasing her, scaring her. Even from the distance, Emily could tell his eyes were dark. Almost black. That moment, it seemed like the devil himself was on her trail.

Go away! She wanted to say but nothing came.

What would it have changed? Soon, the sun would be setting, worsening the already imminent problem Emily had. With the way back down blocked, all she could do was climb up Carlton Hill as quickly as possible. And hope for a bunch of people visiting the summit. It never occurred to her calling for help.

The farther she made it up, the better her technique got, preventing her from slipping, even though it got icier closer to the summit. Checking on her persecutor would've proven difficult. There was no need, either. Emily could feel him, sneaking up on her, closing in on her, almost as if she could feel his warm breath on her neck already.

When she finally made it to the meadow on the summit of Carlton Hill, Emily was relieved to see people, if only for a moment. In desperate need for a rest and catching her breath, she started to run as fast as she managed toward the National Monument.

At one time, she saw a tourist couple looking her way but when she wanted to call out to them, nothing came. The ascend had taken the rest of the wind out of her, leaving her throat bone-dry and sticky at the same time. A strong, cold wind made her realize her clothes were soaked through with sweat.

In front of the gigantic stone structure mimicking an ancient ruin, Emily fell into a cough, unable to run anymore. The second she turned around she was prepared for anything. A blow to the head as much as hands closing around her throat like a vise. A fight. In awe, she realized there was nobody there. Was it all a figment of her imagination? Impossible. Simply impossible. The man from the bus had been chasing her. Nobody would ever convince her of the opposite.

"Excuse me," someone asked from behind her, making her freeze. Emily didn't realize the heavy accent.

Slowly, she turned around, sighing in relief when she understood it was the couple she'd spotted before, the woman holding a phone in her direction.

"Yes?"

"Would you please take a picture of me and my boyfriend in front of the town?"

With pleasure, Emily did as asked. They thanked her at least fifty times, complimenting on the nice camera she still had dangling from her neck. All exhaustion kicked in at once, and Emily sank down on the cold stone steps, facing city center.

With her pants soggy, she couldn't feel the cold at first but it quickly made its way through, all the way to her bones. Emily started freezing even before she'd caught her breath.

Checking for people to the left and right, she saw at least two dozen tourists. The first time she tried getting up, the weight of the backpack pushed her right down again, her legs still too tired. A drink of water would've helped her but she didn't bring any. The second time she pushed herself up, it went smoothly. And then she felt a strong pair of hands, pushing her back down.

"Take some more rest," a dark voice whispered right into her left ear, sending the worst shivers right through her, all her hair standing up straight. All strength was gone from her.

"It's alright," he added, his warm breath on Emily's earlobe, ruffling her hair. "There's nothing to be afraid of."

"What do you want?" Emily managed to say, her voice weak and almost imploring. Hearing the powerlessness in herself made her sick to the stomach.

"I want to be nice to you. Do you a favor. Don't say you don't want me to."

"I don't want you to."

"Poor thing. Look at you. Your dark blonde hair, like honey. Like a field of wheat just before harvesting season. Gosh, how it smells. Beautiful."

Emily imagined him with his eyes closed when he inhaled all of her sweat-infused odor, her hair pulled to his nostrils. She didn't cry. She couldn't cry.

"You're sick. You're a sick man."

"It's not me who's sick. It's the world that allows an angel like you to go to pieces."

"You know nothing about me."

"Darling, I'm a wolf. I know everything I need to know from sniffing you."

"Sick."

"You contracted the disease of our time."

"Deranged."

"It can be helped."

"I know someone who's going to help you."

"Your boyfriend?"

"A real man."

"Not like me?"

"No."

"What am I?"

"Clown."

"Welcome to the circus rink."

He closed his fist around Emily's shoulder-long hair, pulling her neck down. Not yanking at it, but pulling it down with force. Like the reins of a horse.

"I'll tell him about you."

"What's he going to do about it? He and his little pecker?"

"Show you what it means being a man."

He giggled at that, his breath reeking of coffee and red meat.

"Why won't you come to my favorite place? See what it's like being safe and sound. Be a woman again. Here, take this– "

"That's been plenty," a man boomed from right in front of Emily.

Even though she'd been looking straight up, she hadn't seen him coming. Not even the city in the background, framing the scene. All her thoughts had been occupied by the man blowing his breath down her neck and ear and cheek, with a firm grip on her hair.

"Mind your own business."

"Let go of her. Slowly and carefully."

"Or what? You call the hounds of hell upon me?"

"No."

Something about the way he'd said it made the perpetrator reconsider. Talking tough was one thing. Somehow, you knew if someone wasn't only talking smack but could back it. When Emily mustered him, her fears slowly dispersed. His build wouldn't suggest it but here was a man you'd think twice before messing with.

"Mind your own business."

"I make it mine."

"You'll regret this."

"Make me."

He pushed Emily aside, a charge out of the blue, almost making her fall over face-first onto the stone slabs. Despite her limited knowledge on fighting, Emily could tell this stranger coming for her help was experienced. The perpetrator found himself charging at cold air, like a bull missing the torero.

Cursing, he charged again, swinging wildly, catching nothing but air. This was Emily's chance to escape but instead, she straightened herself, watching with growing fascination. No blow ever connected with the mysterious stranger.

Not landing his punches took a lot out of the perpetrator, making him gasp for air.

"Defend yourself!" he demanded.

"As you wish."

A series of blows found his way, handed out much quicker than Emily could've kept track of. The last one drew blood, a thin red line running down the perpetrator's nose.

"You broke my nose, you son of a bitch!"

"Give it up. Punk."

"You made a big mistake."

"How come? You suck."

"Suck this."

And then he drew a stub-nosed pistol from his coat's pocket, cocking it while aiming. But he didn't aim at the man that had broken his nose. He aimed at Emily.

The barrel of the gun was several yards away but it seemed to her as if she was looking right down it, to where the drum was holding five soft-tipped bullets. The world switched to slow-motion, like a movie's climax meticulously drawn out for effect. There was no way of telling if Emily had enough time to react.

The weight on the trigger increased. To a point where a shot was imminent. But there was no shot, no loud bang, no flash of lightning cutting through the air, followed by rolling thunder. No bright lights and sudden blackness, when a bullet ate its way through her head.

The pistol dropped. A red gush dripped on the grass, clogging and freezing solid on the icy ground right away. Only when he yelped in pain and started running did Emily see the knife poking out from his right forearm. The pain must've triggered a very primitive flight instinct as he ran towards the observatory, a red trail marking his route.

"Bloody hell," the mysterious man said, then turned his attention to Emily. "Are you alright?"

"Yes."

"No shot was fired."

"I know."

"I'll secure the gun."

The gun looked even tinier in his big hands. It made you wonder how something as fragile-looking as this could take a life on a whim. He opened the drum and shook the bullets in his palm, pocketing them first, then decocked the pistol. All of this he did with the ease of a thoroughbred professional.

"Thanks for helping me out," Emily said getting up, feeling her strength returning.

"Saw him sneaking up on you. My two cents on it were that something wasn't kosher."

"And you always carry a throwing knife?"

"It's not a throwing life. It's like a k-bar."

"Like the Marines' knife."

"Exactly. How do you know?"

"My Grandpa had one."

"Now that guy has one too."

"Hope it wasn't a collectible."

"Certainly a tad rarer than a Japanese kitchen knife."

"You carry another knife?"

"There's nothing to be afraid of. It's a sick world and a sick town."

"That's what the guy said."

"Only he's the disease, not the remedy. I heard about some strange things going on."

"So did I."

"You need something? A doctor? Cops?"

"To report what exactly?"

"Give a description of the guy."

"Your name. For starters."

"Samaritan."

"Funny. I'm Emily."

"Roman."

"Like in Roman Empire?"

"Exactly."

"You look kind of familiar. As if I'd seen you before. Roman."

"I'm busy all over town."

"Maybe. Maybe not. Anyway, I'm cold. And tired."

"I'm not offering to take you home. All I'm saying is, should you need someone to testify, call."

What he handed to her was a slip of paper, supposed to look sloppy but ripped carefully from a sheet of printing paper. A telephone number was scrawled onto it in almost indecipherable handwriting.

"I'll consider it," Emily said taking the slip of paper. "Until then, I'll try and clear my head."

"Take some rest. I'll go hunt for my knife."

"Follow the dotted line," Emily said and turning on the camera, taking a snapshot of an ice-cold Edinburgh from the top of Carlton Hill.

16

This hadn't gone as planned. Not a bit. Tracking down Arrowsmith and making a connection to someone he was seeing who wasn't one of his regulars had been a challenge. And now that he'd followed her, that creep had showed up. That she'd seen him, knew his name now, was more than just an unpleasantry.

But then, what could have been done, other than intervening and preventing something worse from happening. Roman kept hearing the call of duty, no matter what. The girl was tough, he'd give her that. A tough cookie for her age, more so considering the times she was brought up in. He'd pick up her trace later.

First, he chased away a tourist couple trying to score instagrammable content on the Scottish National Monument. Rather blatantly, that is. One of them had stomped on the evidence but the brown footprint was a minor stain at best. They called him names in a foreign language, or so Roman assumed.

"Go tell someone else," he said waving them off.

The second Roman picked up the evidence he knew it must've been something. A dark red business card with letters in champagne gold. Burgundy Bobcat, it said. Plus, a number: 10558420. Neither an address nor a phone number.

Feeling the cold, Roman put the business card in his wallet and left the scene. The trace of blood ended at the foot of Carlton Hill. Right at a deserted parking space, fresh tire tracks leading out of town. While he could've tried figuring out what tire thread it was, and potentially find the corresponding car, Roman wasn't in the mood. There was no shortage of utility knives in his collection, contrary to what he'd said. A friend of his made them for fun and almost gave them away. Roman knew he'd eventually stumble over that guy again so it wasn't his priority getting his knife back right away.

At a café, he got himself hot breakfast tea and a croissant that tasted very much like cardboard. The waitress was a real looker. She seemed interested in Roman. Every time she tried meeting his gaze, he looked away. First, women meant trouble. Second, she was just too young. Claiming that she wasn't attractive enough would've been a blatant lie. Only discipline had a restraining effect on him. An old man taking a young girl's heart was selfish and foolish.

"Anything else I could get you?" the waitress asked beaming right at him.

"No."

"No?"

"No, thanks."

"I remember seeing you here two weeks ago."

"Maybe."

"Seems you like it here."

"Not the worst."

"Not the worst," she repeated and laughed. "Nobody's ever said that before."

"My apologies."

"I accept. But there's a condition. I wanna know what you're apologizing for."

That slender body, maintained physique, a bit more muscular than your average model-type, the long, dark-blonde hair. Hard not to look. Not to be sold on it. Eventually, he managed.

"I apologize for intentionally being rude to you."

"I was right assuming it was a scheme?"

"You were."

"Never mind."

Roman pulled a twenty-pound bill out and put it on the counter as he got up.

"Didn't work. Sorry."

It got cold on the instant when he swung the door open.

"Will you be back?" she asked looking prettier than ever. Like a deer in the headlight.

"Who knows?" Roman replied, nodding, pulling the door shut.

There was more than one section of his body vehemently refusing when he tried telling himself he'd done the right thing, putting his integrity and set of morale to test. For the first time in a while, he wanted a cigarette, fished one out of his pocket, told himself rather not to but eventually settled for it. There was no point in being a saint in small details.

The phone rang but Roman was in no hurry picking it up. He knew the caller. The ringing hadn't ceased when he took a last, deep drag and flung the butt into the gutter.

"Hi, Joe."

"Got something for me?"

"Hm."

"Okay. I got something for you."

"The red Lotus."

"You should thank me for this."

"Why?"

"There's more than just one red car in Edinburgh."

"How many are Lotus'?"

"It's a 91 Excel."

"SE. Last facelift."

"Someone said that."

"Nice car. Remember seeing it once."

"You might be seeing it again."

"Where's it registered."

"Leith."

"Front."

"Probably. Let's meet there."

"I need to get something done before," Roman said when he spotted Emily getting on a bus.

"Stalker. When?"

"One and a half hours."

"Bring coffee."

The line clicked.

The taxi driver Roman had flagged down was doing a good job following the bus through traffic without raising too much suspicion. The obvious problem was the bus rolling to a stop every fifty yards or so it felt. Anyone poking out the back window must've spotted the taxi. Luckily, nobody did. Or cared.

A Sri Lanka native, the driver talked about cricket as they drove. Not politics. Or how hard life was. A most welcome change to Roman.

"Back home, we played cricket in the street. We had only one ball and a poplar bat handed down for generations. Every time someone knocked a 6, we were raking the bushes together, trying to find the ball. Got a lot of scars from doing that."

"Tigers?"

"You're funny. I hope the younger kids didn't lose the ball after I left."

"Do your parents still live there?"

"Yes."

"Let me send them a box of cricket balls. It'd be my pleasure."

"I'll write their address down for you."

"Don't follow the bus anymore."

"What do you want from that young woman?"

"Nothing, as of yet. Keep the car rolling but don't come to a stop."

The driver was splendid. Roman considered hiring him whenever he needed to tail someone. Emily didn't seem to notice the car when she unlocked the front door and quickly vanished inside a small house. Very inconspicuous. A garage, too.

"Where to now?" the driver asked.

The light in the kitchen was turned on. A dark orange against the falling winter night.

"Leith."

Roman leaned back for a quick nap. The car picked up speed. The driver knew what he was doing.

Two freshly-poured coffees were still steaming in their disposable cups when Roman got out of the car, handing them to Joe, leaning quite casually against her car.

"Gotta pay the man," Roman said.

"Give him a kiss from me."

"For the ride," he said handing a bundle of bills through the rolled-down window. "And a tip."

"Keep it," the driver said handing a slip of paper back. "The cricket balls will be plenty."

"Thank you, sir."

"But make them good quality, they need to last for a while."

"Think me for a cheap skate? Take care."

The car turned around, the exhaust clouds much thicker in the moist ocean air.

"Friend of yours?" Joe asked.

"Been to the 'Nam together."

"Bún chả, beer and bunnies?"

"You're looking good tonight, Joe. Real sexy."

"And you're giving me the creeps."

"My pleasure."

"Who were you stalking?"

It bugged Joe when Roman took a long, good sip from the coffee, extending the effectful pause.

"That's good coffee."

"It's great coffee."

"Guatemala? Or Sulawesi."

"Don't even know where Sulawesi is. Quit the mind games, that's what I think."

"Don't call me a stalker. I'm no creep in a trench coat with a super-zoom camera."

"And a jar of petroleum jelly in your pocket. I know. Who did you tail?"

"Emily."

"Who's Emily?"

"Pretty girl, about twenty-one or so, judging from her looks. Works at a café in Stockbridge for a little more than change."

"Politics major?"

"Don't know. Don't know much else, really."

"But you know where she lives?"

This time, Joe took a big sip of coffee, almost burning her mouth.

"Rather where Arrowsmith is living."

"Now I'm getting it."

"Someone told me they saw the Excel in front of a café in Stockbridge. And a stud hitting on one of the girls serving the tables."

"How did you know it was her?"

"Easy. She's the prettiest out of the bunch."

"Come on."

"It's not even close, Joe."

"That testosterone sure is poison."

"Juice, darling."

"You're assuming she's living with him?"

"Yeah."

"Did you see Arrowsmith?"

"Negative. Nobody seems to have in the past 48 hours or so."

"We have another one missing, did I tell you?"

"No."

"A boy."

"Same pattern?"

"Not this time."

"No blood?"

"Just a wee. Very low key. Someone is trying to keep a low profile."

"What makes you so sure the boy's part of our little case?"

Joe pulled an envelope with photos from the passenger's seat. There were closeups, one showing a bloody, severed fingertip. Not as bloody as you'd have suspected if you hadn't seen the likes of it before and knew better.

"We found this underneath the sideboard. When we looked closer, we also found traces of all the little splatters of blood that had been wiped away."

"Weird case."

"Wish I could make any sense of it. But the more I try getting into night life and sex life and fetishes and all the sick things so many people do on a daily basis for whatever pleasure they're getting from it, the less I seem to understand."

"What about the car?"

"It's registered to a Mr. Hamish O'Rouke. Lives in one of the projects in Leith."

"Working the docks?"

"Used to. Left hip got shattered in an accident some ten years back."

"I'm pretty sure we're not going to see the red Excel sitting in front of one of those concrete blocks."

"I'm pretty sure you're right. Let's go talk, can't do no harm."

"We'll see about that."

Joe drank the rest of the coffee, while Roman poured the cup out, riding shotgun, not fastening the seatbelt for the short drive.

"Tell me something, Roman."

"With pleasure."

"What is it about the male lion, taking a pride of lionesses from an older male, committing infanticide, mating and sending his females to work while he's doing nothing, still ruling as undisputed king."

"Until a younger, stronger male would kill him in a duel, inevitably."

"Why is it so simple?"

"Genetics. Design. Ask God."

"But I asked you already."

"Consider this. The lionesses, strangling the king that's too old to protect them, or impregnate them anymore. You're only king for as long as you can."

"As long as we allow you to."

"Know what's really unfair?"

"Huh?"

"That lion, bulging with muscle from doing nothing all day, except sleep, eat what the ladies drop off in front of him, and mating whenever he's in the mood."

"Someone once told me sleep is anabolic as hell."

"Maybe I should give that a go."

The project was another upright concrete brick, some desolated parking lots in front of it. No classic cars, mind you. Utility cars, some that were good years back and expensive then but worthless now. Like anything else that still worked fine but had no staying power in this world. Some new cars certainly running on financing, salaries stretched thin, leaving little for anything else. The type that looked like a whole lot of even more the same, one undistinguishable from another. No character or soul. Big price tags, though. And the prestige that purportedly comes from riding them.

Their steps were reverberated by the concrete when they climbed the outdoor stairs all the way up to seventh floor. Joe had insisted, knowing what the elevator in a building like that would be like, smell like, feel like. Worse than a pub's men's room. The stairs weren't far above. Someone had puked all over the banister on fifth floor. Trash bags almost blocked the way on sixth.

"I always knew I preferred winter," Roman said stepping over trash that would have been crawling with maggots in summer, helping Joe.

"Animals," she replied. "Only animals shit where they live."

The outside hallway was cold and windy. They passed several gray doors, one as uninviting as the next, until they stopped in front of the right unit. A TV was blasting at full volume. Some action movie, the tell-tale ballet of blue and white flicker dancing on the ceiling. Their knocking was firmly ignored at first. Roman took it to himself, almost kicking the door in at second try. The film was muted, not paused.

"Who's that?" a man called from inside in thick accent they couldn't place, almost a slur.

"Room service," Joe promptly hollered back.

"Police," Roman added right away, not in for the fuss.

"Get outta here, I didn't do nothing wrong."

"Where're here about your son," Joe said.

They waited. They almost didn't dare taking a breath. Suddenly, the TV was turned off. The lights came on. Then the door swung open. Mr. O'Rouke in a tracksuit, a cane in his left hand to support his leg. Not even years of hard work and neglect could disguise his well-proportioned features. A man still attractive well into his sixties, despite a developing baldness and traces of a pot belly.

"Come inside, it's cold," he said moving them from the walk-through kitchen right to the living room.

"Apologies for disturbing your peace tonight," Roman said.

"You're not a cop," Mr. O'Rouke said popping the fridge open, getting himself a can of diet cola. "The pretty lady is."

"Thanks for the compliment," Joe said.

"You're welcome. Now, what about you, mister? Look like a specialist to me."

"Specialist?"

"Bomb squad. No. Paramedic. Maybe. Or mercenary."

"Foreign Legion."

"Too simple."

"I'm sorry. I guess."

"I have a lot of respect for the military. And the rozzers, of course."

"Take it," Joe said with a smile directed at Roman.

"What's the police doing allying with a private dick? Matter of fact, what's the trouble with my son?"

Knowing he liked her over Roman, Joe gave a quick summary of the events, playing with bits and pieces whenever she felt fit. Mr. O'Rouke sat through it, brewing tea for everybody after he'd finished his diet cola, listening without asking any questions. But when Joe arrived at the end, he'd tied the knots all by himself.

"My boy would never do anything like that."

"What makes you so sure?" Roman asked.

"You know people all your life, there's not much they could possibly hide from you. With my brother Clint, I'd always known he wouldn't last. Got into fights all the time. Won a lot of them, too. Ran out of luck one day."

"We all do."

"Heard about it from his friend. They were over in Ireland, looking for work. Funny thing. Clint got into a brawl, like he always did. It was about nothing. Maybe he'd looked at the guy's girl and she smiled back or whatever. Or they were just a bunch of fools, looking for trouble. Guy took some punches from Clint, then glassed him. A shard somehow cut his throat. Choked to death on his own blood in an alley in Dublin. It's a goddamn shame, if you pardon my French."

"Did your boy have a good relationship with your brother?"

"Learned boxing from him. Just like I did. We both saw some success in amateur boxing."

"With those cheeks and nose, you must've been good."

"Quit when it was about time. When I had my little boy and we needed the money and the fights got harder and I couldn't count on pocketing the extra cash for a win without getting smashed to pieces myself."

"Was Duke good as well?"

"Duke?" he asked as if he'd never heard that name before, considering before Joe could say anything further, then went on. "Duke, yeah. That's his ring name. They took it from an American who wasn't even a boxer, I don't know."

"He gave it up but kept the name?" Roman asked.

"Danny never really gave up on anything. Just shifted his focus. Maybe for the worse at times."

"You're aware of how he's making his living?" Joe asked out of the blue. The question stung.

"That's none of my business," Mr. O'Rouke answered as calmly as he managed. "And by God, it's none of yours, either."

"When young men and women are tortured and disappear, I make it my business, Mr. O'Rouke."

"You really think my boy did that? All those terrible things they don't put in the papers anymore."

"Let me tell you something. You never really know anyone. Not even the people closest to you. You never know what they're capable of. What they'd do for pleasure or money."

"There's no need raising your voice. I'm old. But my ears work fine."

"Why's the Lotus registered under your name and address?"

"The what?"

"The red Excel."

"He bought it?"

Joe and roman exchanged glances.

"You didn't know he had it?" Roman asked.

"We didn't talk. Not since he started working for that witch, down at the waterfront."

"Did you kick him out?"

"Maybe he thought me for a fool. But I noticed when he switched from basketball shoes to wingtips. From hoodies to tailormade clothes. How wouldn't you? Said he'd quit at the warehouse and was selling insurance plans now."

"What did you say?" Joe asked.

"I said, well then, what about that witch you're talking to, that's much too old for you, dragging you along like a puppy on a leash. Can you explain? Obviously, he couldn't. No, I'm no fool. I know people here in Leith. I know who's sincere and who's not."

"And who's doing dirty business."

"And what business. I told him, son, you got the brains and the looks, go back to uni, sit down on your ass and hustle through, you'll see it's going to pay off. Not today and not tomorrow, but in a few years' time, you'll be grateful.

"You're so much smarter than me, so much stronger and you got the good looks from your mother and grandfather. You can do anything I never could. All you need is a little faith and direction, that's all. Don't repeat the same mistakes I made. Don't be a fool, like your uncle. Be the best you possibly can. If I could make one wish, it'd be for you to come to your senses, you bloody foolish little boy!

"Pull through and you'll see, the life of a made gentleman is a lot easier than the road you're going down right now. You'll buy that Lotus and we get it fixed together on the weekends, just you and me. And when we're done, we're rolling it downtown, to Old Town and the Castle, along Holyrood Park. And then we go to Carlton Hill, where I carried you on my shoulders when you were a little boy and there was only me and you and I wanted nothing more for you than to be living a happier life than me, son."

It took him a moment to recompose himself. But Mr. O'Rouke, being the hard-boiled man he was, soon continued.

"If you're looking for Danny, I'm of no help. I told him, if you wanna make a living like that, you're not going to make it under the same roof as I do. That's when he left. Talk to Rayne, that witch, because all his friends still live here and they check by from time to time, and neither has seen him."

"Thank you, Mr. O'Rouke," Joe said and they got up to leave. At the door, she stopped, looking back at a desolated man. "Mr. O'Rouke, what was your wife's maiden name?"

"Arrowsmith," he said staring at his hands with empty eyes.

17

Word in the street wasn't getting Duke any farther. Within two hours, he'd knocked off all his contacts close to Midtown, establishing little. The little he established was that the rumors had spread far enough and quick enough to make him persona non grata. Not only with a bunch people. With all of them.

"Duke, you look like shit," Rider said, sitting casually in his thick leather armchair at his office, windows facing out on Scott Monument down on Princes Street.

"Thank you. For talking to me. I had to be persistent with your secretary. What did you tell her?"

"Me? I didn't tell her anything. To be careful, that's what I told her. We can't have anyone waltzing in our doors these days without an appointment. There's strange things going on in this town."

"I didn't have to wait last time I came in."

"When was that?"

"Two months back, Rider. When I did that little favor for Rider Industries, remember? When you had those important clients over from Japan, trying to bag a deal."

"Hm, I don't know, Duke."

"I waited three weeks for my money. Even though I did a great job, didn't I?"

"Duke, buddy, it's rough times. Strange times. You should know."

With his pot belly, flappy meat all over his body, an overall unappealing appearance, and his thinning blonde hair, Rider leaned back even further in the armchair. They'd known for years, doing business whenever Rider needed someone to entertain female business partners, showing them around town, going out for dinner, making sure they were having a good time. Duke had paid a lot more attention to his regular customers for a while now, working with Rider only sporadically.

It hadn't sit well with the business man, losing one of his trump cards. Maybe the most powerful of them all. From then on, Duke had known he'd catered a grudge against him. It was why he had Rider quite far up on his list of suspects.

"I do know, Rider. Very well. I'm not here warming up the past or whatever business association we used to have."

"Uh-huh," Rider said, casually sipping from his tiny espresso, spilling some on his shirt but overplaying it.

"You hear a lot through the grapevine. At least you always gave the impression it was that way."

"Guilty as charged."

"What about the news?"

"What news?"

"The Big Red One."

"Big Red? Oh, got you. What would I know about such abominable crimes?"

"You heard nothing?"

"Nothing."

"You know Henry Pike?"

"Of Pike Pan American Industries and Trading. Sure. We played golf together at Saint Andrews this fall."

"He's good friends with Charlie Townshend."

"Head of Stratton-Moore and Oswald Consulting Group, yeah."

"Charlie has a wife. Rachel. And a daughter. Natalie."

All life suddenly faded from Rider's face. As if his blood pressure had dropped to zero.

"I know nothing about Charlie's wife. And less so about his daughter."

The espresso cup was empty but Rider was sipping off it anyway, with a shaky hand.

"You've never met either of the two?"

"Never."

"And you'd never know what they were up to?"

"Never."

"You have not even the faintest idea what Rachel or Natalie are doing in their abundance of spare time?"

"Listen, Duke. I'm tired of this, okay? If I tell you I know nothing, rest assured I'm not lying to you. I'm a stand-up guy, running an honest business operation, okay? Whatever it is you're implying I should or shouldn't know is bogus. I know nothing. And neither should you, Duke."

"Neither should I?"

"Exactly."

"What did you hear?"

"Nothing. I told you that a thousand times by now."

"You never heard who was entertaining Mrs. Townshend when Mr. Charlie was busy again pretending to do big business and personally making sure the female interns were having a big learning experience?"

"Duke, I- "

"Don't give me that now, Rider. You don't know any of this? Not how Natalie- "

"Shut up!" he burst out. "For once, shut up. You know zilch about anything. And I know even less. Whatever business you're doing with someone is far out of my interest. I'm not going to allow you throwing dirt at the good names of these people."

"These people you call friends and associates, that would push you down the cliff at first chance if it helped them in a deal so small it'd make anyone with their head screwed on right burst out laughing?"

"I don't need to listen to all of this."

"Did you do it?"

"Do what?"

"You've been hanging around with Natalie."

"I knew a girl called Natalie in boarding school."

"Is that all you're going to say for yourself?"

"Yes."

"Where's Rayne?"

"Rayne?" he asked, sliding back and forth uncomfortably in his leather armchair, making the thick burgundy leather squeal.

"You shut up now!" Duke then burst out, the hands behind his back formed to tight fists. "I know you know Rayne. Where else would you be hiring your little schoolboys from? I know you're a regular down in Leith and elsewhere, rubbing elbows with any scumbag that's washed along in Rayne's tide."

"Duke, for the last time, listen."

"Listening."

"I know nothing. Nothing, other than the fact you're running out of friends in this town. You've been pissing off people for quite some time now. What did you expect? That everyone's going to watch you rolling by in your red Lotus, cracking a smile at them, taking their money, their customers, screwing their wives, partners, daughters? You're way in over your head. I'm your friend, Duke."

"Cut that out. Just cut it out already."

"Change that disguise of yours once again, throw away your phone, hop on a train and leave Edinburgh. As long as you can. And forget about that red Lotus already, it's ridiculous."

A moment of silence passed between them. The fists behind Duke's back were clenched even harder, tendons and veins popping out, the flesh turning red. With his heart beating in his temples, anger swelling like a riptide, Duke was contemplating his words. Rider sat in waiting, the tiny cup clicking against the saucer.

"I'm not someone to run away," Duke said calmly, but with authority. "Less so am I going to allow anyone to force me out of my town. Should I ever decide to leave, it's going to be on my own accord. Nobody's going to have a say in this. Least anyone like you, Rider."

"Duke– "

"Shove it up where the sun don't shine."

Duke walked out. Whatever it was Rider called after him, he didn't hear it.

The baboons that made sure people like Rider were save and sound and cozy looked strangely at Duke. The secretary at the desk next to the elevator wouldn't even as much as glance at him. Last time he'd been there, she'd been flirting with him all the time, coy, devouring him with her eyes.

The crowd felt hostile now that Duke was, without a doubt, stranded. The police didn't know, but someone had talked. Someone had spread the news that it had been Duke Arrowsmith, hanging like a thick cloud of thunder over Old Town, New Town, Stockbridge, University, the Meadows. Ripper of his own time and age. A curse on all mankind, sent by the devil himself. To purge all sin and make sinners testify and recognize the Lord and savior. Like it said in the Book of Revelation, the world would end in a climactic and devastating spectacle just before a fresh start. Would the police, or the press, ever know, then Duke was chopped liver on a dirty plate. After all, how much digging would it actually require to unearth all the little, mediocre and big things he'd done in the past few years? If someone like Rider stepped forward, into his personal fifteen minutes of undivided spotlight, it'd all disintegrate with the snap of a finger.

Leith was the only place left to go. Duke knew that. And as much as he knew, he dreaded nothing more than going there and confronting what he should've confronted a long time ago. Like George, who'd simply gone out and slain the dragon, Duke would've been better off taking care of this inconvenience before the ground got too hot to walk underneath his feet. Not right away, he told himself, thinking hi lips moved with his thoughts. Maybe to make him the epitome of madness, mingling with those that had no voice in this world. Homeless people, their stray dogs all they cared for. Like ghosts, forbidden from the afterworld, lingering on for eternity to come, neither here nor there, really.

It didn't take much effort shaking the baboons in their suits and sunglasses, that had followed Duke since he'd left the building. New Town wasn't big. But big enough to get lost if you didn't know it like the back of your hand. Those were easily delt with. Not someone else Duke picked up in the corner of his eye as he passed by the Golden Harpy Pub.

The guy was built like a lightweight lifter, not looking like much at first glance, sporting tight muscle underneath his clothes. You could tell through the jacket he was wearing, a black and not too heavy piece probably picked up from a secondhand store, manufactured back in the 90s. Cocky but handsome face, too. What bothered Duke wasn't how he'd managed to keep up and sneak up on him. It was how he knew him.

"Easy, pal!" cocky face called out when Duke surprised him, grabbing him by the collar. The plea was ignored. Duke forced him hard against a dumpster, denting it. Cocky showed neither pain nor fear.

"Why are you following me?"

"Because everyone's looking for you."

"Who told you?"

"Would you let go of me? Please?"

"Give me one good reason."

"I know Emily."

Duke froze. His grip wouldn't ease up. But he felt the hair in his neck standing up.

"How?"

"University. Nice girl. Pretty. And smart. Wouldn't it be a shame if anything happened to her?"

Duke let go.

"Needless to say, I'm going to cave your head in if anything happens to her."

"I'm Sport."

The hand he offered was left hanging in the air.

"What do you want?"

"Me? Nothing. The boss wants to help. Word is, you're in deep trouble. Defenseless people, heavily molested before they disappeared without a trace. Bad PR. For sure. And the police is about to find out. Someone saw the red Lotus in front of the apartment block, where Agnieszka disappeared. Someone also saw the red Lotus where they found Rowan's fingertip underneath the dresser."

This had to sink in, first. Dukes mouth turned dry, his tongue spongy, a taste of copper somewhere farther down his throat.

"So the boss wants to help me out," Duke said, fighting the dryness in his mouth, feeling as if he would start coughing sand soon.

"Exactly. Wasn't easy, but a strong alibi is available. And– "

"Cut it. Where?"

"Zoo. In an hour."

"Zoo's closed this time of day."

"Let that be our problem, Mr. Arrowsmith."

Cocky-faced Sport straightened his jacket, slicked back his hair and took off, mingling with the crowd in front of the pub. The bad taste in Duke's mouth wouldn't disappear. Even though the guy named Sport had left and was out of sight now, Duke still felt as if he was under surveillance. The whole town had eyes and ears and mouths to devour him. Unable to grasp a clear thought, he had to walk, instinctively in the zoo's direction. Almost all the way down to Haymarket, before he managed to bring out his spare phone.

It occurred to him Emily must've been scared out of her mind over him. None of this had gone as planned. He wouldn't be home for dinner. That much was for certain. All he could think of was taking her in his arms. If she would let him, should they ever see again.

The line clicked. Duke waited. All he could do. Wait. Walk. Wonder. When the phone call was taken, he had to close his eyes and focus before he could speak.

18

Getting the winter cold out of her flesh and bone had occupied Emily for some time. When the hot tea kicked in and the even hotter shower thawed her body, the house suddenly felt empty. It had been empty for a while. It had been empty from the moment she'd walked out in the morning. And it had been empty until she returned. The void hadn't been filled by her presence.

No message from Duke on her phone.

The TV screen had collected dust from neglect, and when Emily turned it on, just for taking her mind away, she understood why. The blue light was driving her crazy. The blaring of young and hot and dumb people blind-dating on a tropical beach talking crap even more so. With the TV turned off, the silence was enjoyable, if only for a moment.

On the camera's screen, she checked the photographs she'd snapped during the day, suddenly reminded of what had happened when she came across the shot taken from atop Carlton Hill.

"Cold World," she christened the shot.

It seemed much too surreal. To a degree where Emily wondered if she could trust herself. It was easily established whether, or rather not, all this had happened. All she had to retrieve was the slip of paper she'd pocketed, dial the number and see what the man would have to say. The man that had come to help her. Seemingly out of nowhere. Much in the same manner as the man that had stalked and attacked Emily.

And then she remembered something else, another slip of paper. Dropped by the attacker. It hadn't meant anything to her back then but now she saw it, clear as day, in front of her mind's eye.

No message from Duke on her phone.

It was dark already, and getting late. Emily suddenly felt her heart beating hard against her ribcage. The photographs seemed good for a fresh start, or so she felt, but she wouldn't dare looking at them on the laptop, since it could've been an invasion on Duke's privacy. Or was that true? Wasn't she rather afraid of finding something better left alone?

"Calm down," she told herself into the silence, her words reverberated by the emptiness. "Calm your nerves."

A shot of bourbon spiced up her Scottish breakfast tea but it hurt her teeth and smelled too strong. In a kitchen drawer, she found a pack of cigarettes, foil still intact, a Bic lighter next to it. Her heart started pounding even faster. It was a bad idea and it was the best idea, and would Duke mind if she smoked and calmed her nerves? Emily broke the foil and popped a cigarette in her mouth, a strong taste of tobacco already just from breathing in. It had been a while.

Ruining the living room seemed like pushing it, and when she entered the garage, it smelled of wood dust and chips, but also a bit of oil, grease and gasoline. The light tubes underneath the ceiling flickered to life, taking their time. The lighter must've looked like a searchlight in the darkness until the electric light overpowered it. Emily inhaled deeply, the smoke stinging her lungs as if poison ivy was shoved down her throat. She almost coughed but kept it in, instant sweat appearing on her forehead, cold and salty, head spinning some. It numbed her nerves, too, a cheap party trick, replacing one pain with another.

Filter pinched between her delicate lips, she got her phone back out, full of messages from people she didn't care about that moment.

"Where are you," Emily said to herself, pocketing her phone.

The red Lotus appeared in front of her when she looked up, sitting in the middle of the garage. The red popped even in the artificial light. It jumped right at her. For the first time, it turned into more than just an old car. The little details, the lines of the bodywork, not curvy but still sexy, like an athletic female physique. Golden trimmings, touching up the lines. Duke had said the car needed a mechanical issue fixed but it was hard to imagine anything wrong with something this beautiful.

More smoke entered her lungs, calming her, but not enough to stop the tears that started rolling down her cheeks. One after the other. Salty and wet and they kept coming. The smoke burned in her eyes when she wiped away the tears. It was irrational and infantile, but Emily knew something wasn't right. It didn't matter to her what Duke had done. All she wanted was to take him in her arms and she knew things would sort out. Everything could be sorted out. Like a mechanical issue, plaguing an old Lotus.

The straightforward fact of the matter that Duke still wasn't there lingered in the back of her head. For the time being, she could cope with it. When the phone buzzed in her pocket, Emily was in no hurry getting it out. Eventually, she did, crushing the cigarette butt underneath her heel, making sure it was out. The wood dust could've turned the garage into a furnace with ease.

D wants to start a conversation, the phone informed her. Emily's heart started racing again as she confirmed the contact.

"Sorting things out, don't be afraid. A friend is stopping by."

Before she could've processed the message, Emily heard the front door. It wasn't the sound of a knob being turned to see if it was locked. It wasn't the sound of someone breaking in with force either. The lock clicked. The cylinder was sliding back. Someone had the key. Her heart turned into a rotary engine inside of her chest.

There were plenty of tools and utensils to defend herself with, only Emily couldn't grasp a clear thought yet. When the door to the garage swung open, she still stood there, sweatpants and hoodie, hair damp from a recent shower, smell of cigarette smoke.

"I saw light shining through the door," the stranger said, cracking a smile at her that wasn't returned. "You must be Emily. I'm sorry if I scared you."

"Who are you?"

"A friend. Trying to help out."

"I don't know you."

"We haven't met before. At least I wouldn't remember. Edinburgh is pretty much a big village, so I'm sure we've walked past each other at some time before. But I digress."

"Tell me who you are," Emily demanded, taking a step to the right, closer to the beautiful Milwaukee hammer sitting on the workbench.

"I'm Jamal. Me and Duke, we're old friends."

"Where is Duke?"

"Good question. I'd like to know that myself. It's hard helping someone out who's pretty much disappeared."

"Disappeared? What're you talking about?"

"Listen, it's a long story."

"Start with the most important information. Where did you get the keys to the house? Did you hurt Duke?"

"I'd rather we talk things over in the living room. We calm down, have a seat. Is that okay with you, Emily? Bring that hammer if you like."

In awe, Emily realized she'd grabbed the handle of the hammer. Ready to deck Jamal if he dared coming too close.

"I'm sorry. I didn't realize I grabbed it."

"Don't mention it. I'm in the kitchen, brewing tea. Join me after you've had another of those camel shit sticks."

With that, he left her to her own device. With the Lotus. With the tools. With her worries. Emily lit another cigarette, sitting down on the workbench, not minding that she got fine dust all over her bottom. She did a terrible job, trying to get things in order inside of her head.

Jamal was sitting on the couch, two cups of tea at the ready on the nice mid-century coffee table.

"Is that your camera?" he asked pointing at the Fuji.

"Aye. It's mine now."

"Heirloom?"

"How would you know it wasn't Duke's?"

"He's got a sense for the arts and film, a cultivated taste. But this camera, getting into photography, that's not him. It must've been you because it fit in here so nicely."

"What are you implying?" Emily asked sitting down next to him on the couch.

"He's not here and he's left a void."

"Hm."

"He's not coming tonight," Jamal said tasting the tea, that was good but did nothing to him. "Duke sent me down to see if you were alright."

"And he gave you the key to house."

"Not quite," Jamal replied, wondering if he'd spoken prematurely.

"Explain."

"Duke had an escape plan. Part of it involved a locker at a boxing gym."

"I didn't know he was a boxer."

"He only did that for himself. The rest of the time, he's working out at high-class gyms, alternating."

"What's with the boxing gym?"

"They have combination locks for their lockers, so regulars can keep their gear. Duke had one too."

"In case of emergency."

"I got the key and came here."

"What else was in there?"

"That's beside the point."

"A Picasso? Photographs of UFO-sightings that have been classified? The codes for starting a nuclear war?"

"I readily understand you're upset. For the time being, I also understand you have no choice but trusting me. To some degree, you already do."

"Think so?"

"You didn't smack me in the head with the hammer when you had the chance."

"Okay. Fine. What did Duke tell you to do?"

"Ask you if someone followed you around town. If someone freaked you out. Or harassed you."

It was the first time Emily noticed some electrical buzzing in the walls, impossible to locate and pinpoint, but still there, working on her last nerve while she considered. Or rather, while she felt nothing, only the void Jamal had been describing, slowly creeping into her, deeper, harder and harder to push back.

"Somebody is setting him up," she said.

"Yes. But you didn't answer my question. Where did it happen? When you left your job in Stockbridge?"

"I guess it's irrelevant asking you how you know where I live."

"We went on a walk together in Holyrood Park."

"A strange guy on the bus tried striking up a conversation when I left the café. And then he followed me after I got out at Waverley Station."

"What did he do?"

"Stalked me all the way up to Carlton Hill. There were people up there and I thought I was safe."

"But you weren't."

"He grabbed me from behind. Said something about being a wolf in a sick world. Wanted to lure me to what he called his favorite place. Suddenly a bloke appeared out of nowhere, trying to scare him away. That creep drew a gun but the bloke got him in the hand with a knife."

"A knife?"

"Looked military spec. Got the palm of his hand with ease. As if he was playing darts at the pub."

"Okay," Jamal said, trying to digest all this. It was tough. Even with the mess he heard all day on his job, this wasn't the same ballpark. Something about it stank.

"Do you believe me?"

"Yes."

"Why's someone framing Duke? And putting pressure on me to break him?"

"We haven't seen in years, I'm not sure what he did. But I'm sure he's stepped on some toes in the past few years."

"Doing what?"

"Did he ever tell you how he's making his money?"

"Does it matter?"

"It matters to the people you're dealing with. They can lift you into the stratosphere, but that makes the crash even harder when they shoot you back down."

"Duke's got a powerful enemy."

"That's not all."

"What do you assume he did?"

"Something bad."

"Tell me."

"I don't know any details."

"You're a bad liar."

"It's beside the point."

"You're trying to evade me. I want to know what they think he did."

Sipping tea couldn't buy him time. It wouldn't get him out of there. Another dead end.

"You heard it from the news."

"Could you be more spe– " Emily said and stopped. "Oh."

"I only see any mitigating circumstances if he's leading the cops to the victims."

"Wait a minute, you really believe he did it!"

"Beliefs are for churchgoers."

"Sure. What a great friend you are. Showing up after years when Duke needs you the most and– "

"How dare you? You know nothing. Nothing. You're still counting the hours since he's reeled you in with those blue eyes and blonde hair and the way he talks and behaves himself. With that darn red Lotus! I've known him all my life. It doesn't matter how many years have passed in which we didn't see each other. People don't change and you're too young to know that already."

"I've seen his true colors."

"True colors. How he put you in danger, waiting for him to come home. What if the police kicked the door in, huh? Finding you next to evidence. Or if one of those thugs on his tail decided to– "

"If that's all you've got to say, you might as well leave now, Jamal. Please leave the keys on the kitchen table when you're seeing yourself out."

"Listen, Emily. I'm trying to resolve this situation. If he's guilty, he has to be put away. If he's innocent, then what better way washing his name clean than working with the police? Please, come to your senses."

"Don't forget calling the cops and telling them to look for him elsewhere, other than his home. Good night."

"Is that your last word?"

"Thank you for being so concerned over the well-being of your old friend."

"Thank you for your hospitality. Good night."

Jamal got up, put his coat on and left the keys on the kitchen table just as requested. Soon after the door clicked shut Emily heard a car's engine roar to life, some 90s junk box with a fart can for an exhaust pipe. Her face was still a dark red with anger.

For ten minutes, she couldn't do anything, think nothing, only sit on the sofa and stare into the abyss of a worn wallpaper. It was a battle between her and the faded colors, the blurring Mandalay of lines she couldn't quite see for the buzzing inside of her head. For the tears in her eyes. But the tears would have to dry up, she knew. They weren't worth their salt for sure.

With all other options adamantly out the window, Emily knew she was only left one thing to do. Her jacket hung from a nice brass hook next to the door. Duke had salvaged it at a yard sale and installed it on a beautiful black cherry wood board. Digging through the pocket, Emily found what she was looking for. And when she pulled it out, she suddenly froze. It wasn't the slip of paper the man had handed her on Carlton Hill.

"Oh," she said to herself. Then it dawned on her. "Oh."

It was the business card Sport had handed her. Emily turned it around in the artificial electrical light emitted from a single light bulb above her head. In her memory, the business card had been a dark red, almost burgundy in color. But now she saw it was a perfect shade of burgundy.

"Burgundy Bobcat," Emily read. A number was embossed underneath in champagne gold letters. She traced it with her delicate index finger: 10558420.

It took her tremendous effort, trying to remember what Sport had said to her. It hadn't been much, nothing of great substance. Something about having fun and painting the town. Something that clearly wouldn't have been for her.

Burgundy Bobcat. And a number.

"Where?" she asked herself. "Where would you want me to go?"

Sport. She'd firmly refused going out with him, glad she'd so thoroughly blocked his advances. Now she wondered if it had been a mistake after all. Knowing his phone number would've enabled her to at least inquire about the Burgundy Bobcat. That was out, though.

Going to bed and sleeping things over wasn't an option. But beating to death a whole sleepless night was the least appealing prospect Emily could've imagined. She knew it was a bad idea and couldn't help it anyway. Resisting the urge of putting another cigarette in her mouth, she rummaged through the other pocket of her jacket, retrieving a crumbled slip of paper, then dialed the number. The line clicked its robot dance tune.

"Hello?" a man's voice came on.

"Roman?"

"Emily?"

"Aye."

"Are you alright?"

"You didn't show up by chance out of thin air, did you? Don't lie to me."

"No."

"I'm not sure if you're George or the Dragon in this tale. But for the time being, it's not giving me choices."

"What's your plan?"

"Burgundy Bobcat, does it ring a bell?"

"Yes."

"Where can I pick you up?"

"National Gallery. I'll come from the Christmas market. How will I find you?"

"You'll notice the car. Just assuming you know a whole lot more than you ever should've."

"Can you make it in half an hour?"

"Yes."

Click. Emily hung up on him. Half an hour was pushing it, so she got dressed in a hurry, not really caring. On her way to the garage, she stopped. In the kitchen, she found a steak knife with a zig-zagging edge just small enough to be concealed inside her jacket. When she checked the edge, it took off some of the callused skin on her fingertip. With its profile, it would rip the most terrible wounds imaginable.

The only thing she knew about old cars was that their engines would have to run and heat up before being put under load and gunned into traffic. Holding the key of the Lotus inside the ignition lock, Emily said a quick prayer, hoping. The engine caught right away when she turned the key, roaring to life, blowing vast amounts of exhaust fumes out the back pipes against the garage door.

"You'll hold up just fine," she told the car, tapping the leathered dashboard softly before getting out and opening the door like a lion's cage at the circus.

19

In pitch-black night and devoid of people, the zoo was a different world. By no means would it resemble the place Duke remembered so fondly from his childhood, when his father, sometimes his uncle, took him to see the baboons and the big cats. The kangaroos had always been his favorite, for reasons unknown. Not everything in life was easily determined, making such memories all the more valuable, Duke riding on his uncle's shoulders, trying to convince him a kangaroo was a much nicer and better animal than a lion.

As much as he would've imagined the zoo to be more relaxed without the ever-flowing stream of people and children screaming and tapping on glass and dripping ice cream on asphalt, it was the exact opposite. Duke felt watched with every step. Stalked by creatures helpless against their primeval instincts, encoded in their DNA even before they'd evolved into their current shape. Enclosures the equivalent of prison cells. The same kind people tended to erect around themselves. Invisible to unsuspecting spectators.

A gate at the entrance hadn't been locked, with nobody waiting either. There was no need telling him where to go. With quick steps, somewhat stiff from a day's walking, he made his way across the compound. Most of the animals were resting or sleeping. Only the baboons were putting up a spectacle, hard to make out in the darkness of a Scottish winter night.

As he approached the enclosure of the Asiatic lions, Duke could see a shape in the darkness, a brighter gray than the rest of the now almost indistinguishable scenery. Not until he got within sixty feet could he spot the delicate details in front of him.

"You haven't forgotten," Rayne said, leaning on her elbows against a balustrade as casually and elegantly as only a lady could. "Hi, Duke."

"You haven't gained an ounce. Someday, you'll have to share your secret."

"Let me look at you. Gosh, you look like a bum in those clothes."

"I look like a craftsman."

"Yeah, right. Still chasing that old romantic dream of making a living crafting things with your hands, like any other poor slob with the brains of the scarecrow."

"I've never appreciated your presumptuousness."

"You've never told me that before. To my face, I'm assuming."

"You're assuming right."

"Something I never liked about you. You're a cocky, unreliable, sneaky little bitch."

"Only you would say that about me," Duke said leaning against the rail right next to her, their sleeves touching. "Where are the boys?"

"See that shadow over there?"

"Uh-huh. That's a rock behind a bush."

"Got me. I told them to let the boys go on an empty stomach for a day longer so they'd be hunting tonight."

"And willingly putting up a show for you."

"You may keep that undertone to yourself."

"Apologies, you reminded me of one of my youthful sins."

"Awfully funny of you, Duke. Nothing about your attitude has changed. Which makes me wonder how someone as smart as you could maneuver himself in such a, what do the French call it? Cul de sac."

"All these years and you still don't know me."

"I know you better than you know yourself. I know every inch of you. Look at me, you know it's true. You can't admit it to yourself. But you know it's true."

"I've become a man. That's my biggest sin. You never forgave me for it. Not that I ever asked for your acquittal."

"What has being a man to do with the things you do?"

"How would you understand, preferring to play with boys."

One of the Asiatic lions rustled in the undergrowth, actively for a big cat at night, moving swiftly, like the king of the jungle should. Even against the darkness of the night Duke could see all the bulging muscle this elegant monster packed. They'd always filled him with some irrational sense of envy.

"Let's go inside, I don't appreciate the cold," Rayne said.

Duke made sure he was walking right next to her as they went into the building lit in the same light as a cricket ground during night games. The other lion was prancing in front of the grated fence.

"Where are the zookeepers?" Duke asked.

"I gave them a night off. We can handle this."

"Who's here with you? That guy Sport?"

"Sport is out on a special assignment."

"I have questions concerning the guy."

"I thought so."

Just when Duke was about to continue, the Asiatic lion they'd seen stalking outside shot through the hatch into the building, coming out of nowhere, proving how easily civilized people would fall to the simplest tricks of the predators out in the wild. The lion was big and graceful, even more muscular than Duke had assumed, now that he could see him clear as day. At first, he didn't realize why the lion had come for his companion, joining into the procession march. Then he saw it, someone sitting at the fence, swinging what looked like a giant turkey leg in front of the two lions. You could see the rage burning in their eyes, glowing like kindling, even brighter than the LED lights.

"Who's that?" Duke inquired.

"A friend of yours."

"No."

"It hasn't been that long, eh?"

"It can't be him."

"I thought you'd be glad."

"No," Duke repeated himself.

His right hand was masculine and feminine at the same time, an oddity in itself, neither spoiled by hard work nor the digital age. The redness of a single finger was easily distinguishable against the light skin of the turkey leg. The red nothingness of a whole link missing.

"Rory, darling?" Rayne addressed this young man, looking strange in his expensive clothes, the fur coat, the million-dollar haircut, sitting on the floor littered with hay and cat feces, swinging a giant turkey leg.

"Hm?" he asked back without looking.

"See who's come to join us for kitty night. It's Duke. Now, won't you say hello to your old friend and mentor? Be a good boy, will you, and come over here?"

Carelessly, he tossed the dead meat at the two cats not starting a fight but sharing it brotherly. When he got up, he wouldn't even brush the dirt from the bottom of his pants.

With elegant steps, he approached Rayne and Duke, his hand turning into a bloody hook, swinging it like a pirate.

"Hi, Duke."

And he offered his hand, extending it like a well-used meat hook, looking grotesque, out of proportion, simply hideous, and Duke's mind started playing tricks on him, the wound crawling with maggots, blood seeping out from it, flies and worms eating away at the exposed flesh, where the cut hadn't healed up, where it would never heal up but leave evidence of pain and despair and failure.

"I thought you were dead," Duke spoke his mind.

"He's not," Rayne replied, putting an arm around this young man, his eyes still cold as ice. "I took him in, helped him readjust."

"Reeled him in like the rest of your boys. I should know."

"Sport found him. Cold. Alone. Wounded. The way you left him."

"What he did was his own crime, not mine."

"Rowan, honey. You got something to say to this? To Duke?"

Rowan closed his eyes, forming his disfigured hand into a fist, squeezing hard enough to start bleeding through his fingers.

"It's excitement all the way," he started, "It builds up until uncontainable. You feel it when you're alone. But it's worse among people. When you see someone that gets you going. For me, it was bad when I got my hair cut. The barber using the razor around my ears, down my neck. It sent shivers down my spine, making me long for more."

The blood dripped and formed a small puddle on the floor. The lions smelled it. Their instincts took over. Both of them started prancing faster, forcing their heads through the bars as far as they could, using their enormous paws, knowing their prey was out of reach but still trying, that rush of blood to their heads, up their nostrils, sparking insanity.

"I should've known better," Duke said. "I should've trusted my instincts telling me you were bad news, kid."

"You're in trouble," Rayne said, and Duke couldn't tell what she had on her mind.

"They're looking for him. I'm wondering what they're going to do when they find him with you, not dead in a ditch, his limbs chopped off."

"I can tell you what they're going to do. Press charges against the guy in the red Lotus that was seen parked in front of the house when Rowan was molested and disappeared."

"They'd need evidence to press charges."

"Don't worry about that."

"It's just a car."

"I beg to differ, this car is you. All the way. All the way down, too. In all its beauty and its wonderful smell and the grace and the flaws. They've seen it."

"Who?"

"Plenty of people. People I know."

"The very same people swearing under oath you're running a reputable business, paying taxes and never trafficking any people."

"Yes, the same people," she said and couldn't help but smile that long-necked hyena smile. "They've seen the car in front of Agnieszka's house. Don't say you weren't there, Duke."

"I- "

"Excuse me, what was that?"

"I wasn't- "

"Can you say that again? You weren't what?"

"Where is she? Playing with the tiger?"

"Anybody's guess. Rowan?"

"Huh?"

"Did you read about that girl? You know, the young blonde from Poland that disappeared in a puddle of blood, probably chopped up to little pieces by some unsuspicious beau that couldn't control his impulses?"

"It was on the news."

"You're right. It was on the news. Other than your disappearance. Look how much they care for you. For young men. These days, they're worth shit, it's the zeitgeist, that's all. But you deserve better, don't you? I took you in. I provide for you. Because you deserve better and you reap what you sow."

"Yes, Rayne."

And she kissed him on the mouth, forcing her lips on his'. All the while Rowan extended his hand away from her, as not to get any blood dripping from his disfigured finger on her.

"Does the police know he's okay?" Duke asked, trying to be calm when he felt like screaming at them. At both of them.

"They'll know. In time. Which doesn't get you off the hook."

"Where's the evidence I did anything to him?"

"I wasn't referring to that. Rowan's alive and kicking. But what about the girl?"

"I didn't do anything to her."

"Where's the evidence for that?"

"You know darn well where it is."

"I didn't send them on your trail."

"If it wasn't you, someone else talked. A snitch."

"There's no snitch anywhere near me."

"What makes you so sure?"

"Don't play mind games with me."

"Can you find her? Yes or no?"

Surprised at the question, Rayne hesitated. It seemed as if she was really wondering if she could find a girl presumed dead, gone missing and, thus far, without a trace.

"No. No, I don't think so."

"Why are we even talking, then?"

"I wanted to see you."

"Farewell, now that you've seen me, for the last time."

"Stay. Just a second longer."

"Give me a reason. A good one."

"I can clear your name. Oh, now you're listening. I got your precious attention just for once."

"It's not giving you choices," Rowan threw in, and Duke looked him right in the eyes, unable to see any humanity left in them. It was as if the rest of the person he used to be had just gone out like a spirit out of a bottle.

"You lured me out here to clear my name. Rayne, I didn't see that one coming."

"I'm still feeling responsible for you."

"Sentimental attachment at best."

"Splitting hairs."

"What would you want in return?"

"Nothing."

"Nothing."

"The status quo."

"The status quo that has me working for you. Exclusively."

"A family reunion. So to say."

"Bringing home the beloved family dog. To look after the children, chase the predators away."

"Duke, please."

"Put a collar and a nice, good chain on me. Not a short chain to yank at, only short enough to pull me back close when I stray away too far."

"You're embarrassing me."

"Make me your puppy again. No will of my own. Living off of the bones you throw at me to pick the flesh from."

"Enough."

"Knowing perfectly well I could never break free again. Because, should I ever dare making that mistake, you'd send the hounds of hell after me. A phone call, that's all. The snap of a finger."

"Shut your mouth, you rabid mutt! You'd be nothing without me and you're nothing now! I have all the cards in my hand and you better relearn your place quick before I lose the last of my temper with you!"

Again, Rowan showed no emotional reaction to what happened around him. Fear would've been an appropriate reaction. But there was none. Duke collected himself, knowing the noose was pulling tighter around his neck. Whatever it was he would have to do, he'd take all the necessary steps. For the time being, though, he didn't know how to get out of this. The only thing he knew for certain was that he wanted to put as much real estate as possible between himself and Rayne.

"If you don't know where she is," Duke continued, "I'm asking only one thing from you."

"What would that be?"

"Inform Rowan's family and the police that he's not dead. If you want to tell them anything else, go ahead and do as you please."

"You're not coming back."

"No."

"You won't take your spot at my side? The way it was always supposed to be?"

"I'd rather die a man than live like a mouse."

"Is that your last word?"

"The last you'll ever hear from me."

"I have one more advice for you."

"Listening."

"If you didn't do what I believe you did, you better find her yourself. They'll lock you away either way. But you're too pretty a bird to be behind bars for twenty years or so."

Duke turned around to leave, walking towards the door, already feeling the winter cold creeping in. A stark contrast to the nice, tropical heat inside the building. The big-cat smell was intense. It had evaded his notice at first. Behind his back, the two lions were done with their turkey leg, not satisfied with eating what was thrown at them without a hunt and a fight to death. The wound on Rowan's finger still occupied their attention and desire.

"Find that snitch," Duke said without ever looking back, feeling his heart pounding, ready to be jumped by a tiger.

20

When she got out of the car the wind caught the door, forcing it open much harder than advisable. Joe took a look around, hearing the seagulls squeaking above her head, gliding in the wind almost in a standstill, not doing more than minor adjustments to their wings to stay on top of the current. This small fishing village instantly reminded her of what she hated so much about the country and village life. Somewhere not far off, a flock of sheep was minding their business, bleating a characteristic song while growing wool and meat and making milk.

The salty air did her lungs a world of good but the cold wind was cutting at her exposed throat like a hunting knife. A smoke was out of the question. She walked straight into The Whaler's Retreat, the only pub in town. They had a nice wood fire going in the stove and it smelled of roasted meat and pie. Several brands of beer on tap, most of them Scottish ales, only one or two industrial lagers nobody cherished but everybody cared to drink these days.

"I'll be right with you," a man's deep and friendly voice boomed from somewhere beyond the bar coated in a fat layer of chocolate-colored lacquer. They had two armchairs set in front of the fireplace. Joe took the one to the right, from which she could be seen, and could see all of the small pub. The fabric was worn thin in places but still held up fine. A nice, classic Scottish pattern almost like Harris tweet.

On the coffee table they had a big and heavy and high-quality book on art deco architecture in New York City, something she wouldn't have expected to see anywhere near a place like this. The illustrations were marvelous, printed in thick coats of colored ink, almost as rich in texture as a postmodern acrylic painting. Joe got hung up on the chapters about buildings she'd see so many times before in movies but never had paid any attention to.

"Beautiful, aren't they?" she heard the recognizable voice of a massively-framed man, sporting a classic beard, gray already, and short salt-and-pepper hair.

"All of them," joe replied and closed the book.

"Keep browsing as much as you like. What can I get you?"

"Scottish ale and a sandwich, please."

"We got ham and salad, tuna with onions, bacon and– "

"Surprise me. Oh, and add some chips."

"Certainly."

"I'll come over, sit at the bar."

"No, please stay. This season, it's best in front of the fireplace."

It wouldn't take long until he returned with a massive tuna, bacon, salad and tomato sandwich, topped with hollandaise, as thick as a phone book, a big ceramic bowl filled with chips seasoned with crushed pepper and vinegar, and a coppery Scottish ale that smelled perfectly of earthy hops.

"That's what the doctor prescribed," Joe said starting with the beer, downing half of it in one gulp.

"You must be thirsty and hungry, driving all the way down from Edinburgh."

"In summer, it would've been a nice drive. Everything's changing with the season."

"Enjoy your meal."

The sandwich was savory, the hollandaise complementing the taste of the tuna. It didn't take Joe long finishing it all. One of her habits, whether good or bad was for someone else to decide, was to begin a meal with the main attraction, having it all before giving her attention to the sides.

"Another beer?" she heard from the bar.

"Same again, please."

"On the way."

She was back at the book she enjoyed so greatly, making sure she'd wiped her hands thoroughly before picking it up, wondering how it would survive in such pristine condition in a pub environment.

"Are you an architecture buff?" Joe asked when he returned with two fresh pints of beer, taking the armchair on the other side of the coffee table.

"One of my childhood passions that carried over into adulthood."

"Playing with Lego blocks too?'"

"Nay, they're still too restrictive. These days, they remind me of video games."

"Interesting comparison."

"Did you enjoy your meal?"

"Best I've had in a long time."

"I'll drink to that. Cheers."

"This beer is amazing."

"Yet you didn't come for the beer. I've seen the license plate when I looked out the kitchen window. The car speaks volumes, too."

"I wasn't quite sure how to start this off."

"Yes," he said pondering. "It's not easy being you, I feel sure." Then he added. "No offense intended."

"It's alright, Mr. Stapleton."

"It's about my boy," he said and drank again, preparing for the worst while hoping.

"He's alive."

"Alive? How do you know?"

"We got a call late last night. Unknown caller, unregistered number. Explained to us Rowan was fine, apart from minor injury. Said he would come to the police office in the morning to prove his well-being."

"Sure enough, he did."

"I saw him myself. Rowan told us some of it. Very cryptically, but he did. You want to hear any details?"

"Spare me the details if you don't mind."

"There's one thing I need to tell you."

"Go ahead, hit me with that garbage truck."

"Part of his ring finger was severed. Poorly, that is. Pretty nasty wound. Looked inflamed to me. It's never going to heal up well. When we asked him how it went down, he said we should imagine whatever we please."

"Sounds like him."

"Self-evidently, we offered medical assistance. He declined."

"Him all the way."

"The last bits were the most interesting. At least to me."

"He wouldn't file any charges."

"Right. But he also said he'd found a home. Someone to take care of him. Nothing to worry about."

"Okay."

"Worse, your son was of no help regarding the missing girl."

"I read it in the news. If he says he doesn't know anything, he's not lying. That much I know about my son."

"We asked him if we should inform his family. He shrugged. I'm sorry."

"Don't be sorry. I lost him a long time ago. I'm glad he's alive. That's all I'm hoping for. It's his life to live, not mine. You should know when you have to let go."

"It must be tough."

"When they're young, you'd never expect. It looks like a good life ahead of you and your family. Then there's disaster, one after another. Eroding everything you worked so hard for. You have to acknowledge your dreams would never come to materialize. Otherwise, you're lost as well."

"Cheers to that."

They both finished their beer.

"I know you want to understand more about it," Mr. Stapleton continued. "But I'm afraid there's little more to it. Not much more than you already pieced together. Yes, with Rowan, there's been signs. Different magnitude, yet foreshadowing what happened. It's no surprise he came into contact with the wrong type of people in the city. It's no surprise either his tendencies went from bad to worse under that influence, nourishing them."

"I've noticed his arms, his neck, that he's hiding underneath a stiff collar. His ears underneath his long hair."

"I blamed it all on myself. Not anymore, no. I forgive my son. As long as he won't do any harm to anyone that's not asking for it. Now that I've done that, I'll forgive myself."

"Good man."

"Let's have a whiskey."

At the bar, Mr. Stapleton got his oldest whiskey from the top of the shelf. Glenlivet 12 years old, bottled in 1968, which was important to him because that year, Jim Charles lost his life in a Lotus formula 2 at Hockenheimring in Germany. It was the best whiskey Joe ever tasted. After that, lingering on felt like an act of courtesy commonly called for, but clearly off in this instant. There was nothing more to say. No charges were filed. No further information could be extracted. Most importantly, the father had forgiven the son first, himself second. It was, given the circumstances, the best outcome anyone could've hoped for.

Mr. Stapleton saw Joe to her car, skillfully keeping the rain at bay by help of an old but sturdy umbrella. They said goodbye and he stood there, looking after the car leaving the village until it went out of sight behind the first bend, with a flock of sheep grassing to the left.

21

The big house felt silent and deserted. This hadn't changed. Not with Charles, pretending to be home when all he did was talk on the phone or in front of the computer. Not with Natalie, who'd returned to her old bedroom for the time being. Whenever Rachel referred to the room as Natalie's children's room, she soon stood corrected. In fact, her daughter had made it look like a freshman's room starting at the age of fourteen, and when she'd moved out to the apartment at the Meadows, the room had already been the blueprint for the interior design concept to come. From the library, where Rachel was trying to read for days but failing miserably at it, she could see the door to Natalie's room. It looked odd, closed up like a barricade.

No news had materialized. The man was still at large. Unimaginable how anyone could go into hiding effectively these days. Especially a man like that, driving the most flamboyant car. For a second, Rachel couldn't help but remember the scent of his skin, the touch of his hand, what it stirred inside of her. Footsteps on marble floor, light and elegant, removed her from the thoughts she'd vowed never to allow herself again. Natalie was standing in front of her, dressed up like a model for Paris fashion week, even though she hadn't left the house in days.

"Honey, hi," Rachel said forcing a smile as she closed the heavy book.

"Making progress with Pynchon?"

"Yes, some," she lied, glad she hadn't been caught with her thumb still stuck between pages 15 and 16.

"If you care to enjoy Pynchon, you have to learn how to read Pynchon. It takes effort, of course."

"I'll get there," Rachel said, wondering what this was supposed to mean and if it was knighting Pynchon that his prose was so heavy and unreadable that enjoying it had to be learned under effort.

"You will, eventually."

"Did you get some rest?"

"Plenty," Natalie said looking rejuvenated, which was contradictory given her young age. "You want to go outside, have some coffee?"

"Mr. Sykes said we oughtn't do that."

"Yeah, concerning that Mr. Strykes."

"Sykes."

"Sykes, then. Well, what exactly does he have to show for himself until now?"

"Several leads, some bad mud dug out from Edinburgh's underbelly."

"Not Duke."

"Duke's clever. Apparently. And he knows people."

"We're calling it off."

"You want to hand it over to the police?"

"Haven't you seen the news, mom?"

"No. No, in fact, I haven't. I– "

"You don't care for these things. I know."

Natalie turned on the TV set that was built into the faux fireplace. It did its circus trick illusion of a bad campfire for a second before Natalie tuned it to a local news network. They were running it up and down the news band in the bottom of the screen.

Missing college student returned – no charges filed.

"I don't understand," Rachel said. "What's it to us?"

"There's been more than just me."

"Yes, that poor Polish girl that went missing."

"There was also one boy. At least."

"A boy?"

"They found his room empty. Deranged and bloody. His fingertip got severed. Some cop retrieved it from underneath the dresser."

"How would you know all these things?"

"If you're well-connected, you always get informed. It wasn't in the news, you know."

"If I understand you correctly, you want him to get away with it."

"What exactly did he do to me?" Natalie asked with the greatest of confidence. It shook her mother to the core.

"You know exactly what he did to you. I can still see that black eye shining through the makeup, no matter how thick or expensive it is."

"That doesn't matter. What matters is what we can prove. Nothing."

"Testify."

"There's no evidence."

"The apartment looked like a battlefield."

"It's been cleaned thoroughly."

"The photos."

"You burned them."

"There's Sykes."

"What does he know? Only what you told him. No, it's time to move on. That Sykes is pretty expensive for what he delivers. And if you ask me, we've seen the last of Duke Arrowsmith."

"Why would you be so sure?"

"There's nowhere he could go in this town. If he keeps out of the spotlight, they won't be able to tie the missing girl to him. Less so now that he's off the hook with that Rowan."

"Rowan?"

"The boy he molested."

The words sent shivers down Rachel's spine. They were of a different kind. Long forgotten.

"We go talk to the police. Maybe there's even more victims, afraid to come forward."

"Face it, mom. We blew daddy's money on Sykes. And we blew our shot along with it. They're not going to find Duke Arrowsmith. They're not going to find that missing girl either. That's the end of it. If I testify now, with the news of Rowan's return and him not pressing charges all over town, what're they going to think of me when I accuse Duke? They'll rule me a copycat and send me on the way. No, all I can accomplish now by talking is damage our family's good name and reputation."

"I can't believe you're saying this."

"I've made peace with it. You should do the same. Look at daddy, he's got a head start on you."

Through the light well they could see Charles walking up and down the living room, headset clipped in his ear, looking at something flickering over the phone's screen. When she looked at him, Rachel knew Natalie was right. Even in great crisis, Charles was who he was. Successful, yes. But not the man Rachel literally stumbled into in a hallway at university when she knew nobody, fumbling her stack of books, a scene right out of a cheap summer romance flick, helping her pick them up, their hands touching by chance, lightning flashing through her, through him, asking her out for coffee, holding her hand after ten minutes, vowing never to let go.

"I'll call, Sykes," Rachel said pulling her phone out, almost dropping it on the hard maple floor she disliked so greatly for its lack of character and color.

"Thank you. Are you coming?"

"No, I'll stay, try learning Pynchon."

The smile she forced fooled nobody. There was nobody to be fooled anyway. Natalie walked out. No change of atmosphere. Rachel dialed, then hung up again. Before she could talk on the phone, she would have to recompose herself. Wiping the tears out from her eyes was a start.

Natalie drew a deep breath before she descended the stairs down to road level, devouring the fresh winter air. So cold and cooling and refreshing in her lungs, taking the fire out. The city looked the way she remembered it. The same way it had looked from her former bedroom window, where she'd exiled herself. For her mother's sake, not her own. And clearly not for her father's sake, who hadn't seemed all that worried about the whole affair, least about his wife's near breakdown or the fact they'd decided not to involve the police. To keep their good family name out of the tabloids. That had been a decision much to his pleasing, for the responsibility had been taken off of him convincing his wife it would've been for the best anyway. It was one of the reasons they were still married, since Rachel tended not to concern herself too willingly with inconveniences.

It must've been why she was so blind to the things happening around her, making sure never to notice anything she'd rather not to. A mechanism of self-defense. But at the same time an attempt at upholding the pretty picture of a noble, filthy rich family that had come up in the world, only to always put the family first.

Just thinking about all this, Natalie smiled. Not because there was anything funny to it. But because it wasn't giving her choices. It had never even in the remotest occurred to her mother to question who her father was constantly talking to on the phone. Something Natalie herself had learned quite soon from working student jobs and unpaid internships was that the top dogs could do a great deal of talking without saying anything, excelling in pretending they were indispensable. It was a secret Charles had kept from his wife, not his daughter. It wasn't the first time Natalie would've had all the right reasons being mad at her father.

Lisa this time, a month younger than Natalie. Beautiful, athletic, sporting a body easily suitable to the swimsuit editions that weren't made anymore. A girl much too attractive not to notice. She could kick Charles' ass too if she wanted. Academically, she ranked with honors, though only because she was good at studying and passing tests. As contradictory as it seemed, her intelligence just wasn't quite up there. Lisa was a lot more the country bumpkin as was good for her. Always able to recite the textbook-perfect answer to a clear question, struggling with anything out of the box calling for creativity and intelligence.

It hadn't been by chance her father had noticed her, making sure to check on her daughter's surroundings every once in a while, ever since she was sixteen. It had also been his habit using his larger-than-life persona to impress the easily impressed. A play of power and dominance, and more than anything, exploitation.

There was no need for talking on the phone with an intern for hours. Accounts of pending deals were blended into their talks occasionally, as to give the impression they were more than two lovers chatting. This had neither worked nor sit well with Natalie. With her mother, it had been all that was needed. It was the reason her father hadn't been to the apartment in Old Town in years.

A cute man in his mid to late thirties passed her, making sure to come close enough so she could pick up the scent of his expensive fragrance. It wasn't anything off the shelf, a nice surprise over the ever-same smell of boys of all ages, overestimating their appeal to the other sex.

"Hi," Natalie said on a whim, stopping him on the sidewalk as if she was flagging down a taxi.

"Hi," he said smiling cutely, without any hint of insecurity. "I have the feeling I know you."

"Really?"

"Yeah, from a party last October."

"There's been many parties in October."

"A fair amount, I feel sure. Wait, I'll remember your name."

Natalie giggled as he tried pretending to be raking his brains.

"Claire, right?" he said blinking at her, the giggles getting higher-pitched.

"Natasha," she said extending a hand that was swiftly grabbed.

"David. Call me Dave."

"You're a funny guy. Dave."

"You don't know the half of it. Say, are you free for coffee?"

"Me? Why, sure. But what about you? No meetings this afternoon?"

"Nothing that couldn't be postponed."

She said she knew a café nearby, a hidden gem no tourist would ever stumble into. Walking, she hooked to his left arm, giggling at his jokes, delivered with the confidence of an experienced man dealing with a girl.

"This way," she said pulling him into an alley that stank of food waste even in winter, trash and newspapers on the cobbled path.

"You weren't lying when you said nobody would ever find this gem."

"It's just around that corner, to the right, at the dumpster."

"Okay."

Dave went right down after they turned the corner, and Natalie had let go of his arm in time not to be dragged to the ground along with him. He wasn't as heavy as she would've anticipated. Another impostor that knows how to dress, she thought, then retreated to the brick wall on the other side of the alley.

"Hey," Dave said weakly, rubbing his right temple.

"Who's that?" Sport asked, wearing his signature jacket and the hawkish smile, arms crossed in front of his chest.

"That's Dave," Natalie said.

"Hi, Dave."

"Natasha, don't talk to him," Dave said from his knees, checking his hand for traces of blood. They both laughed at him.

"You look like a Natasha," Sport said.

"That's right. I assumed he'd buy into the Eastern European thing."

"Clever girl."

"What's going on here?" Dave asked, now from his feet, straightening his expensive coat, trying to regain his posture.

"You've entered a boxing competition," Natalie said. "And the prize is – drum roll!"

Sport did as asked.

"Me!" she finished, posing like a bikini girl in a 90s car ad.

"You're crazy," Dave said faking sincerity when he was still in for it.

"You win," Natalie continued unphased, "you'll get me. One day, one night. I'll do anything you want. Hell, I'll be your slave! Your little harem girl. I'll wash your car topless, tell you how nice your abs look, how delicious you taste. Anything."

"But there's a catch," Sport continued.

"What?" Dave asked. "You'll knife me if I lose?"

"Gosh, no! How absurd."

"He's right," Natalie delivered the punch line. "It's much worse. You won't be allowed to tell anyone. And you'll have to limp home with your tail between your legs like the little useless puppy you are."

Despite his head aching, his heart beating in his temples, Dave wouldn't run or outright refuse. First, he looked Natalie down. Head to toe, then back, assessing her.

"You guys are crazy," he concluded. "You set me up."

"Maybe so," Natalie said. "But what're you going to do about it?"

"I'm out of here," Dave replied and started back to the busy street, only to find his way blocked by Natalie.

"That's no option, sorry."

"Step out of the way, gorgeous."

"You don't want me?"

"I want you bad."

"You want to caress my body?"

"I wanna do things to you no man has ever done before. Show you what a real man feels like."

"A real man can hold himself. Defend a girl. Fight for a girl."

"See ya."

When he tried pushing past her, Natalie connected a jab with his jaw, bringing him down to a knee again. This time, Dave was lost.

"You bitch," he said weakly.

"I'll help you up."

"Don't touch me!" he cried, pushing himself up, turning around, away from her, only to see Sport, coat sleeves rolled up, ready for a fight.

"Round one," Sport said before darting at Dave.

He wouldn't attack right away, only take his stance.

"Come on," Natalie said, "lift your hands."

"I'm not fighting."

"What part of, you have to fight, didn't you understand? Lift your hands, defend yourself. Wouldn't it be a shame if your pretty girlish face was smashed to little bits and pieces?"

Succumbing to his fate, Dave lifted his hands like someone who'd seen fighting in movies but who'd never done it himself.

"First punch is free," Sport told him, smiling, lowering his arms. "Come on, right here, right at my chin. Payback for what she did to you."

Rage started crawling up inside of Dave, from the stomach right into his head. You could see fury in his eyes. With a battle cry, he threw a strike, catching only air. Sport had easily dodged him.

"Missed me!"

The first punch went right into the liver, knocking the wind out of Dave. This time, he couldn't take a knee. Sport caught him. As he stumbled back, Natalie shoved him forward. Right into the second punch. It found the pit of his stomach, making him sick. Again, Sport caught him, mid-air, put him back on his feet. Doing all he could, suffering what he had to, Dave went for Sport's torso, his shots blocked. They went into an inside fight, Sport flexing all the tight, steel-cable muscle in his body.

"Give it to me, daddy! Harder!"

The punches got harder, still missing their purpose. Gasping for air, Dave did his best. It was nothing.

"Pathetic," Natalie said. "If I was a docker, I'd spit on the ground."

"Try again," Sport urged Dave on.

He did as told, the swings getting weaker, more pathetic, until he tried clinching but was easily repelled.

"Weakling," Natalie said. "Feel ashamed of yourself."

When Dave turned around to say something, he couldn't, his heart racing like a bad engine, sweat running down his neck, fear in his eyes.

"He's done," Sport told Natalie, rolling the sleeves of his jacket back down.

"Finish him," Natalie said and turned around, leaving the alley.

It took no more than two seconds for sport to do his excellent footwork just for show, launch forward and knock Dave out with a single blow right in the face. It wasn't hard enough to shatter bone. But it came pretty darn close. As he sank to the ground, it was like the end of a chapter. A dispensable episode, easily forgotten. A point proven, neither for the first nor for the last time.

"How did everything go?" Sport asked, wiping his hands nonchalantly.

"As smooth as I expected," Natalie said as they were on their way back to the street, where life went on without taking notice.

"Does that mean that private dick is out of the picture?"

"We'll see. What about the blonde?"

"She's been looking for Arrowsmith."

"What else would she be doing?"

"Give up on him," Sport said. They turned the corner towards Old Town.

"She'd never do that. I can see it in her eyes."

"You're not going to believe what she's doing."

"Huh?"

Sport stopped, putting a finger to his lips. To silence Natalie. Make her listen. There was the white noise of any city at daytime. But there was something else in the mix. Natalie closed her eyes. Her ears picked it up.

"Know the sound?"

"It's that souped-up Lotus."

"She's been rolling all over town in that red atrocity."

"Stubborn little thing."

"Guess who's riding shotgun."

"It keeps getting better."

"Exactly. Private dick, tagging along."

"Why'd he do that?"

"Beats me," he said shrugging, starting back down the sidewalk.

"Why didn't you go get her?"

"It's against the rules. You should know."

"I made that rule."

"I didn't dare asking for an exception."

"Good little puppy," she said stroking his head, enjoying the fondness she received.

"What now? We don't have all day."

"She'll come to you."

"For him."

"Yes. For him. She'll come. You'll see."

"Arrowsmith?"

"What about him? He's got nowhere to go. What would you think he's going to do next?"

With that, she left Sport to doing what he was best at. A game he was perfectly suited for. If for not much else. Natalie enjoyed the walk to the apartment in Old Town. It felt like homecoming. Finding her confidence renewed, she dialed a number. Just like she'd promised to. To arrange an appointment.

22

The engine was still humming its wonderful song, driving through night and day without any mechanical issues, using nothing but air and fuel, running low now. The carbs were slurping the high-octane gas. Emily's nervous foot on the throttle hadn't helped the mileage. Feeling tired and exhausted, she checked through the side window, spotting Roman still talking on the phone. Whoever it was he was talking to, they were arguing. Without any way of knowing, Emily understood it was bad news.

"Son of a rabid dog," was all she understood from his cursing when he got back into the car.

"Bad news," she said.

"That wouldn't begin covering it."

"Don't talk around it. Why'd they get you off the case? I'm no genius but not a fool either."

"They wouldn't tell me."

"Try again."

"Seriously. They told me to send the invoice covering my expenses. That's it."

"Their reasons are theirs alone."

"Now look, I'm as disappointed as you are. Probably even more."

"But what?"

"But nothing. Everyone's entitled to their own opinion."

"You're out?"

"You bet."

"The second the money well is drying up."

"Watch your mouth, Emily. I did everything I could trying to help you and crack this case."

"What about the missing girl?"

"It's a shame."

Emily wondered if she could believe him.

"What about Duke?"

"A real man wouldn't have split once the ground got hot beneath his feet. Now I've said it. You ask me, he's long gone. All this driving around was for nothing."

"Now you watch that tongue or I'll rip it out of your filthy mouth."

"I'm sorry."

"Don't be."

"You're young. In ten years' time you'll know better."

"Thank you for your time and help, Roman. Farewell."

Hand on the door handle, Roman hesitated, making up his mind.

"Farewell."

With that, he left her banging the door, car idling, a song of a time past and gone, singing against the noise of the city. Emily checked her phone, hoping, wishing, wondering when she found yet again no word from Duke.

The clock was ticking. She knew that better than anything else. For a split second, a thought crossed her mind. What if Roman was right? In that case, her heart would burst and shatter into a hundred million little shards, impossible to mend. The thought was banned quicker than it had popped into her head. Emily would never accept it. After all, she needed a beating heart to keep on going.

A dozen possible places to keep on searching flickered through her head like shots in a movie cut in quick succession. But none of them made any more sense than all the places she'd been to before. There was no way. Duke had disappeared. That much about the equation was correct. To protect her and himself, until viable evidence clearing his name was available. It took her past the crossroads. The final crossroads in her head, leading into a dead end.

Dead end. Here it was. It felt bad to the touch when she traced it with her fingers. Like poison, diffusing through her skin. Into her flesh. The blood circuit. Washed into her nervous system. Invading her mind. The business card. Emily pulled it out.

Burgundy Bobcat.

No street address.

No phone number or email.

Only a number, printed in finely embossed champagne gold letters. Her number.

10558420.

Emily pocketed the business card again. The gear lever felt wonderful to the touch when she pushed it forward into first. She had no trouble beating incoming traffic from behind, speeding down the street. All those familiar streets, their appearance altered through the new perspective from behind the steering wheel, all the shapes and lines and colors filtered through glass.

The drive to Stockbridge was a blast. The only one she knew she would be having that day. All the worries disappeared from her mind. At an apartment block, where a friend of hers out of college lived, Emily pulled into the parking lot out back. 13 was reserved for her friend for reasons unknown to Emily. Since she didn't own a car, and didn't rent it out, nobody would mind the Lotus sitting there for a while.

The cozy warmth inside the car, mixing so perfectly with the smell of leather and whatever material they'd used for the rest of the interior, was replaced with the sharp, cutting cold of another winter day when Emily got out. On the radio they'd said the sun would be coming out in the afternoon. There was nothing but grayness when Emily started down the road, cutting a path through Stockbridge like a sharp knife.

Kate looked astounded upon the door to the café swinging open and Emily stepping inside. Last night's hardship had left visible marks on her. Not enough to diminish her beauty. But plenty, still. There were a few people inside, drinking coffee and whatever olive tea was supposed to be, staring into their phones. No talking.

"Hey," Kate said cold enough to rival a winter storm.

"Hi."

"Want something?"

"Glass of water and a lager."

"It's early in the morning."

Are you my psychiatrist, Emily wanted to snap at her but didn't.

"Exactly. I'll be sitting over there."

It was the table she spotted Duke sitting at for the first time. Emily took the seat on the other side of the table, facing the back. A vintage piece delicately formed out of what seemed like little more than twigs, looking like it had had been stolen right out of a café in Vienna. Facing the back wall of the café, with its decorative wallpaper, Emily felt she had her thoughts to herself. The massive window front to the right was only mildly fogged over. This time, Stockbridge looked like a caricature all messed up.

"Here you go," Kate said putting a glass of water and a small bottle of lager in front of Emily. "Can't grant you the employee's discount. Because you quit, you know?"

"Thanks, Karen. I'm sure someone else is going to pick up the tap anyway."

Walking off, Kate mumbled curses Emily didn't catch. The water looked tempting. The beer even more so. In one big gulp, she downed it, finding her thirst quenched. Hand on the glass of water, she sat and waited.

People finished their hot drinks, heading for work, someone coming in for a vegan donut to go, a pensioner who'd probably gotten up around three in the morning, wrestling with himself for weeks until finally having the heart to push open the door to this café and try something new, for goddamn's sake. All this happened as a reflection in a mirror hanging from the wall, where Emily's glance drifted from time to time. It was impossible for her to tell how long she'd been sitting there. The only indicator she had was her fingers and palm warming again as the glass of water slowly lost its chill.

And when she heard Kate giggling from behind the counter, Emily knew it was about time. Nothing was required of her. Wait. Only wait. Be pretty as you wait. Nothing you could do about it. Be pretty all the time, can't help it. Trying not to look, she only caught what seemed like a single frame in the corner of her eye. But what she saw was familiar in the creepiest sense of the word. A jacket she'd found tasteless and suggestive from the start, that she wished she'd never seen at all.

"I'll call you," an attractive male voice said, the giggles getting louder.

The water tasted stale in her mouth. It did nothing to wash away that taste of cotton and copper. Whatever level of sovereignty she'd retained slowly faded from her grip, leaving only a void so intense it induced physical pain.

"Is that seat taken?" Sport asked sitting down on the other side of the table, casually leaning against the window.

"There you go, Sport," Kate said putting a small espresso cup and a tiny glass of water in front of him with a smile.

"Thanks, darling."

"It's on me," she said, beaming.

"I'll make it up to you."
"I bet you will. I'm free tonight."
"I'll give you a buzz."
"I– "
"Would you please excuse us?" Emily said in a voice making herself very much clear. Kate understood and retreated back behind the counter, checking her Insta and TikTok while sneaking peaks at Sport, jealousy burning in her eyes.

"Emily, it's been a while," Sport began.
"No while would've been long enough."
"You didn't call."
"Think I should've?"
"You refused accepting my number."
"Exactly."
He smiled into his cup as he sipped espresso.
"How does the espresso taste? Thin and tasteless?"
"Thin. And stale."
"It's not the beans. And neither the expensive equipment, mind you."
"You put up quite the show, running all around Edinburgh."
"A show? I was going for a circus."
"Circus?"
"I wanted to attract a clown. Worked out just fine."
"If I didn't know you were a literature major, I'd suspect it now."
"Other than you, right? You're not really studying literature and reading Faulkner, do you?"
"Nay."
"That speech you gave. On Pylon. That was straight bullshit, wasn't it?"
"Straight from the prairie. But they're buying it. What can I say. They're always buying it."

Sport shot a smile at Kate, melting her brains, almost making her drop a bowl of oatmeal swimming in oat milk a vegan customer was craving for.

"I didn't buy it. Not an inch of it."
"You're one tough cookie. It's part of your appeal."

Sick of talking to him Emily produced the card. It looked pretty and fake on the oak table top.

"10558420. That's my number."
"Aye."
"I hope you're not counting up."
"It's a code I don't understand. It's beside the point."
"The point is, this somehow connects with Duke."
"You want to see him again?"
"Yes."
"Let's go, Emily."

Without hesitation, Emily followed Sport to the exit. Everything around her looked like a movie set. The coffee cups, the furniture, all props. Kate seemed like the worst cast actress in the world, chosen for her good looks, not talent. Sport sensed her disdain, quickly crossing over and pressing a kiss on her earlobe, whispering words to her. Any sugar-coated words would do.

A car had been waiting, a British racing green Jaguar from the 90s, V12 running as smooth as a stalking tiger.

23

Five pages of Pynchon had been the result of her efforts. Rachel had found her eyelids turning heavy as lead. Too heavy to keep them open. The house was dim and silent and, she felt, empty, when she woke up from the doorbell's persistent ringing.

Charles had gone off to work and Natalie hadn't returned. Rachel shifted in the armchair, wishing the ringing had been nothing but a fragment of a bad dream already and quickly fading from her memory. The images, so clear and vivid when she dreamed, turned to dust. They were slipping away.

The ringing got more persistent. If that made any sense at all. Nothing seemed to be really making sense anymore. Then Rachel realized her daughter was gone. Case closed. No word from her. On the way to the front door, she asked herself if Natalie was alright, if someone was keeping her safe. A friend, maybe. That someone she'd mentioned. A distinctive name Rachel couldn't remember for the life of her. She was still looking for the name when she understood she'd arrived at the front door, in time for another ring.

"Who's that?" Rachel asked.

"Police."

"Police? Can you show some credentials?"

"Come to the peep hole."

Did she say peep hole, Rachel wondered when she positioned her left eye to look through the small glass circle, only to see a police badge. It looked legit. But what did she know?

"What do you want?"

"Talk to you."

"Congratulations, we're talking."

"Witty."

"I don't recall committing any offenses."

"You're Mrs. Townshend?"

"Yes."

"I'd rather you let me step inside and we talk in confidentiality. You know, nosy neighbors and all. It's cold."

Reluctantly, Rachel removed the chain from the door and opened it, amazed at the well-trained and beautiful police officer pocketing her badge.

"I have no idea what you need from me," Rachel said, arms crossed in front of her chest.

"Call me Joe."

"Joe?"

"Joe. As in Josephine."

"That's a beautiful name. It shouldn't be abbreviated."

"Only a mother would say that. Can we talk? Won't take long."

Rachel saw Joe to the library. It was the only room in the building she could bear. When she returned with two cups of coffee, Joe was at the coffee table, reading the blurb to Pynchon.

"One heavy book. Like a brick."

"It's some 800 pages."

"I didn't mean that. Thanks for the coffee. Oh, it's strong."

"If it wasn't, what would it be good for?"

"We're on the same page. Pun intended. Not with the Pynchon, though."

"What do you mean?"

"You didn't make it past page five. Me, I pushed all the way through."

"You like it?"

"Hello, no. I'm just too stubborn to ever give up on a horse ridden to death." She replaced the book, taking another sip of coffee.

"So," Rachel said, intent on cleaning house, "to what do I owe the pleasure of your visit?"

"It's your daughter. Claimed she fell victim of a crime. You bypassed the police, hired a private dick. Guy straight out of a pulp novel. Marloweish. Doesn't look the part, though. He was hunting for a man he never caught. Your daughter called it all off. But there's no closure. Actually, it doesn't even add up. Am I missing out something yet?"

Cotton in Rachel's mouth. Even if she'd attempted to speak, it would've been tough.

"Okay," Joe said and continued. "Moving on. I'm not going to ask you where you first met Mr. Arrowsmith and why seeing him was habit-forming. With your husband, it isn't hard. Don't get me wrong. Upholding the lie, that's hard. Relating to your choices? Less so. Sorry if it comes out straight and hard."

Cotton turned into thick spiderwebs.

"I don't judge. Really, I don't care. I know people and they have certain needs and don't they just love betraying each other. I have a question for you."

Rachel took a sip of coffee. It mixed to jelly with the spiderwebs.

"Go ahead."

"Did your daughter ever mention a Polish girl named Agnieszka?"

"No."

"What about Angie?"

"Maybe. I don't remember. She didn't bring any friends home in years."

"Angie's a poor girl from Kraków. Smart and beautiful. Studying on a scholarship, working her back to the bone too. To stay afloat. So her parents wouldn't have to send any money. When she's not in class or studying, she's waiting tables. She's got three jobs. Neither paying a whole lot of diesel. When she met Natalie, Angie was still so naïve."

"Naïve?"

"Yes. Naïve. She felt they didn't have anything in common. After all, they're from different worlds. She didn't even understand why Natalie was taking that course in commercial writing. It wasn't down her alley, while it was exactly what Angie wanted to do. Nobody would ever hire a Polish native speaker writing copy in Scotland. At least not if her English wasn't pristine."

"Probably."

"Angie knew getting a break in managing would be tough. Writing was that niche, just for her. Where she'd bring together economics and what she considered her greatest talent. Writing. She's written a book of poetry in Polish. It's good, from what I understood from the transcript. But that's beside the point.

"Nobody would ever care. That's the point. A girl like Natalie, with a father running a multi-million-pound sterling operation, would clearly get her a break. Knowing her was a foot in the door. Angie didn't mind helping Natalie with her writing. Not that she felt Natalie would ever have to write anything worth a damn herself. They became friends. Mutual benefactors, rather."

"What are you getting at?"

"I'll be brief. Your daughter's influence on Angie? Well, let's say it wasn't ideal. She gave her ideas."

"What ideas?"

"Marketing herself. Inside her niche. You understand?"

Silence first, then nothing. Joe saw it. It was time to call it.

"Mrs. Townshend?"

"Yes?"

"You don't know anything about Angie?"

"No. But I hope she's safe."

"I don't know if she's safe. At least she wasn't dismembered. Remember the girl that vanished from the dorm?"

"The abattoir? I remember."

"It was Angie that went missing. Mr. Arrowsmith was our prime suspect. Scottish Psycho. Losing his bearings. Turns out Angie left the country on the private jet of a South African gentleman in his fifties. If there hadn't been confusion over a custom's affair at Glasgow airport, we wouldn't have known she was back in Scotland."

"What's the punch line?"

Joe had rehearsed this inside of her head. Over and over, picking her words. They'd sounded great then, but when she looked down the black abyss of her coffee cup, she lost all confidence in what she'd planned.

"The point is, you knew something and never cared knowing enough. You're a victim, like many. Even though you don't look the part. You're the accumulation of circumstances. I don't blame you. I don't hail you, either. It's your very own demons you'll be fighting for the rest of your days. No charges will be pressed. And thanks for the coffee, it was delicious."

It sounded like a bad joke but it was all Joe had to say. As she waited for a reaction, Rachel wondered if she wanted to hear it at all.

"A bad dream," Rachel said in a voice barely more than a whisper, much too quiet even for a library.

"Make your own choices."

"How?"

"Beats me. Did Arrowsmith reach out to you?"

"What's it to you?" Rachel asked, her head hanging down.

"It should be nothing to me. And yet it feels like everything. Have a nice evening."

"I'll see you out."

As she descended the stairs back to the street, Joe wondered if that majestic feeling would ever come, or if it was destined for people so much not like her. There was no unprecedented feeling. Devastation. But that was normal.

"Hi, Roman," she said without looking the moment she stopped at her car.

"You beat me to her," Roman said and stepped out from behind the shrubbery, where he'd been doing surveillance.

"Figured she'd prefer hearing it from another woman."

"Had you said lady, you'd have had me laughing."

"What makes you laugh at me calling myself a lady?"

"Nothing."

"Nothing speaks volumes."

"Why didn't you call?"

"I knew you'd find me anyways. Arrowsmith?"

"A ghost."

"Thought so. It's like the car is everything he ever was. A red shadow, zipping through town."

"I don't know a thing anymore."

"Want to talk over a cup of coffee? For old time's sake?"

"Fish and chips and a beer."

"On me."

They sat in mutually agreed upon silence, spearing bits of battered and deep-fried haddock with tiny wooden forks, sometimes adding fries soaked in vinegar to the mix. They washed it down with cheap lager, like any other simple man or woman would've after a hard day's work.

"Got paid?" Joe asked, pushing the paper tray aside and wiping her hands on a thin, brown recycling napkin.

"Plenty."

"But you feel like a thief."

"Like a cheat. What exactly did we accomplish? It was all a scam."

"Right. It was a scam."

"Why?"

"Sounds like you're disappointed."

"Don't tell me you didn't expect to unearth some sinister place deep in the bowels of Edinburgh."

"Those sinister places, you don't have to look for them. They're in plain sight. Behind drawn curtains. In the back of an apartment block. Behind the most beautiful eyes you've ever seen."

"A girl with all her life still ahead of her."

"Does it surprise you? In a world like this."

"Sodom."

"Babel. Or Rome. Carthage. Shanghai. Make your pick."

"What about Arrowsmith?"

Joe rolled the recycling napkin into a ball and tossed it into the bin some ten feet away with ease.

"Joke's been on him all the while. Don't tell me how the dots connect."

"I got a suspicion."

"I'm beyond caring."

"What's that supposed to mean?"

"It means, I'm done with all this. I've had it."

"Hand in your gun and badge?"

"Now that I know she doesn't need me to come for her, there's no need going on."

"Not for yourself?"

"I've overstayed my welcome, so to say."

"Huh."

"No, don't do that now, Roman. I didn't mean to change your mind or anything."

"You'd never do that. There's nothing else I want to be. I wanted to be a soldier. To help people, at first. Which was foolish and hypocritical. I wanted adventure. Being a private eye is the next best thing, apart from becoming a mercenary or hitman."

"You'd be a terrible hitman."

"True."

"Ever considered picking up pottery?"

"With hands like mine? Forget about it."

"One of us is going to stay, keep an eye on everything. Make sure the Royal Mile is safe in my absence."

"Where'd someone like you be headed?"

"The Hague."

"The Hague?"

"Need a map?"

"It's just the least possible place I could've imagined."

"Wanna trade for Burkina Faso?"

"What're you going to do there?"

"Go for a walk at the beach in Scheveningen, get some bitterballen and live my life. For a change."

"If that's so, I won't be keeping you any longer. It's been a pleasure."

"Pleasure's been all mine."

A formal handshake evolved into a hug. Quick but intense, soon broken, a moment savored in memory but irretrievably lost. Roman said he had to go, tailing a man purportedly cheating his business partner out of money and a lover. It was what kept him going. Walking away, he knew it was the only life he knew. He never looked back.

Joe turned her badge in her hand. The only thing she'd ever desired, and now felt lifeless and cold to the touch. On the way back to police headquarters she got lost twice, turning left when she had to go right, with confidence. When she walked inside, she couldn't remember the name of the officer at the front desk, a person she'd seen almost every day for years. It was embarrassing. It didn't sit well with her. Her head felt numb as she ascended the stairs, still loathing the old creaky elevator that smelled of piss. Francis walked right at her.

"Joe," he said in a voice making her wonder if he was glad to see her.

"Hey, Franny. How's everything going?"

"Business as usual."

"I never said I was sorry. "
"Don't say it, it's alright."
"I'm not sure it is."
"What did you get for lunch?"
"Fish and chips and lager."
"Want coffee?"
"Only if you brew it."

Whatever he did to the coffee was beyond Joe. All she could say for certain was it tasted better when he brewed it. Special. They stood at the small tea kitchen, drinking black coffee, Francis out of his Batman – The Dark Knight cup, Joe using one of the many unassorted cups that had been floating around the inventory. Chatting and talking about private matters made Joe feel somewhat better. Eventually, she had to pull the pin from the grenade.

"I'm here to return my badge."
"You understand we don't live in a Hollywood movie?"
"After this last debacle, I'm not so sure."
"Your reasons are yours alone. We've worked together for, what? Five years?"
"Six."
"There's one thing you need to do before you return that badge and six-shooter, Annie Oakley."
"What would that be?"
"Come."

Francis led her to interrogation room five. All of them were free but using five was one of their tricks, pretending to be much busier than they ever would be.

"Who's in there?"
"See for yourself."
"If this is a bad joke on my expense, Franny, I'll kill you."
"Oh, screw you, Joe. Go inside already, close that chapter. If you want to go on afterwards, I'll be working with you again. If you feel like quitting, I won't ever hold it against you. And I'm sure as hell not going to talk you out of it."
"What good father would ever stand in the way of a wayward daughter, huh?"

Francis didn't see anything funny in it. Joe realized this but said nothing. Opening the door, she didn't know what to expect. But then she recognized the person instantly. Seeing her made her feel like a harlequin at a medieval court. A defeat, completed.

"Are you Joe?" Agnieszka asked in a polished but still thick Polish accent.
"Aye. How did you know?"
"They said you were easily the prettiest woman around."
"If that's so, I'll thank them on the way out. They never told me."
"At least not when you were in earshot."
"True love."
"Can I smoke in here?"
"Have one for me, too?"
"Sure."
"Thanks."

Joe flicked her lighter open. A big flame like a camp fire appeared, and she lit their cigarettes with it, almost burning their eyebrows off.

"I like the print on the lighter. What's that?"
"The logo of my ex-boyfriend's favorite football club."
"You support the team as well?"
"I watched the games together with him so we'd spend time together. I was fresh on the police squad, working the graveyard shift. Figured we could be together before I headed off to my shift and he went to bed."
"How did it go?"
"He liked drinking beer with his friends and flirting with other women better after a while."
"Why? You're gorgeous."
"I was very fit and my deadlift put his to shame."
"Little boy, crying his heart out."
"Some will never get it."
"That's why I prefer men over boys. Only there's not that many left anymore."
"They must've said that in Sparta. Why'd you come seeing me?"
"Thank you for coming out and looking for me. I shouldn't have left town in a whim."
"You mean with a bed soaked in pig's blood?"
"Yeah," Agnieszka said and shrugged as if it explained it, "maybe that wasn't the best move."
"But a chance presented itself and you went for it."
"I know where you're going. He's a real gentleman."
"And twice your age."
"That's beside the point."
"It's none of my business. You're old enough."
"You sound disappointed."
"Perhaps I am."
"My life's better than ever."
"Are you happy?"
Agnieszka pondered the question.
"Yes. I phoned my parents. They were glad I didn't get killed and chopped to pieces. That didn't last. When I told them about Nigel, they got mad."
"They're your parents."
"Does that mean they don't want the best for me? After all, it's not for them to decide what that is."
"That's true."
Joe carelessly crushed the cigarette out on the table top. Agnieszka threw hers to the floor, stomping it out under a high heel worth a fortune.
"You're not interrogating me," Agnieszka continued. "I appreciate that."
"Case's closed."
"You're not interested in all the little details? How it's tying together?"
"How Arrowsmith is fading into the picture."
"Yes."
It was an opportunity right there, within hand's reach. All she had to do was grab it. Joe hesitated. She pondered.
"No," she eventually said.
"No?"

"I know what you're thinking. The answer's still no."

"If I told you I was going to a meeting and all you had to do was tag along and–"

"The answer would still be no."

"That surprises me."

"Maybe as much as it surprises me you're snitching on the people that made you. Here's something we've got in common."

"They deserve it. Not for the outcome. For who they are and why they did it. You understand that?"

"Yes."

"It seems there's nothing more to say between us."

"I'll see you out."

People watched their every step on the way across the building. It got to Joe she felt so little sympathy for the person she'd been trying to save, sacrificing her days and nights. No further evidence was needed.

"Thank you again, Joe," Agnieszka said when she put on her oversized rhinestone sunglasses, already watched by the greedy eyes of a hungry wolf leaning against a Mercedes parked at the curb.

"All the best."

Joe let go of the door. It closed softly.

"Are you mad?" she asked sitting down in the worn-out office chair in front of Francis' desk.

"I don't know," he said without looking up from the computer screen.

"There's nothing to be done. You know me."

"I know you for sure."

"What're you going to do?"

"Carry on. Someone has to."

"Not me. I don't have to."

"No, not you, Joe."

The gun felt heavy in her hand, almost unwieldly. She removed the clip, pushing out the bullets one after the other, carefully lining them up on the table top. Once she was done, her hands smelled of gun oil and smoke and death.

"She in?"

"Uh-huh. Charge inside, full blast. Like Custer's cavalry at Wounded Knee or something."

"I'll come see you some time."

"No, you won't. It's okay. I'm not even sure I'd want you to."

You could feel the cold hovering across the table like winter fog over a loch. There was nothing there to salvage, she knew that much for certain.

It didn't take long with the chief, some yelling, some appeasing, followed by yelling and cursing. None of the words and curses touched Joe. After fifteen minutes of not giving an inch, she had the chief signing all the necessary paperwork. When it was finally time to put the gun and badge on the table, Joe felt like the Blarney Stones were lifted off of her shoulders. Another nod for a goodbye was all she gave, leaving the building hoping not to bump into anyone. It didn't work. But the ambience did the speaking for all of them.

For the first time she remembered, Edinburgh smelled different. Burgers for dinner, a Pepsi to go with it, some good night's sleep. In the morning, Joe would know for certain if she'd go ahead and carry out her plans or if she'd stumbled from one delusion into another.

24

The crowd wouldn't bother Duke as he made his way across Waverley Station. Knowing where he was going, he avoided everyone. Including the passengers queuing for the Highlands Express, enchanted by the brass band playing The Saints Are Marching In. At the lockers, he wouldn't even check for anyone watching him. With quick hands, he removed all the items and shoved them carelessly into a linen bag he'd bought at the Guinness Brewery in Dublin, disappointed in the experience but thrilled by the merchandise.

Temptation was big and mounting when he approached the exit, knowing he was running out of time. Emily. She crossed his mind like a fast train coming in. There was no way keeping his thoughts off her. Not being able to tell her what was going on was killing him. To Stockbridge first, then Old Town.

When he caught a glimpse of himself in the reflection of a shop window, Duke felt he looked no different from the beggar on the other side of the street. It wasn't just the worn-out clothes. It was the expression on his face. The sadness in his eyes, sunken in deep. For the rest of the way, it was hard on him avoiding the reflections chasing him like the hounds of hell. How many reflections there were, scattered all around the world, making a fool of him.

Mad Dog Boxing and Gym was hidden behind a squeaky metal door, up a narrow flight of stairs. It was the steepest staircase Duke had ever seen in Edinburgh, the likes he'd only encountered in Amsterdam. A beefy guy carrying a stinky knapsack pushed past, forcing himself and Duke against fading wallpaper on adjacent sides of the staircase.

"Sorry, pal," the guy said and continued his descent on legs toasty from the leg press and hack squat machine.

"Don't break your neck," Duke said automatically.

The entire gym was in full swing, with all three boxing rings occupied, one with two girls throwing punches like the biggest guys. Duke went straight for the locker room in the back, avoiding everyone. Those that saw him, not really acquaintances, just people you talked to between sets, didn't say anything.

A woman in her thirties beamed at him as he passed, not caring about his less than dapper attire, which so uncharacteristically contrasted what Duke usually represented. Duke was her unrequited gym crush. He forced a smile, settling for not crushing any more delusions.

It was dim at the locker room but manageable because they kept a window open to let out the sweat and man stink. It had sold Duke on working out there. The atmosphere was one thing. He'd always loathed gyms, overcrowded and underfunded. But the stench at the locker rooms, that was something else. Running that thought back in his head was clearly one of his mechanisms of coping with this situation. With shaky hands, he tried opening the combination lock. It wouldn't work.

"Let me get this for you," Jamal said, getting up from the dark corner where he'd been sitting on a ring stool. It took him one try to get it right.

"I didn't expect you here," Duke said.

"The cops don't know."

"Don't know what?"

"Don't you follow the news?"

"You didn't sit over there all day just to tell me this, did you?"

"Are you expecting an apology? I tried all I could."

"But it's never enough, is it?"

"I've been to your place."

"Did she talk to you?"

"Yes."

"Cursed you."

"Yes."

"Told you to get lost if you didn't mean to get my neck out of the noose."

"Don't you pretend you know her. She's just a girl and you've been with her for, what? Hours."

"Don't you dare giving me the victim and exploitation routine."

"You're asking for it."

"Whatever any grown-up person is doing by their own accord is none of my business. And it's none of your business either."

"I'd have expected at least some degree of respect."

"You've been mistaken."

"The cops paid your father a visit."

"The car," Duke said packing his gear from the locker."

"That stupid car. Why'd you keep it?"

"Why wouldn't I?"

"It's like pinning a bull's eye on your back. Like screaming, come and get me, to the entire world."

"Come and get me for what? You're living in a strange world, buddy. Like plenty of people these days."

"Yeah, we're all crazy and you're the victim. Didn't I hear that before? Too many times."

"The cops dropped the case. Turns out she wasn't cut to little pieces and dumped in the Fifth of Forth."

"You make it sound like she did something wrong."

"Didn't she?"

"Oh, screw you."

"Now I get it. Old friend my ass. You think I'm guilty. You believed it when they said I chopped her up and messed with that other kid as well. And when it turned out I didn't, you're disappointed. You want to know what else I did to them. To save face. Because to you, I'm a predator. I wrap them around my little finger with my sweet-looking face and my charming talk and then I exploit them to the bone. It's my nature, I can't help it. I'm as much a dinosaur as the skin and flesh and bones turned oil my Lotus 912 engine is burning into fire, smoke and propulsion. I should go extinct. If I didn't by myself, I should be judged and taken out of commission."

The way he looked at Duke spoke volumes.

"You messed them up," Jamal came forward. "I know it. You did it to them. It doesn't matter it wasn't as cinematic as it appeared. You killed them."

"And people like you reanimate them."

Duke slammed the locker door. Hard enough to unhinge it. The hair he'd straightened somewhat presentable was rustled again.

"Turn yourself in."

"Or what?"

"I'm sick of people like you."

"Do me one favor. Take your attitude wherever you want, it's a free country. But make sure that place is at least fifteen miles from me."

"Someday, you'll see what you did. Who you are. And then you'll be ashamed. What would you mother be thinking?"

For that, Duke popped him right in the mouth. Much quicker than Jamal anticipated. He sat down on his bottom, trying to get back up out of reflex but finding his jaw connecting with another swing. Two teeth chipped. Another one broke right off. His nose snapped. When he went back down, he crushed the ring stool underneath himself, barely slowing his fall. Jamal was dizzy, fighting to stay conscious.

"Shut your filthy mouth," Duke told him, his eyes wet with tears. He threw his unwashed gym towel right at Jamal's face, walking out, leaving him in the corner of a poorly-lit and stinking boxing gym locker room.

25

Crossing North Bridge, he had a beautiful view of Old Town. In the early morning, it was his favorite view of the city. Next to Carlton Hill. The buildings looked like stone skyscrapers. Majestic and aesthetic. They seemed much taller than they actually were. Duke could see the one building he was headed to. Nothing had changed. An eternity without change.

The stone skyscrapers were the same they'd been for hundreds of years. But were the people behind their walls? Would anyone ever suspect what happened behind closed doors? Behind drawn curtains. What strange things people were doing. These thoughts occupied his mind as he walked, past a group of students, some tourists snapping bad pictures, good and bad and average people.

Since he'd changed into a fresh pair of chinos, blue Oxford shirt, Paisley tie and brown leather jacket matching his belt and Brogues, Duke could feel the stares of the women creeping up and down on him, his chest, his thighs, resting on his eyes. Just for a moment, then wandering again, meandering. The transformation had been complete. Duke Arrowsmith, back in his prime. A well-respected member of society. Not a poor slob drifting through the streets like a shadow of his former self.

The door was unlocked. Duke pushed it open, climbing the stairs to the top floor. It wasn't taking anything out of him. He wasn't breaking a sweat. Something had changed. The transformation had affected every single fiber in his body.

The apartment spanned the entire top floor. When Duke arrived at the double door, it swung open.

"Mr. Arrowsmith," Sport said, grinning in his signature jacket.

"You could've at least dressed up for the occasion."

"I beg to differ. Dress code clearly said: Be Yourself! Someone had to adhere to it."

"Where is she."

"At the parlor. Waiting for you. She's been dying for you!"

Sport took a step to the side, ushering Duke in. There was no need leading the way, though. Duke knew the apartment in and out. Sport tailed him, walking casually with no worry in the world. The interior was richly decorated. Victorian age reproduction of much older chic. A blend of neo gothic, Venetian gothic, which in itself was a recycling of Byzantine aesthetics. Several other influences that flowed seamlessly together. It had always astounded Duke how such a beautiful interior could feel so cold at the same time.

They quickly crossed the mirrored hallways, with themed rooms to the left and right. The pool room. The library. The study. The parlor was a dead end, looking out over the city. Egyptian revival themed. A homage to Cleopatra. Or rather, how she was fantasized over in the 19th century. A big mirrored wall to the right, a book shelf up to the ceiling to the left. At the window front in the middle sat Natalie, sipping tea as she gazed down at Waverley Station. In the light of the city and the station and cars crossing North Bridge, she looked beautiful. Despite all, she looked beautiful.

"Isn't it nice," she said, "seeing someone again you thought you'd lost for good."

"I can't relate."

"Have a seat."

"I'm fine."

"No, you're not. Please."

"I'd rather stand."

"Duke, please."

"I told you I'd rather stand. Thank you very much."

"As you wish, then. I wasn't prepared for this level of hostility, to be honest."

"What would you expect?"

"Some degree of gratitude."

"For feeding me to the birds?"

"For making you learn a lesson you should've learned years ago."

"You're not one teaching others lessons, Natalie. Not by a long shot."

"What makes you think you have the right reprimanding my actions?"

"That I've seen it with my own eyes."

"I've never forced anyone into anything."

"Other than me, you're implying."

"Duke, you're putting words in my mouth."

"Want me to put something else there? Is that what you want? Duke Arrowsmith on a leash, licking your heels whenever you desire?"

"You should know better."

"There's nothing less desirable than a man who's not a man."

"Bingo. What now? The police aren't after you anymore. No need playing cops and robbers in a beggar's rags anymore."

"You know exactly what I want."

"Hm. Maybe I do."

Natalie shifted in her seat, sipping tea, legs crossed, all casual, eyes fixed on a train departing. It was impossible not to add the thick clouds of vapor puffing from a smokestack never attached to this electric train to complete this Victorian Age fantasyland.

"How much?"

"Don't make me laugh. As if I need a penny from you."

"I wasn't asking about money."

"All you have to do is stay here with me and watch. Would that be agreeable?"

"Agreeable?"

"Duke, you're sweating. Are you okay?"

"I'm okay."

"Why won't you take off that leather jacket, huh? Loosen that tie, just some. Step out of those heavy Brogues, change into a pair of my father's loafers. Those loafers, they're not even broken in just yet."

"Natalie?"

"Huh?"

"I'll let you know if I ever care wearing your father's loafers again. Is that understood?"

The tea was stale. It almost burned her mouth. The pain was good. It woke her tongue.

"Do you agree to my terms?"

"It's not giving me any choices."

"Frankly, it does. Leave. The way you always do. Walk out this door and don't turn around. Be gone. Like the Roadrunner. Poof! Mep-Mep! Gone with the wind, like Tuesday."

"You know I can't."

"If only I did know that, Duke. I'd be a happy little camper. Sport?"

"Yes, Natalie?"

"Please close the door behind you. The show's about to begin."

"Of course, Natalie."

And Sport bowed. Much deeper than any free man ought've. Then he left the room, closing the door behind himself. Duke listened for a lock clicking. There wasn't any.

"Duke, you make me uneasy, standing there, staring me down."

"Once this is over, we're divided people."

"That was part of the equation."

"Natalie?"

"Yes."

"If she gets hurt, I'll kill you."

The expression on her face solidified. Natalie understood Duke wasn't joking.

A bell rang, quite subtly. It could've been easily mistaken for some random sound. Without saying anything further, Natalie produced a remote control and pointed it at the mirrored wall. With the click of a button, the mirrors turned translucent, revealing the parlor modelled after an oriental harem on the other side. Duke stood there, looking handsome and cultivated, a subdued scent of cologne and aftershave around him. The Paisley tie matched his brown leather jacket wonderfully.

From then on, all he could do was watch, and keep himself from shutting his eyes or looking away.

26

The purple satin cushion supported her little weight easily, adjusting to the shape of her buttocks. They'd given her a rather short skirt to wear. Never before had Emily worn a skirt. At least not that she remembered, except for school uniforms. They'd made her wear that, too. The blouse was much nicer, though. The colors weren't right. The concept was still the same.

Fatigue was sinking in, making her eyelids heavy as steel shutters. Hard keeping them open. The sweet scent of the oriental room made her sick to the stomach. Worse was the light, tainted in the richest shade of burgundy from the decorated windows. It was reflected by the mirrored wall to the left. Laser beams, flickering, stinging her eyes.

There had been no instructions, so Emily was playing with the idea of what would be happening next in her head. Not much came of it, though. The sole emotion she felt was desire for Duke. It hadn't diminished. Nothing had ever reduced it in any way. As much as she knew it was irrational, immature, dependent, she found no way of standing between her heart and what it wanted.

Terror shot through her, if only momentarily, when suddenly the door swung open. In the dim, burgundy light, it was hard to see who was approaching her, more so when the door was shut behind him again, no light shining in anymore from the hallway. It was a man, alright. The leather heels of his shoes were clanging and banging as he crossed the acacia wood floor, coming for Emily.

"My apologies for making you wait," he said with a smile that was distorted by the light into a grotesque clown's mask.

"Who are you? Just assuming you know who I am."

"Oh, certainly you can't see my face in this light."

But once he was close enough, taking a seat on a red cushion right next to Emily, she did recognize him.

"I know you. You've been a regular at the café."

"Let's say I didn't just come for the Angel Stain. I'm Hunter."

"That's why you never had dessert. You had plenty watching me walk across the shop floor, devouring me with your eyes instead of a cupcake or slice of pie."

"I'm not going to lie to you. It's even better than apple pie with a slice of melted cheddar topping."

"Disgusting."

"There's no question all this had been a big inconvenience. To you as much as to me."

"To you? I genuinely doubt that."

"You're a wonderful person. I couldn't just stand by and watch– "

"Watch me being taken by the black knight? So you polished your armor, mounted your horse and sent someone else doing the dirty business on your behalf?"

"Emily, please," he said reaching out for her hand.

"If you touch me, I break your hand right off and beat you with it."

"There's no need for hostility."

"Where's Duke?"

"Close enough."

"What's that supposed to mean?"

"We'll get to that, I promise. When it's time."

"Stop waffling and cut to the chase."

"Excuse me?"

"You're here to offer something. To buy me. Okay, go ahead with your pitch. Sell yourself to me. Get me to buy into you. Whatever you like best. Let's get it over with."

"I wasn't prepared for that."

"You're not going to get out of this the easy way. Start your sales pitch already, I don't have all day."

Hunter turned his head, looking at the mirrored wall. But there was nothing there, only the reflection of himself, grotesquely transformed and disfigured by the burgundy light. He sighed.

"It's far from easy. Bu I'll try."

His performance sounded very much like a job interview. A freelancer, selling skill to potential customers. How he studied engineering and business simultaneously. How he'd advanced through ranks, making more and more money, working long hours. How he'd topped it up with highly-speculative investments that made him a fortune, admitting to some insider trading that could've gotten him into trouble, but didn't, not without hints of pride in the guts he'd displayed in pulling through without ever cracking up. A brief episode in Dubai. Some affairs with fitness models, luxury girls in luxury management, all of them trying to use his connections in exchange for favors. Good favors, mind you.

"There was never any emotional bond, you know?" he commenced. "I never felt anything past desire for any of those women. One day, I walk into a café in Stockbridge. Some girl I met online suggested it for a first date. I was there early, picking a random table when I saw you. Boom! Blew the back of my head right off. I couldn't take my eyes off of you."

"I didn't notice you."

"How could you have noticed me? I was blown to bits and pieces by you. Reduced to a little schoolboy. I knew right away. This is it. Right here."

"Why wouldn't you say anything?"

"I didn't have the heart. Add to that, this gorgeous woman walking in, all charms, fascinated with me, trying to persuade me to accompany her to her apartment. But I didn't see her. I saw the guy at the next table lapping his tongue for her, imagining what he could do to her. Me? I was sneaking peeks at you all the time."

"You came back, time and time again, never saying anything past Hi! and Angel Stain, please."

"My apologies for being so rude."

"I'll summarize this now. Just to make sure I'm getting this right."

"Okay."

"You're a handsome, athletic overachiever. Well-trained. Spare time genius trader. All gorgeous fitness influencers in town crushing on you slept with you and referred you to their friends and customers. Still, none of it ever meant anything to you. You fell in love with me on the spot. You're willing to provide for me. Correct thus far?"

Hunter hesitated, then nodded.

"You want me to consider this a good deal. In exchange, I need to find some soft spot in my heart for you, be a good wife to you, make sure I take care of my good looks and that's that. That's the conditions to this deal."

"The way you say it, it sounds like a bad deal."

"It sounds like the kind of deal a girl in dire straits with big ambitions and no interest in a boring, conventional life would take. A girl that's sick of working her back to the bone without ever being properly compensated for her efforts."

"Listen, I understand this is all a bit much."

"We're not done yet talking. Let's talk about Duke."

The look on his face spoke volumes. Hunter stared at the mirror, seeking something he couldn't find. Emily was about to lose her temper, thinking this charade had gone on for much longer than she should've tolerated. Within her head, she started counting. The time she gave him before the executioner entered.

27

Duke stared at the see-through mirror. At the man sitting next to Emily. The man who'd tried taking her hand, finding himself rebuffed. Their eyes met. Neither of the two knew. It bore no meaning, either.

"Who's that yuppie clown?" Duke asked Natalie.

"Your rudeness isn't being called for."

"Answer the question."

"It's Hunter. Smart. Successful. Handsome."

"Debatable."

"Witty as well. I wish you could've heard the beautiful things he said. I was reading his lips."

"I'm sure you could crank up the audio as you wish. Assuming you've done it before, sitting here, watching."

Natalie's face turned the color of a good Bordeaux instantly.

"You're right. I've seen plenty from out of this seat."

"Hasn't your mother taught you not to peek and spy on people."

"No. My father did that."

"Your father, a man of high standards."

"Don't you dare running your mouth on my father."

"It is astounding you went at such length just for teaching me a lesson."

"This is far more than a lesson."

"Punishment."

"Now you understand."

"Agnieszka's been sitting here too."

"On the other side of the mirror."

"And you've been watching as well."

"Yes."

"Did it give you any satisfaction at all."

"The most intense satisfaction. Stronger with every time."

"Building up to the climax, which is now."

"I was wondering if your suffering would give me satisfaction."

"Does it?"

"I can taste it. Lap it out of the air. Thick. Dense. Like heavy cream."

"You ruined my good name all over this city. You terrorized innocent people and their families. You messed with the police."

"So?"

"I could've let all that slide. But nobody's messing with Emily."

"It's too late for that. You've thrown your cards on the table and now that I've seen them, I'm amazed I was ever fascinated with you."

"That craving you've been having since your teenage years. Since the first time you've snuck into this outpost of your father's filthy empire. Spying on your mother."

"Oh, shut up."

"Wouldn't it be easy, putting your father on that pedestal? Turning him into that hero you know he never was."

"Shut your mouth."

"Did you ever really believe he started chasing girls your age because your mother was keeping herself entertained with someone else when he wasn't home?"

"Quiet!"

"Or did you understand yourself he did it for his own pleasure? For he knew Rachel would never actively look for someone to give her what she wouldn't be getting from her husband?"

"Shut up!"

"How would you think your mother and I met in the first place? By chance, when I walked over saving her from a tedious conversation at an antique auction, where some old cougar was trying to rub elbows? Or by default. Because I was supposed to be there?"

"You're lying."

"And you really believed your mother was paying me, huh? We were joking about it. But she never knew. She never knew I was sending invoices out to her husband."

"You're a big, fat liar!"

"It was tough seeing her, wringing her hands when she had a touch of bad conscience. When she should've known it had been his idea all along, giving her something to keep her occupied with. To get himself out of the spotlight."

"You're making this up."

"Here's the worst part. You didn't even know this wasn't the only room with see-through mirrors."

Natalie was stopped dead in the water.

"Come, I'll show you."

"I'm sick of your lies."

"I'll prove it. Come."

Duke reached for her hand. Natalie pulled it away. Trying to regain her composure, she was struggling. The complexion on her face hadn't changed. The burgundy wasn't doing her delicate, beautiful facial features any justice. It made her the look-alike of a Vaudeville artist.

"We'll see about that," she said and pushed a button on the remote control.

The light inside the adjacent room changed as the mirrors reflected the flicker of a TV screen coming to live. Duke was watching, but then Natalie got out of her seat, taking his hand.

"You're coming with me?" Duke asked.

"Anywhere you'd take me."

Duke led her away. Neither of the two saw what happened in the other room. When they exited the Egyptian Revival room, Sport reached into his jacket.

Natalie shook her head no, and he assumed his almost militaristic stance, hands folded behind his back.

"It's over there," Duke said leading the way across the hallway.

"The broom closet."

The tiny closet had been cleared years back. Natalie only knew it empty, even as a kid. Sometimes, she'd used it as a retreat for playing with her dolls. Duke pushed a concealed button and the back wall popped open. Suddenly, the small room was tainted in flickering light, all blue and green and white. Natalie froze.

"No," her lips formed the word more than saying it.

The see-through mirror went from floor to ceiling, giving the impression there was nothing separating these two rooms. A chair was place close to the mirror. Wood worn, pillow used up, almost mangy. Without thinking, Natalie sat down, supporting her weight with a firm grip around the arm rest. Duke stood behind her, seeing every frame of film on screen. They both watched. Neither said a word. But Natalie's hands were unsteady. She grabbed something, her fingers closing around a silk handkerchief. It had the signature pattern of her family insignia, with a set of initials stitched into it. Champagne gold thread. With her fingers, she traced the letters. CT. The fabric was all stiff and tough.

"There's no satisfaction," Duke said.

"No."

"That's why they keep coming back for more. Trying to quench the unquenchable thirst drinking more."

"It doesn't feel good."

"No."

"It doesn't feel right."

"It never did."

"How would you do it?"

"I do what's in the cards for me."

"That makes you a slave."

"You'd never consider me a victim."

"Never."

"You won't forgive me?"

"Never."

"I won't forgive you either. We're even."

"It ends here. Tonight."

"We'll be divided people."

"I tell Sport to call it off."

"We've gone too far. There's no need stopping now."

"As you wish."

Natalie pushed herself gently out of the seat. Duke put a hand on her shoulder, pressing her back down.

"What's the rush? Stay, watch the show. You've written the script to it after all."

"Did you know I hate you? From the very first moment I learned about your existence?"

"There was something right there, when I touched you. Too dense to know for sure."

"What was it?"

"Desire. Fear. Attraction. Suspicion. Modesty. Pride."

"You made me feel many things."

"You enjoyed it, too. Those climaxes."

"The body is a primitive machine."

"If I learned anything, it's that it won't suffice pleasing the body. You don't get under the skin, you might as well just walk away from it."

"Take that hand off of my shoulder."

"Or touch you here."

"Duke, don't."

"Or?"

"I swear, I'll kill you."

"You've blown your chances."

"Duke."

"This'll edge into your memory. I'll give you something you won't ever forget."

"Your hands are hot to my flesh."

"It's blood, rushing to your head. Through your body. I can feel your heart pounding like a ten-pound hammer."

"Duke, let me be."

"I will. Once it's done, I will."

28

It was difficult at first, understanding what was going on when the big screen came to life, showing film that appeared to be patched up out of single snapshots, frames in strange and unnatural colors, almost as if a silk scarf had been drawn over the lens.

But Emily did understand. Very well. Eyes fixed on the screen, she watched. It tripped emotions, only she wondered if they were those intended by the makers. Hunter sat next to her staring, too.

"Hey, Hunter," she said shoving his shoulder when it was over and he hadn't come to.

"Excuse me."

"You seemed intrigued by it."

"Me? No. It's disgusting."

"Yeah, for sure."

"How could you ever feel drawn to this man?"

"When there's someone so clearly better for me?"

"I'll show you a world you could only dream of. With or without him."

"What makes you think I ever wanted to be part of that world?"

"It's logical."

"Logical, sure. For guys like you, planning their lives ahead in Excel sheets. This year it says go find a girl, settle down, doesn't it? When will you have to be married? Get me pregnant? One thing's planned for certain for me. Shut your mouth. It spreads across all columns."

"I was hoping you'd understand."

"I was hoping you'd understand love can't be bought. It can't be learned or taught or explained rationally. Love is. Period. You'll never get that."

"Okay, then," Hunter said.

You could tell his heart was racing. Much quicker than it ever had. Worse than during the biggest company presentations. Those make or break deals. In shaky handwriting, he scribbled a number on a sheet of paper, then handed it to Emily.

"What's that?"

"I've taken the gloves off. It's a down payment."

"That's a lot of diesel."

"Take it as a compliment. It's yours. You can do whatever you want with it. Later on, there'll be your private account."

"An allowance."

"I'm not going to elaborate on that."

"You're tempting me, you know."

"That's my intention. I was sure you'd eventually change your mind."

"I have."

And Emily got up, giving herself good leverage before she smacked him right across the face, bringing him down, cheek glowing. Hunter didn't know what to say. Emily crumbled the sheet of paper and threw it right at his forehead.

"In this world," she told him, "you're a winner. In my world, you're a clown."

Emily walked straight for the door, not knowing what to expect. Somehow, she felt it'd be locked. That the door handle would move but nothing happened. But the door swung open. What she never expected was to walk into Duke's arms.

"Emily," she heard him say.

"Duke?" she asked, still unsure. When his arms closed around her, she knew. A meteor shower inside of her head.

"I thought I'd lost you."

"Never."

There they stood, embracing each other, Duke stroking the back of her head, Emily putting her ear to his chest, listening to his heart beating. It was a fleeting moment but felt like infinite joy.

"I'm sorry."

"Don't be."

"Let's get out of here, what do you say?"

"I say I've had plenty anyway."

Taking his hand, Emily led the way out. They wouldn't look back. Not at Sport, leaning at a wall trying to look casual. Not at Hunter, running numbers and stats through his head trying to cope with the clearest of defeats. Certainly not at Natalie, sitting in her father's chair, silk napkin in her hand. The flamboyant, luxurious and expensive interior suddenly appeared, more than ever before, to be nothing but redundancy.

"I took the Lotus," Emily said as they walked out the front door into another Edinburgh night. "I hope you're not mad."

"Of course not. Where'd you leave it?"

It was then that Duke saw Rachel standing on the sidewalk, trying not to meet his gaze but in vain. Her face was a caricature of its beautiful self.

"So this is the bottom of the rabbit hole," Rachel said.

"Not how I wanted it."

"No, of course not."

"There's a lot I could say now, and nothing I feel needs saying."

"I'm sure you've recited all of your lines one time or another, whenever convenient. I don't blame you."

"I didn't have to pretend we're friends."

"I never pretended anything."

"It could've been different."

"Yeah, but it wasn't. You changed your mind, that's fine. Didn't make a bad pick. After all, she's still here, holding your hand."

"You did the same for the man you love."

"You're wrong there. But we digress. There's no substance in warming up the past. The past is what it is. When there's no future to it, it might as well be gone."

Duke let go of Emily's hand. When he approached Rachel, she took a step back. But he caught her, took her in his arms even though she told him not to, petted the back of her head as she pressed her face against his shoulder, weeping, crying her heart out, her eyes, her everything.

"It's alright," he told her

"Don't say that. Liar."

"This is one end. You'll make it through."

"What makes you think so."

"I know you. Better than your husband does. Hell, sometimes I think I even know your husband better than you do."

"What if you're right."

"Rachel, promise me something. When there's a storm and you're trapped at sea, in the cold, dark waters, reach for that lifeline when it's tossed in your direction. Will you do that for me?"

"Yes," she said without hesitation.

"You never deserved this," Duke said trying to smile at it, finding himself unable to blink away the tears welling in his eyes.

"Don't cry for me," Natalie told him, wiping a tear away with her delicate finger. "I forgive you."

They kissed. For the last time. It was quick and intense. It did everything it was intended for. Soon enough, it was over. They broke from their embrace in perfect synchronization.

"I hope you'll be fine," Emily said sincerely.

"I wish the two of you all the luck in the world."

With that, she left them, wiping her eyes dry, pushing the door open and vanishing behind the heavy oak wood, richly carved with the family coat of arms of people long dead.

29

Three days of solitude and peace did them both a world of good. Duke's house felt like a voluntary exile. They wouldn't go out. They wouldn't work, or do much of anything else. When they felt like it, they watched old cartoons Duke had on disk. Sometimes they sat on the back porch, sipping hot coffee against the winter cold, wrapped in bathrobes and a thick Scottish lambswool blanket.

"The air smells so good," Emily said, her eyes fixed on nothing in particular.

"I'll repair the 912 this afternoon, it's been three days now."

"Oh."

"Don't worry, I'll call it quits before our binge-watching night."

"I think I'll be reading in the meantime."

"You want to help me?"

"What do I know of engine repairs?"

"It doesn't matter."

"If it doesn't matter, I'm in."

"The last time I've worked on a car with someone else has been a while."

"Hard to trust someone else with something you love so dearly."

"You can say that again."

Duke gave her one of his coveralls, with Lotus stitching on the chest and all. It was much too big for her, all saggy, so they rolled up the pants legs and sleeves until it was okay. Emily started the 912 and put on the gas once it was warmed up. Shoulder-to-shoulder, they stood in front of the engine bay.

"Listen," Duke said.

"I don't hear anything."

"It's a clicking noise."

"It comes from here."

"The valve pulley? No. But you might be on to something."

Leaning in closer, Duke almost touched the valve cover with his ear. Emily did likewise, trying to understand how it worked. What to listen for. At times, Duke pointed at one part or another. Emily quickly improved.

"We need to take this off," she said and tapped the valve cover when Duke cut the engine.

"I second that."

"Where's the socket and ratchet?"

"Over there. No, take the 3/8 drive."

"The what?"

"The intermediate one. That's the smaller one, that's ¼. Bigger one's 3/8 drive. The even bigger one is ½ drive."

"Okay, got you."

"There's ¾ and 1 inch drive as well but we shouldn't be needing those on a car like this. It's not a lorry."

Eventually, she found the right socket and removed the valve cover, amazed at the mechanical secrets it had kept from her for such a long time.

"Beautiful," Emily said. "I never knew it was so sexy underneath."

"Sexy?"

"Sexy, yeah. Sort of. What's wrong with that?"

"Nothing. It's just that girls usually don't pop off valve covers calling it sexy."

"You have any idea what we're looking for?"

"If we're lucky, it's a valve's clearance. That'd be addressed rather quickly."

"And if we're out of luck?"

"Then it could be anything, really. It's usually something you've never had before and didn't see coming."

The engine oil had a light golden flicker to it, indicating some part was wearing. It couldn't have been long since the damage occurred. Duke had changed out the oil just one month prior. And then Emily spotted a thin crack on one of the rockers.

"Good job," Duke said, kissing her. "You're getting the hang of it."

"Oh, it was nothing, really," she replied and blinked. "I got a feeling this is a bit more complicate of a problem than, what was it again? Valve clearance?"

Dismounting the valve train took the rest of the afternoon. It could've been a faster repair, hadn't it been for Duke explaining every step to Emily before watching her carrying it out by herself. Duke had all the spare parts at the ready. They also had to change the oil and filter.

"Here goes nothing," Emily said before she turned the key and the engine roared back to life.

"Sounds good," Duke said.

They listened for any odd noises as the engine ran and heated up. But there weren't any. The 912 was good to go.

"This was fun," Emily proclaimed. They were standing in the kitchen, drinking tea out of cups smeared with engine oil and grease on the outside.

"Getting things done is always enjoyable. Only it takes resilience and stubbornness to get there."

"I know this is the prelude to something. Don't claim otherwise."

"Not tonight. Tomorrow."

"I want to know."

"Sorry to say you've got to wait. One more night. Been looking forward to this one."

Something she understood, as much as she needed closure, was there was no point pushing it. It gave her some sense of serenity. Almost a naïve state of mind, avoiding the inevitable. Was it something she would have to be afraid of? That was anybody's guess. Emily had a suspicion. She wouldn't attest any more relevance to it than was necessary.

"Okay," she said, finishing her coffee. "Off to the shower."

That night they watched "Batman Beyond: Return of the Joker", a film Emily had never even suspected could exist. They had nachos with cheese dip, a beer, another one. Duke lay with his head in Emily's lap, watching with eyes fixed on the screen. Neither said anything. Once the credits rolled, Duke had already fallen asleep. Emily wouldn't wake him up, only pet his head. Soon enough, she fell asleep, too.

"Perfect timing," she heard the next morning, waking to the sound of bacon sizzling in the pan and a heavy, yet beautiful scent of an oversized Scottish breakfast. Emily rubbed her eyes.

"What year is it?"

"Year of the Lord something."

"You're surprisingly cheerful in the morning," she said and sat up, stretching and yearning, slowly coming back to life.

"Slept like a dog. Did me good. Coffee or tea?"

"Chai, if that's on the menu."

"I'll tag along."

Everything was neatly set on the table when Emily returned from the bathroom. A single rose, red and thorny, stood in the center of the table in an art deco crystal vase.

"This is beautiful," Emily said sitting down.

"Thought you'd appreciate it."

"Because we've never done anything of the likes back at the café, got you."

"I wasn't coming at that."

"The chai smells rich."

"Got a spice mix from a local Indian shop."

"They know their stuff."

"You care for a ham and cottage cheese croissant fresh out the oven?"

"Is that really a question?"

"Here you go."

"What about you?"

"Full Scottish will do for me."

"Would you please tell me what's going on?"

"No beating around the bush anymore?"

"I'd rather not to."

"Should you have any concerns, you'll let me know?"

"I'll sure as hell do."

"After breakfast, we'll take the car out to the Fifth of Forth, go for a walk on the ocean."

"And we'll talk."

"Yes."

"You're going to tell me everything I need to know."

"It's not an interview. It's something you need to know. It'd be unfair if I withheld it from you."

"If I told you every little lie I told, every sin I committed, about the people I disappointed, we'd be talking for quite some time."

"It's not a confession, either."

"Why's it necessary then?"

"Because I need to get it off my chest."

"You're aware people tend to run away from problems? All they want is to be sitting on cloud nine, dreaming their marshmellowy dreams, never even consider how they got there. They don't care what's buried in the backyard."

"Those free of sin cast the first stone."

"Sometimes I feel it's a much cleverer book than they're willing to acknowledge."

"I'm not trying to scare you off."

"I didn't assume that."

"I'm not trying to win you over."

"I'll go with you. And I'll listen. Maybe I'll ask you a bunch of questions. But I'll never point my finger at you."

"I was wondering if– "

"Why'd you pause?"

"It's not easy leaving all this behind. I didn't live two lives, that'd be an overstatement."

"But you built a façade to hide behind and we all have secrets."

"Sort of."

"You'd take my affection for you as a secret well kept," she said taking his hand, her forearm touching the vase with the thorny, red rose in it.

"I sprayed this rose with water and put it in the freezer. The leaves thawed just when you woke up."

"What would you've done if it died instead of recuperate?"

"Leave it alone."

"With its leaves spread across the breakfast table."

"We'll go whenever you're ready. Deal?"

"Done."

It was a wonderful breakfast. Only it left a bad taste in Emily's mouth. Duke barely more than poked at his fried eggs, eating about half of it on toast, spearing the crispy ham just to look at it. His stomach felt as if a giant snake was lurching around inside of it. Somehow, he'd have to fight the urge to pour hot water down his throat to cook and kill it.

Emily took the Lotus for its maiden drive after the valvetrain repair, giving her mixed feelings that soon turned to dust. The car was a real pleasure. She didn't even realize they were rolling across North Bridge, from Old Town to New Town, down Princes Street and into Stockbridge. This time, she never had the feeling they were watched, rather it seemed as if nobody took any notice.

Out at the Forth, a strong wind was blowing about the beautiful red bridge, which seemed so sturdy and solid it was almost unimaginable it could ever follow the fate of its predecessor.

"Scotland really used to be an engineering country," Duke said getting out from the passenger's side.

"What happened?" Emily asked.

"Time. People. If I ever know, I'll write a book about it."

"These things are hard to figure out."

"I have a hunch I can't pinpoint. Anyway, are you ready?"

Emily eyeballed his stretched-out hand, so strong and masculine, at the same time as tender as a drawing by Dürer. Everything about Duke struck her as contradictory. One of her professors certainly would've called it juxtaposition.

"I have a feeling we need to go through with this."

"I wish we didn't have to."

"I wish we had to but it was over already."

"Is your mind playing tricks on you?"

"Cranking out images like crazy."

"I'm not going to say anything to that."

"If there's anything I consider pathetic, it's a man apologizing all the time. As if that would fix it."

"Take my hand."

Walking for a while, they wouldn't say anything. The wind wasn't sparing them. Neutral grounds made it better, if only a tad. It took Duke a while to get started. To find the words to begin. Once he found the beginning, he knew he'd make it to the end.

"It all started when I was fourteen," he said and sighed, even though he'd tried not to. "There's a lot that happened before. A lot I've forgotten. All beside the point. Childhood is the prelude to those formative years."

"Yours started at fourteen."

"One event. We can single it out."

"What was it?"

Duke sighed again. A lump formed in his throat. Something clicked when he tried speaking. His mouth felt as if it was stuffed with cotton balls.

"When Jamal introduced Angélique to me," he said. The story began.

30

Duke and Jamal had lived in the same building since they were born, mates from the very beginning. Separated by only a month, they shared a lot. Jamal's mother had studied French before dropping out. She'd made friends there despite being an outsider. Chloé was the daughter of wealthy French immigrants. And her daughter, Angélique, was only two months younger than Jamal. They'd known forever, playing together until they were old enough to realize the differences between boys and girls.

Duke hadn't really taken Jamal seriously when he'd been talking about the girls he was spending time with, all of which he knew through Angélique. Up to that point, he'd done everything in his power keeping her away from Duke. It wasn't for any vicious or sneaky reasons. It was for separating the two spaces he was occupying. With Duke, he was a boy. With Angélique, he was something Duke couldn't imagine. Certainly, he was imagining the wildest things, anyways.

In February, these two spaces collided. By chance and with force. Duke had been with Jamal, checking cricket bats only when Angélique had waltzed in the door. She'd dropped by with her mother on short notice.

"Hi there," she'd said. "I didn't know you had company. I'm Angélique. Who are you?"

"Duke, say something," Jamal had urged him, shoving an elbow into his belly.

"Ouch. I'm Daniel."

"Daniel?" Jamal had asked.

"Hi Daniel," Charle had said, awkwardly shaking his hand hanging in the air like a dead fish from the hook.

"Everyone calls him Duke."

"Why not Danny? Or Dan?"

Duke had no time listening, being occupied with this mythical creature right in front of him. Angélique was smart, tall, slenderly built. Not the type of girl to stun boys right away. Her appearance was more subtle than the straightforward beauty of the girls from school Duke had been falling for, smacking you in the face straight at full force. It had a lasting impression on him.

What Duke had always failed to notice was his impact on girls. Good, bad and ugly alike. It wouldn't boost his confidence. They sat at a distance, talking about music. Just for a lack of anything else to be talking about.

"You like pop music?" Angélique had asked.
"I like pop," Jamal had replied.
"I know about you. I want to know about Danny."
"Duke."
"What do you like?"
"Detroit Techno."
"Say that again."
"Electronic music."

He had to elaborate on that. Angélique was sliding up on him. Jamal stopped it by sitting between them suddenly.

"Duke, you didn't tell me what you thought about Hibernia's last game."

It was all a decoy, and Duke was falling into the trap. When Angélique's mother had poked her head into the room, the show had been all but over. They'd said their goodbyes, with Duke's heart racing like a race horse crossing the line at the downs.

"Thanks for that, jerkosaurus," Jamal had come at him right away.

"That explains a lot," Emily said trying to weigh in on the talking instead of listening all the time.

"I didn't see the hostility back then."

"Oh, that was the spiderwebbish crack that broke eventually sometime later. I feel sure."

"Back then I thought friendship was for life. Boy, was I wrong."

"Did she call you?"

"You bet. At home. I almost fainted when my mom called me to the phone, holding it out saying: It's Lique, she sounds nice."

"Were you clumsy? You were clumsy, right?"

"Aye."

"Why's that?"

"Why do I sometimes think of the old lady living out at the water, calling for the cats, shaking that huge bag of kibble like a shotgun? There's things you can't figure out."

"You can explain it quite easily. You were afraid."

"I liked her. A lot. But I was afraid of everyone else talking trash."

"Did they say she wasn't pretty?"

"Yes."

"Did they say she was boring?"

"Much worse things. One day I stopped Jamal making fun of her. She had a pimple rash, nothing extraordinary. But he made fun of it anyway."

"What did you say?"

"I told him to shut his face and go get a mirror. It confused him. I believe he connected the dots back then."

"Did you date her?"

"Not exactly. We went on a date. Kind of a scam, she mustered my help delivering newspapers for a friend. We held hands. No kiss. I wanted to. Blew it."

"All that gossip in your head."

"Looped and on full blast. It was stupid, because she was the only person I could really talk to. Open up to. On the phone, when we talked. When we used one of those stupid messengers on desktop PCs and chatted, the world was an iced peach in summer. In the real world, it didn't work. I wouldn't wanna live in the real world back then, it wasn't a nice place."

The way he said it sent shivers down Emily's spine.

"What was the problem?"

"Me. I was the problem. As if I blew a lot of things on purpose. Because I felt I wasn't worthy."

"Self-flagellation."

"The reality was, and I realized it much too late, I could've had a good time. I didn't allow myself. And Lique suffered from it. Much more than me, I should think."

"Did she say the words?"

"Yes. Some months after I tried cutting ties in the cruelest way."

"How did you react?"

"Played it cool," he said kicking a rock, burying his hands in his coat's pockets, shielding himself from the wind. "Told her I knew all the time. Shittiest Han Solo of all time. I told her I liked her. As a friend, you see?"

"Yeah, snapped her heart in two."

"Stomped on it, too. We knew everything about each other. It was scary. I'm the one to blame. Because I wasn't brave enough to admit it to myself and back it up. Be a man about it."

"You were still a boy."

"The boy she fell in love with. I surmised she'd move on, go find someone else."

"She did."

"We cooled off some. Mostly because I ignored her. Some day in May, she gives me a call. She tells me about that guy she's been seeing. Thought I didn't know him. Matter of fact, I did. Such an idiot. Fat and slow. Slow in the head and slow on track. We played football once. Wiped him out, rubbing his face in the dirt when he tried tackling me. Just a slob. A bad pick for sure."

"They kissed."

"That guy robbed the bank. Not because I couldn't have beat him to it."

"Because you were an idiot, much too insecure underneath your skin."

"I guess you're right."

"Why're you telling me this? It's not uncommon being insecure in your youth and putting it behind you later on. Neither is it uncommon to be rolling in your youth and choking when you're getting older."

"Me being insecure is not the point."

"What's the point then? If you're trying to tell me you've been a ladies' man from the get go, then you might as well stop talking now."

"Look how the water's moving. Always in motion, ever-shifting. Such a wondrous sight."

"You missed out on her. I understand that. Having regrets? I guess so. We're all craving fucks we missed in high school."

"Life's not so much about what we did but rather what we missed out on."

"That's a grim way of looking at things."

"I didn't mean that. Better you learn not to miss out on things instead of always wanting everything for the sake of wanting alone."

"Which is not the punch line of your story either."

"There's no punch line. It's not funny."

Emily considered apologizing.

"Go ahead, please."

"I coped with my feelings. We put it to rest, so to say. I put her behind me. Sometimes, I thought about her. It didn't last. Life struck and I got older. Took me years getting back to feeling myself. To feel confident. To go out, have fun, be charming and nice and interesting. I got into literature. I was good at writing but never really sold anything. Worked poor jobs, no way up or out. Kind of a dead end early on. A back alley to die in."

"Sounds like life in your twenties, realizing a head full of dreams and nothing to show for won't cut the cookie."

"I was strapped for cash. Walked by a haberdasher. They had all these beautiful Harris tweet pieces on display. Beautiful hats. Jackets. Vests. I had about five-hundred pounds in cash on me. Had another five-hundred in the bank for rent. I remember seeing Harris tweet jackets as a kid and always wanting one. But my father had told me this type of fashion was for people other than us. I think he saw me in boxing, wearing trainers and hoodies, making some on the side while working a steady job, which was at the docks instead of an office."

"It was all he knew."

"I don't blame him. That day, though, I forgot about his reservations towards Harris tweet jackets. I waltz into the shop and a beautiful woman of about forty-five approaches me with a smile on her face. She had style. Marvelous makeup. Not ordinary, the way it looks when your idea of style is off the Insta and you have not a single stylish bone in your body. I must've looked pitiable, wearing faded jeans and a boxing gym hoody that had seen better days."

"She smiled anyways."

"We start chatting. I try sounding all grown-up and mature, contrasting my looks, compensating for them. I point at a green Harris tweet jacket, asking if they carried my size. They did. As she hands it to me, I try slipping it over my hoody before she stops me, explaining I should try it with a dress shirt. I don't object and she unfolds a very nice shirt. Size 41. I wore that back then. She helps me out of the hoody, into the shirt, pulls and plucks and brushes at it, shaping it on me, tucking it for me, her hands working swiftly."

"A real professional."

"Already I catch a glimpse of myself in the mirror, in bad need of a haircut. I see myself turning into someone. She tells me this looks fine, almost half the way, with a charming laugh. And then she gets the Harris tweet vest I never asked for. I slip into it. With her manicured fingers, she buttons it, brushing it straight. I feel the warmth of her hands. The softness of her skin. She smiles at me again. We're standing close. So close. I can smell her breath. Then I shudder, figuring she could smell my breath too. She helps me in the Harris tweet jacket. I see the prize tag dangling from it, which had alluded me before. The numbers weren't legible. They were dancing up and down, back and forth. I shudder again."

"Three-digit number, easily starting with a three."

"I know I could never afford it. I wouldn't say that, obviously. When everything is tucked in place, she takes a step back, looking at me. That smile on her face again."

"What did she say?"

"Gorgeous."

"Did she?"

"I have nothing to say to that. All I do is look at myself in the mirror. I wouldn't hear her coming back with a Paisley tie she puts around my neck, standing behind me, tying it into a Pratt so effortlessly. Her breath is brushing my ear, sending electric shocks down my spine. I think she feels it. Once she's done, she steps back, calling the tie the finishing touch."

"What about the pair of faded jeans?"

"We never talked about them."

"They must've looked out of picture."

"For all I remember, it wasn't that bad. Why'd they concern you this badly?"

"Oh, I don't know," she lied. "Go ahead, please."

"Well, I'm standing there, looking at myself. She's raving about my good looks and all, finding it a lot more charming than I do."

"Because you know you don't have the money on you."

"She said I looked like a real gentleman. The kind every lady would desire to go to dinner with. I missed that hint right there. I tell her, look, I love this attire and what it does to me but I'll have to give it some thought. It must be exceptionally expensive and all. With nonchalance, she drops the number. My heart is sinking like a stone. I worried about tearing a seam or something, getting out of it."

"And then she told you there was another way."

"What she suggested was a business deal. She needed someone to work for her, so I might as well earn these clothes. At a discount, of course. And there was more money to be made. I asked what it involved and she smiled, telling me we should discuss it over dinner that night."

"As the saying goes, the rest is history."

"On the way home, I bought a pair of beige chinos and a coat from Marks and Spencer's, some shoeshine for my Brogues. The rest of the day, I sat around, doing little, just staring at the wall, smoking cigarettes. By the time I took a shower, did my ruffled hair the best I could and left for the restaurant, I didn't feel prepared. But the moment she approached me when I waited on the sidewalk in front of the restaurant, something clicked in place."

"What did she look like?"

"Neat dress, stylish 20s overcoat. Lips painted red, eyes so bright they were beaming like headlights. I say hi, put a hand around her waist, the other around her neck, pull her close, gently press my lips on hers, chew her bottom lip. I feel her tongue inside of my mouth, the sensation inside of her entire body, inside of me, like a riptide rushing through us."

"She made you that day."

"She made me realize my potential."

"What happened to her?" Emily asked, stopping for the hell of it. For not feeling like walking anymore.

"I worked for her, then branched out. When she shot me down, it was for practical reasons. The elderly gentleman she'd been seeing for some time had decided to close the deal, make her his wife and there was too much risk involved.

"Did you ever pay for the Harris tweets?"

"No."

"I've never seen you wear them."

"You never will. I liked her and the tweets were giving me some really bad feelings. I gave them away."

"What happened next?"

"I was struggling for a while. Not like before, mind you."

"You met Rayne."

"Yes. I met Rayne."

"Looking for another sugar mommy after your first one dumped you."

"Emily, please."

"Did you enjoy being handed over to benefactors like a present to victorious conquerors? The likes that sacked and burned down and raped ancient cities?"

"It wasn't like that."

"Oh, please. What about Rayne? How did she do it? Wait, come to think of it, spare me the details."

"I didn't mean to hurt your feelings, telling you all this."

"You're not hurting my feelings."

"Well, it appears to me, I did."

"Forget about it."

"For me it's important telling the whole story."

"I'd rather you'd not to. Have you never heard of Hemingway's iceberg theory? Omit the obvious. Emphasis by implying things and omission? No? I'm wondering what you were doing in college."

"Emily, stop please."

Emily did. In time before saying any nasty things she had on her mind, and rather wouldn't say, but was about to utter anyway. Her heart was pounding. Ready for battle.

"Okay, then, Duke. Please do me a favor and cut to the chase, alright? Because I think if you just keep talking like this I'll start screaming at the top of my voice."

At first, he couldn't say anything to that. After all, his intentions had been good. Hurting her had been the farthest thing from his mind. But he'd forgotten what strong feelings could do. It dawned on him he should've tried compassion first. When he put himself in Emily's shoes, he knew where she was coming from.

"In my late twenties, I'd been around," he continued. "I think I've found a self of mine I could live with. Maybe not what I'd aspired to be. But someone who was making a comfortable living. Enough to enable me to do the things I wanted to do in my spare time."

"Then you remembered what it was like before that. What it could've been. Lique popped into your mind."

"Like a djinn out of a bottle. I hadn't wasted a thought on her in years but there she was."

"Stalked her online?"

"Yes. Took me a week mustering the courage to write to her. Gave her my number. It's all I did. An invitation. She could've turned it down."

"But she didn't."

"When the text popped up on my phone, I couldn't look at it until the evening. Nothing, really. Small talk. How're you doing? How's this and how's that? Oh, I'm sorry. What about you?"

"Like meeting someone out of middle school at the grocery store."

"It was nice until I asked her about that buffoon she'd been seeing back in school. Some shrewd part of mine had anticipated the typical, corny love story. Falling in deep in school, sticking together throughout college, no screwing around, getting married, kids and boring jobs at twenty-five. Teenage dream bullshit."

"It wasn't that pretty, huh?"

"He'd found another girl, another fat slob or something. I didn't say she was a better fit anyway, quite obviously. Then she told me she'd been struggling for a while as well back in college. A revelation at first, college soon turned dry and dreary. She'd been with men, even tried dating girls. It wouldn't cut it. When she told me she'd gone through therapy, and advised me doing the same, I almost dropped the phone. It was only text but it stung as if she'd said it right to my face."

"Everyone needs therapy these days."

"Don't dismiss it so soon. You don't know her."

"Neither do you."

"One night, I was unsettled. I couldn't go to rest, so I went for a walk. Bought myself a pack of smokes and sucked them in, one after the other. It was nine pm when I decided dialing her number. I wanted to talk to her. Explain to her whatever it was she needed to know."

"Clean house."

"The phone rang but she didn't pick it up. I lit myself another smoke when she texted."

"What did she write?"

"I merely wanted to know how you were doing but that's about it. I don't need to talk. Please respect that."

"Unbelievable."

"What do you mean?"

"She's unbelievable. What a privileged prat."

"I never thought that."

"Because your conscience is clouded with guilt. Which isn't called for. She needs therapy and all you want is talk and she's too much of a privileged coward to even pick up the phone? Why'd she even text? Because it's easy. You have all the time in the world to ponder over your response. Or don't respond at all. And then she's got the brass neck telling you to do therapy. Of all things. Just because she's weak. Look what therapy did to her after all. It wouldn't even make her grow up and answer the freakin' phone. Cowardly and despicable. Nobody has the right to be forgiven but at least the chance to utter an excuse.

"Did she ever think of you? What it would mean to you to tell her the things you've never said before? To apologize if you feel like it, even if you don't need to? Close that chapter and go on? No. She's just another selfish snowflake that can't function normally and blame it on themselves. Therapy. Don't come at me with that horseshit."

Purifying silence. The ocean breeze smelled fresh and salty, and Duke felt a certain clearness in his head like he hadn't felt in a long time. That millstone around his neck wouldn't pull him under anymore. It snapped off, sinking by itself.

"I'm glad I told you," Duke said. "I think I was biased on the matter. Hearing your take on it was golden."

"Listen, I never wanted to know any of this."

"Are you mad at me?"

"No."

"But there's something you need to know anyway?"

"I'd never even considered asking you about it. Hell, I wouldn't even have given it any further thought, hadn't been for all this mess."

"If it weren't for me, telling you about Lique."

"Exactly."

"Okay, then. Here goes nothing. What would you want to know?"

"Angie."

"Angie."

"Now that I've seen it, I can't unsee it. I need to get this straight."

"I see."

"Duke, please. I need to know."

31

Following this old professor rambling on over economics, Reagonomics in particular, and how they'd single-handedly forced the Soviet Union first to its knees, then out of commission, had been a challenge from the first day on. The Glaswegian accent was one thing, despite the professor assuring them he'd be speaking his best English. The other thing was keeping your eyes open after a long day in college that had started after a nightshift at the call center out near Edinburgh Airport.

Work hard, Angie's father had always told her. Don't complain, her mother had told her. She'd followed both. But the fact of the matter was, she was losing herself in the process. The scholarship had been a blessing. And yet, independence and financial freedom for her meant she had some pounds to spare in the bank at the end of the month. Even after working her back to the bone.

The professor took it to overtime, as per usual. Five to ten minutes dragging along like being trapped in quicksand. Angie would walk home, maybe get fast food she couldn't afford along the way because the microwave was broken, and eat it standing up because if she sat down, she'd fall asleep instantly and maybe run late for work. On a reasonably-filled stomach, she'd study for an hour before going to bed and getting some five hours of sleep before the alarm clock would wake her for work like a rooster from digital hell.

Press. Play. Repeat.

It was all she knew, and only thinking about it made her sick to her stomach. In the corner of her right eye, she caught Derek sneaking peaks at her, the way he was constantly doing ever since the beginning of the semester. In week two, he'd mustered all his courage, walking up on her, trying to play it cool, chit-chatting, casually but clumsily, asking her out for dinner. Angie had kindly declined, citing her tight schedule. The reality was, she didn't like Derek. The much bigger reality was, she didn't like anyone anymore. Not even herself, come to think of it.

But then, the prospect of an evening off, scoring a free meal at a restaurant or pub, suddenly enchanted her, no matter what. There was a certain temptation to it. Angie looked his way. Out of curiosity. Derek quickly looked away, blushing with embarrassment.

He's having it bad for me, Angie thought and blushed herself. Back home she'd been with boys but none of them had ever really kindled the fire of passion inside of her she'd so desperately hoped for. Not after the excitement of the new and unknown had worn off. What she knew for certain, though, was that boys hadn't stopped looking her way.

The professor opened the last point of the session, oil prices, and Angie decided to give it a shot. Just for the hell of it. A night off wouldn't throw her off-schedule. If she decided it wasn't worth her while, she could jump ship any time. After all, this was a free country.

"Hi, Derek," she said waiting for him at the aisle.

"Cheerio, Angie," he said in a dry voice getting dryer with every syllable. "Tough session, eh?"

"Dry as pumpernickel."

"What's pumpernickel?"

"Never mind. Say, are you free tonight?"

That caught him off guard.

"Free? You mean as in, free to go somewhere?"

"Somewhere, yeah," she said beaming at him. The smile was faux. It did the trick.

"I'm about to see someone. I mean, we discussed it."

"Who're you seeing?"

"You don't know her."

"How would you know?"

"I don't know, I'm awfully sorry. I wasn't meaning anything."

"Is it Becky? I've seen you two talking."

"Yeah, it's Becky. She's got a knack at economics. I figured she might help me out."

"Sure, you two have a date tonight."

"It's not a date. Gosh, I mean, it's studying and company, you see?"

"Too bad. I'm in the mood for Italian food tonight."

Blinking twice instinctively, she changed his mind. Derek shot Becky a quick message on their way out. Finding something to talk about on their way to New Town proved challenging, but Angie managed to keep him talking as if she really cared about his childhood dream of becoming a famous rugby player. Which was so far out of the picture, given his arms were even thinner than hers, his weight estimated at a whole lot less than 200 pounds.

When he talked, he seemed less insecure, and asking redundant questions every once in a while, and giggling at his bad jokes raised his spirit enough to make it bearable. At the restaurant, they had to wait to be seated, and the somewhat heavy waiter kept making jokes about the two of them looking like the sweetest couple, what anniversary they were celebrating, oh and by the way, where's the flowers, Mal? We can get you a nice bouquet, 30 pounds a pop. When they asked what they called him Mal for, the heavy waiter explained it was short for Mal Carne before laughing and slapping Derek's shoulder.

"In Poland," Angie said sipping red wine, "we don't eat out a lot. There aren't many Italian restaurants. Not like they're having over in Germany."

"How is Poland?"

"It's beautiful."

"Why'd you come here to study?"

"Opportunity."

"Uh-huh," he said drinking his Peroni much too fast for comfort, given they were charging seven pounds a bottle.

"I wanted to see something new."

"Uh-huh."

"Challenge myself. See if I could stand on my own two feet."

"How's it going? Are you working on the side?"

"Call center. Out at the airport."

"Sounds rough."

"It's not. Not really. It's the nightshifts that're taking their toll."

"Sleep's so important. If I don't get enough sleep, I feel I'm not growing as much."

"Growing?"

"Growing. As in muscle growth."

"Oh, sure. I noticed those firm arms you're sporting. I guess you need them, playing rugby and all, competing against all those big guys coming at you."

Derek blushed, drinking beer, unable to say something to that. Angie noticed, placing her hand on the table past the imaginative line of demarcation right down the middle. And while he realized, his face turning from red to crimson, Derek didn't have the heart to reach out and take her hand.

"I have two beautiful pizzas for you two lovebirds," the heavy waiter said, putting down two enormous plates taking up pretty much all of the space. "Enjoy!"

"This looks gorgeous," Angie said. "Spinach and egg, that's my favorite."

"It better had be good at twenty pounds apiece," Derek said slicing the mushroom pizza he'd ordered because someone had told him mushrooms were beneficial to muscle growth.

Maintaining their conversation during dinner was much more difficult, and Angie noticed the second Peroni wasn't taking any detours anymore, going straight to Derek's head. It did something to him, which was clearly not good for his confidence.

"Do you care for dessert?" Angie asked. "We could share tiramisu."

"Tiramisu? What's that?"

"It's best tasted, not described."

They had espresso with it. Angie tried sipping it like an Italian Contessa in Rome while Derek downed it in one gulp like a porter from East London. The waiter had thoughtfully brought them two cake forks, but Derek didn't make a move.

"Try it," Angie urged him. "It's good."

"I'll wait for you."

"Your call."

The tiramisu was delicious. Rich and creamy. The way it was supposed to be. But that second fork resting on the edge of the plate spoiled her appetite much quicker than she would've anticipated.

"Care for another drink?" he asked.

"Try the tiramisu first," she said holding out her cake fork across the table with a mouthful of tiramisu on it. Derek looked at it as if she was strangling a cobra.

"No, thanks."

"You don't want to eat from the same plate as me?"

"That's not it."

"What is it, then?"

Trying to conceal her anger, Angie wondered what she was angry about in the first place. She couldn't quite comprehend it. Derek couldn't say anything to it. Again. All he did was shrug. Even though Angie stopped eating halfway, Derek never touched the tiramisu.

"You didn't like the tiramisu?" the waiter asked busing the table.

"Oh, it was delicious," Angie said with a fake smile. "Only a bit much for one."

The waiter said something in Italian as he walked away. Derek was staring into his phone. The meal had been free but it hadn't done a thing about the void inside of Angie.

"Would you excuse me for a moment?" he asked. Angie shrugged.

There was little keeping her in her seat. The prospect of him coming back, of thanking him for the invitation and, out of politeness, lying about how nice it had been wasn't appealing to her. Should I leave, she asked when she heard a female voice behind her.

"Is that seat taken?" Natalie asked pointing at the vacant seat Derek had so carelessly shoved out from underneath himself.

"Not currently."

"I'll take it. If you don't mind, of course."

That smile. So much depth to it. So many facets. Like autumn light, dancing on the surface of a small duck pond. There was no way of seeing what lay underneath it.

"Go ahead, please," Angie replied turning that almost empty glass of wine in her hand.

"What grapes are those?"

"Bardolino. I think. I don't know a thing about wine."

"Good grapes. Pressed correctly, they make wonderful wines. None of which should be wasted on bad company."

"Do we know each other?"

"Maybe we've walked past one another."

"College. Economics?"

"I'm Natalie."

"Angie."

"I like your accent. Czech?"

"Polish."

"Hard to tell the difference for a non-native speaker."

And then she asked her in Polish how the evening was going. Angie smiled and replied it hadn't been the greatest but at least the pizza was good and she wouldn't have to pay.

"Yeah," Natalie said, "a small victory. But let me tell you, a girl like you shouldn't be asking for the crumbs from the table. Least so when they're thrown by an imbecile."

"Could you explain?"

"Come, let's have a drink and we talk. What do you say?"

"I can't just walk out on him like that. I'd be– "

"Rude?"

"Yes."

"The way he's been rude to you all night? Let me cheer you up. Make the night worth your while."

Natalie stretched her hand out across the table. Almost the way Angie had done it before. The difference was, after a moment's consideration, she took it.

"Okay, then. I got some hours to kill anyway before heading to work."

Natalie settled the bill on the way out, telling the heavy waiter to put it on her account. Simple as that. A couple of words, a smile and a handshake.

"Why'd you pay for him?" Angie asked

"You'll understand soon."

You could only imagine the expression on Derek's face when he returned from the men's room, finding his company gone, the table set for another couple to dine, the tab already picked up. It must've been a fleeting disappointment still, after he'd phoned up Becky from the stall at the men's room, treating Angie like forgettable side catch.

"Have you ever been to the finer bars in town?" Natalie asked Angie as they were strolling down Princes Street, past drunkards stumbling and tumbling home.

"I wouldn't have the money for that."

"Didn't anyone ever tell you a girl like you won't require funds to go out?"

"Not like you."

"You assumed it'd be a possibility."

"But I never tried it."

"Why?"

"It'd give me a bad conscience."

"About what?"

"Spending someone else's money."

"Even if they gladly spent it?"

"Yes."

"Is that your traditional upbringing speaking?"

"I don't want to feel as if I owe the guy anything."

"Yeah. The fact of the matter is, you don't owe anyone jack for buying drinks or food. Contrary to what you're assuming, you're the one doing him a favor."

"Even if I won't go home with him?"

"Yes."

"How exactly am I doing him a favor?"

"Men need to feel in charge. Money is giving them that feeling. Even if they're buying drinks for a woman easily making twice as much money as they do. The feeling's the same. It's a fallacy, thinking they can buy you. Believe me, you're doing them a favor."

"It makes them feel good."

"Exactly."

"It's only a Pyrrhic victory."

"I like your wits. Here we are."

They stopped at a noble pub and night club at Frederick and Rose Street. Chic people were lining down the block waiting to get in. Pretty girls in mini skirts and dresses, no stockings, no jackets, only their arms crossed underneath their breasts to shield against the cold. Guys with fancy haircuts and gold chains and sunglasses. It was all perfectly orchestrated, no need for a conductor.

"I'm not dressed for this," Angie said. "They won't even let me in."

"You'll be fine. Don't remember what you look like with your clothes on. Remember what you look like without them. The boys will imagine that."

The bar was slow but the dancefloor was in full swing. Beautiful people moving to the music blasting from the speakers, making sure you'd feel every bass line like a shockwave right through your body. None of this had any particular appeal to Angie, who was having a hard time remembering what Natalie said.

"We'll take a tour," Natalie screamed into her ear.

"Say that again."

"We'll circle the dancefloor first, then go to the bar for a quick hello before we sit over there."

"Okay."

It never appeared as if anyone was looking in their direction. But suddenly, Angie could feel the stares, the eyes running down her body, lust seeping into her, penetrating with ease the barrier of her clothes. They circled the dancefloor counterclockwise, with Natalie shaking hands with the DJ. It seemed as if they were the nearest and dearest and oldest friends but when they took off, Natalie motioned as if she hated the guy's guts.

"Good DJ but such a jerk. Come, we'll score free drinks."

Angie was about to ask how that would go about but decided to take a back seat instead. Just standing at the bar did the trick. Within less than two minutes, they were hit on by a guy hammered already, mid-fortyish, bundle of greenbacks in his hand emphasizing the gold and diamond rings. Natalie talked to him before turning to Angie after a moment.

"He really likes you."

"Tell him I said he's welcome."

Natalie smiled.

"This is boot camp. It doesn't work that way."

"Boot camp?"

"Angie, meet Harry. Harry, this is Angie. She's from Moscow."

"Moscow, eh? City of beautiful people."

"That right," Angie said faking the thickest Eastern European accent so overdone it fit the occasion perfectly. "We party day and night. Lots of vodka and– How would you say?"

"Fun?"

"Fooling around."

"You bet, yeah. So, what're you two gals doing in town tonight?"

"Looking for drinks. For starters. We're thirsty."

"What would you like?"

"Mocow Mule for me, Screwdriver for Natalie."

"Sounds right."

And he flagged down a bartender with his bundle of cash, attracted by the prospect of a generous tip. A man like this usually wouldn't be served before the beautiful girls they were trying to hit on but the money had a mind-changing quality.

Making sure to tip the bloke nicely, Harry got them their drinks, leaning against the bar casually. They cheered to the gods of entertainment and drank before he tried starting a conversation about men in Moscow and if they were treating the ladies right.

"Angie," Natalie called out, pulling her sleeve, "that's Franny over there, you gotta meet her. We'll be right back."

Before he could say anything, Natalie pulled Angie into the crowd on the dancefloor, skillfully evading everyone without spilling their hard-earned drinks.

"Who's Franny?" Angie asked on the other side.

"Ever read JD Salinger?"

"Catcher in the Rye."

"Franny and Zooey."

"Does that mean you like Zooey better than Franny?"

"It means I was sick of asking for Jane Doe."

Natalie never mentioned it, but she made sure they avoided Harry like the black plague for the remainder of the night. It seemed to come so naturally to her, while Angie kept checking her back. There was still no shaking the feeling she owed him something for the Moscow Mule she'd sipped from before dumping it into a palm tree. After a while, though, she developed a feeling for knowing who was watching her and who wasn't. This took some stress off of her. As did acknowledging the fact she could barely, if ever, remember the names of people Natalie introduced her to.

"Hot night," a girl named Clare said, looking gorgeous in her silver roaring 20s dress, sucking a mojito through a glass straw. "Place's buzzing."

"Any interesting people?" Angie asked when Natalie was talking to a mid-aged lady she'd mistaken for someone much younger she knew from work.

"Most people seem interesting only from a distance. The reality is, they're a bore."

"What did you say you do for a living?"

"I'm a travel influencer."

"Oh, that sounds interesting."

"It's such a grind, finding those places not every average Joe and Gonzo's been to over Easter."

"Places like what?"

"Tangier. Bali. Singapore. All those places, beaten to death over and over again, where you meet everyone you know here in Edinburgh."

"Sounds terrible, yeah, travelling for hours just to see someone you already know."

"Such a bore."

"It's like riding the streetcar out to the airport to work nights on a shit job like every other Gonzo."

"Angie," Natalie said throwing an arm around her, rescuing her. "Would you step out with me for a moment, catch some fresh air?"

"Thanks for helping me out," Angie said on their way out back, where nobody was allowed but nobody cared if you went either.

"Spoiled, rich people tend not to be the most entertaining."

The sheet metal fire door swung open, and there she was, wearing the nicest mink fur, rocks the size of a cricket ball, all the accessories that looked so cheap and phony on anyone who couldn't wear them, which was almost everyone.

But she could wear them. They did nothing disguising her age. There was no need to, anyway. Nobody would ever dare throwing a table sheet over Monet's Rouen Cathedral.

"There you are," Rayne said, smiling as she checked herself in a small, handheld mirror. "I've been eyeballing you all night."

"Angie, this is Rayne."

"Nice to meet you, madam."

"Please, call me Rayne. Everyone does."

"With pleasure."

"Such good manners. And that accent. Delicious. It melts in my ears like butterscotch toffee."

"Rayne has something to offer to you," Natalie said, cutting to the chase with 2 AM approaching on its dark, leathery wings of doom.

"What would that be?"

"Something that's worth your while," Rayne said. "Oh, I'll sure make it worth your while."

32

The alarm clock was waking Angie for work. But despite the ringing being the same it had always been, opting to ignore it had turned into a formidable challenge over the past few weeks. Opportunity. It had done that.

And yet, with opportunity will come a chance to blow it, time and time again. This was tormenting Angie when she was sitting on her bed wondering if she should throw the towel right away. Then again, she remembered sitting at the job just last night, thinking what a bore it was. A train bound for Dead End, Middle of Nowhere. A knock on the door.

"Come in," Angie said, trying to look busy with the unsorted array of week-old scripts from college flying around her desk.

"Hi there," Hailey said. "Aren't you running late for work?"

"Swapped shifts with a co-worker."

"I saw you've been out nights."

"Uh-huh."

"I'm on my way meeting friends, eating out. Nothing fancy, just fast food on the go, maybe grab some drinks."

"Uh-huh."

"Care about tagging along?"

"I got a lot to do here, so, thanks. But I'd rather stay in and get some of it done."

It was easily understood Hailey wasn't thrilled about her answer. What Angie suspected was, she was suspicious of, and curious about her change of habits. But it was none of Hailey's business anyway.

All those social obligations had started weighing down on her like Atlas stones on her shoulder. The change had come as suddenly as it had been drastic. Every time someone she knew had asked her to come here or go there or do this or that, Angie had felt as if they'd asked her to go snake hunting or bird watching.

There was one person though she felt she needed to meet. Half an hour later, she saw Natalie at a pub so uncharacteristic of her they might as well have met at a burger shack. Natalie was leaning against the old-fashioned bar top drinking Belhaven Stout as black as a raven's beak.

"Coming up in the world, beautiful," she said when she saw Angie wearing her new attire. "Beautiful scarf. Irish?"

"Yes. Hi Natalie."

"Did he pick it out for you?"

"I picked it out for myself but it was– "

"Don't say it. I don't need to know. How's everything going between the two of you?"

It had been good, with Angie assuming he was feeling considerably more comfortable about it than she did. With that one little flaw in the equation. A spicy detail, complicating things.

"I'm not sure what to do about it," she said sipping pale ale she didn't want, trying not to look in the direction of the table of working-class guys eyeballing her like one of their free online videos.

"Did you tell Rayne?"

"No."

"Why wouldn't you?"

"I didn't have the heart. She's done a lot for me. Not as much as you, though."

"While I firmly believe you should stop being so grateful towards everyone already, I see where you're coming from. And maybe how to help it."

"Are you sure?"

"Why, of course, my dear. It's actually quite straightforward."

"I'm curious."

"You know what they say. Practice. Practice. Practice."

With a smile, Natalie borrowed a biro and a heavy and stiff white napkin from the bartender and swiftly scribbled a phone number on it, kissing it before handing it over. The burgundy lipstick had tattooed her perfect lips on the rough white napkin.

"When should I call?"

"Oh, there's really no time when it's more convenient than another."

"Okay."

"Why not try it right away? You're much too late for work anyway."

Natalie put thirty pounds on the bar, got up and kissed Angie goodbye on the cheek. With her gone, there was no protective shield, and leaving unsuspiciously was the best she could do.

But going back didn't feel right, so she wandered about town, drawn towards the castle for whatever reason. Standing at the gates locked for night after walking the entire length of Lawnmarket, there was nowhere else to go. Her heart was pounding against her ribs. It was unfathomable why she'd be so nervous about making a phone call. After all, what was the worst case scenario?

Before dialing, she checked the number two, three, four times, getting the figures all mixed up. The terminal at Edinburgh airport on the day of her arrival popped into her head, exhausted from only a two-hour flight, somewhat sick to the stomach, lonely and lost, the first thing she'd buy was Irn Bru from a vending machine, its taste reminding her of nothing, yet giving her something to cling on to, something that calmed her stomach, and something to come back to whenever she revisited an emotional beatdown.

The taste appeared on her tongue. Irn Bru. Angie hadn't had another one since, even though she'd been tempted to buy one from the grocery store every once in a while, when she saw that orange bottle in the cooler. The line clicked.

"Hello?" the man said, his voice lovely and warm.

"Is this Duke?"

"Yes. Who's there?"

"Angie"

"Angie, huh? My apologies, but I seem to fail to remember where we've met."

"We haven't met yet."

"Are you free tomorrow forenoon?"

Silence.

"Angie?"

"Yes? Oh, well, I guess I'm free, yes."

There was a law class she'd skipped enough times now not to make any further absence count.

"Let's meet at the Botanic Gardens at ten-thirty."

"How will I recognize you?"

He laughed. Angie was baffled by the joyfulness. The warmth surpassed everything previously known.

"Don't you worry, there's no way we're going to miss each other. Okay?"

"Okay."

"Have a nice evening. See you tomorrow."

Click.

It was as if the lights had been turned off. The castle was always dark and sinister at night. But during their conversation, everything had lit up in the warmest of lights.

Something haunted her, made her overstay her welcome, feeling the place was growing increasingly hostile towards her. At least in any way places would become hostile towards people. The way home took her much longer, taking turns to the left and right, seeing streets and alleys she'd never visited before, walking over cobblestones and asphalt and grass never felt beneath her feet. Avoiding people, you could almost hear the city talk, telling the stories of its past times to those that cared to listen.

Angie couldn't stop those voices in her head, hearing people she didn't know, and had never even heard about. By the time she arrived home, it was past midnight. She was exhausted.

When she woke up around eight in the morning, she felt rested. That face looking back from the mirror seemed much closer to the person Angie remembered from happier times. Applying the makeup didn't take long, tracing the contours of her eyes in thin, black coal. True beauty never called for much attention. With her wardrobe growing significantly within the past few weeks, both in quantity and quality, Angie wondered what to wear. Eventually, she settled for going by feel, not thought. The result was stunning. Classic Scottish patterns, adapted to the needs of the 21st century. Already when she left the building, she was turning heads.

At a café in Stockbridge, she stopped in for a quick breakfast, remembering the bundle of bills she'd stuffed down the pocket of her new tweed coat. They'd get her as far as she'd ever want to.

"What can I get you?" a beautiful young woman asked Angie after she sat down at the fogged window, looking out over the busy street outside.

"Black coffee, orange juice and a croissant."

"We have stuffed croissant, if you care for that."

"What is stuffed croissant?"

"Croissant stuffed with ham, Chester cheese and cottage cheese."

"Baked in the oven?

"We put it in the panini iron."

"Sounds great, I'll have that."

"Be right back."

As she retreated to the enormous Italian coffee machine, which was clearly incapable of making straight black coffee the right way, Angie looked closely at that young waitress. College student for sure, not a day older than twenty. Maybe twenty-one. Not even trying to show off that God-given gorgeous body that needed minimal maintenance, if any.

It was so unfair. Some gave their all, upholding that façade of fragile beauty, while others blew them out of the water not even trying. Angie felt sure plenty of people failed at telling the difference. The same poor slobs failing to tell a Cézanne from a newspaper cartoon.

"Here we go," she said returning with a tastelessly chic mug and plate. "Orange juice is coming right away."

"The fruits put up a fight? Just kiddin'."

"You wouldn't believe it."

"I feel like we've met before."

"Sorry if I fail to remember."

Only then she spotted the plaque with her name on it.

"Emily, huh? You're at university?"

"Nailed it."

"Did I say something wrong?"

"It's just those nameplates."

"Does it make you uncomfortable?"

"Yes."

"Because of men?"

"Uh-huh."

"They make you wear it?"

"Company policies."

Angie smiled.

"Take it off. What're they going to do about it anyway?"

"Sack me."

"Are you good at this?"

"Fairly good."

"See that co-worker of yours? No, that fat gal. Look how clumsy and slow she is. They're not going to fire you either way. A dressing down, maybe. But what's that to you?"

"I'll give it a thought. And I'll be right back with your glass of orange juice."

In the farthest section of the café sat a man keeping an eye on that young waitress. Another poor slob, much too old and gone now, who'd never really had the heart doing the things he'd wanted to do.

The stuffed croissant was good but the coffee wasn't humble enough to get Angie excited. At the same time, it lacked finesse and the taste of the unknown. Passing by, Emily put the orange juice in front of her. It was too sour to be good for anything. The longer she stayed, the more Angie felt the urge to leave. There was no reasonable explanation to it. That emotional playing ground had turned from a compact, juicy pitch of grass to something more closely resembling the

Kalahari Desert.

"How was your coffee?" Emily asked when she came back busing the table.

"I would've preferred filtered coffee."

"We rarely ever get to hear that."

"People don't know what they're talking about. The stuffed croissant was good, though."

"Care for another one?"

"No, thanks," she sat getting up, feeling the weight of the bills in her coat's pocket, pulling some out. "Keep the change."

"That's generous, thank you."

"I didn't say that to him. Remember what I said about that name tag pinned to your chest? Like a billboard, inviting anyone to make the sale."

"Have a good one."

There was no chance Angie would ever return to that place. It felt too small, hip, too mundane to ever amount to anything. Especially since it tried so hard being something that it clearly wasn't. Would that apply to the people as well? The farther she got away, she understood, the less she cared about such nonsense.

It was other thought keeping her mind occupied on her way to the Botanic Gardens. When she ran a red light, a car almost hit her, the driver slamming on the brakes, blowing the horn and throwing slurs in Scots at her through the rolled-down window, none of which made any impact on her. For whatever reason, she wondered if there was a way monetizing Bactrian camels in the Scottish Highlands. The idea fascinated her. An old cottage or castle, converted to postmodern, pre-apocalyptical standards. Stables for horses and said camels, providing plenty of income carrying tourists too lazy to walk or hike around the countryside.

Angie could easily picture herself standing at the second-floor window on a rainy day, cup of Earl Grey tea in her hand, with saucer, looking down at her employees and customers struggling against the wind, enjoying the view of the mountains, the sparse green and gray and blue, as beautiful as it is hostile to the human condition. She understood the contradictions and all the absurd ramifications coming from it. They excited her. The mundane, though, was something she had little to no time to spare for. All but a waste, living the very typical, normal life everyone else was aspiring to. After all, it was like living the lives of others, something she considered cowardly at best.

33

The Excel was in plain sight, looking gorgeous parked at the curb right in front of the Botanic Gardens' entrance. Time and time again, Duke enjoyed looking at this car. It never got old. It never lost any of its sex appeal. Imagining anything prettier was illusional.

Leather jacket and tie gave him a stylish, yet classy but still casual appearance. It had been months since his last cigarette but now, he wanted one. He slid one out of the pack in his chest pocket, flicked that old lighter, setting it ablaze. The first draw tickled as it went down his windpipe. The second felt like homecoming.

"What a beautiful day, huh?" he said to an elderly couple passing by and they smiled at him in unison, nodding their heads.

The nicotine made him sweat some, prompting him to adjust his haircut. He'd told the barber to make him look like Sean Connery in Goldfinger. Despite Duke's wider frame, it didn't come out crooked. It drew looks left and right, the way he'd anticipated.

Something had boosted his confidence to unknown levels in the past month. That was clearly something to keep an eye on. One thing he'd learned about life was it knocked you down the hardest when you felt like you'd been soaring too close to the sun. Last night had both been wild and wildly successful. In the early morning, after he'd worked out like he always did, he'd pulled out The Complete Short Stories of Ernest Hemingway, choosing a short story at random. Papa had never disappointed him. Reading Hemingway always uplifted his mood for the remainder of the day.

Duke wasn't done smoking when he caught a first glimpse of Angie. There was something unmistakable in how she held herself, walking in shoes meant for posing, not walking for longer distances. That fox hair scarf, complementing her tweet jacket beautifully. No ordinary girl or woman would make it work. Even over the distance, she was stunning.

"You must be Angie," he said the moment she got into earshot.

"That makes you Duke."

"Guilty as charged. I told you we wouldn't miss each other."

They embraced. She felt his right hand on her hip, at exactly the right height to make her know it without giving prompting her to smack him right across the face. The left hand he placed farther up, just shy of her bosom. When he kissed her on the cheek, she could smell his aftershave. Unknown fragrance. Refreshing, yet masculine. Not even faintly ordinary. Cedar and hints of tobacco.

"It is very nice to meet you," Angie said.

"Pleasure's all mine. I felt the need for a cigarette, I hope you don't mind?"

"Where I'm from, people smoke around children. The elderly smoke all the time. We smoke at nightclubs. People cough when they're not smoking."

"Care for one yourself?"

"Despite the fact these are quality cigarettes that don't smell bad, I don't want to spoil the fox."

"It's a lovely fox."

"I had to have it."

"I'm glad you didn't feel the retribution of some animal rights activist, spraying you with red paint."

"Luckily, Edinburgh is a place of people minding their own business."

"I bought two tickets already, so we're good to go."

With his arm offered to cling on to, Angie was still undecided whether or not she liked this man. There was something classic about him. Almost antique. She wondered if that was due to his manners. Meeting someone cherishing manners like any gentleman ought to was a very refreshing experience. Leaving him hanging until he couldn't help but fall was rude, so Angie took his arm with a heartwarming smile.

"Okay, here we go."

Duke Arrowsmith was at ease making Angie feel as if they were knowing each other since their childhood days even when they were doing the mandatory talking trying to get acquainted. The worst part about meeting new people, at least to Angie, was asking and responding to the same questions, over and over again. Almost like a job interview. Once you figured out a successful strategy, all you did was learn the lines by heart and recite them, with only slight variations when under pressure. It was the worst kind of bore imaginable.

"You're good at this," Angie admitted after a while.

"Good at what?" Duke asked innocently.

"Making me feel special. As if I was the world and you were my satellite."

"What's your favorite flower?"

"Dandelions."

"Well, then we shouldn't have come for the Redwoods and palm trees."

"I love this building. They weren't trying to hide anything when they called it the Palm House."

"That tropical heat and humidity, so lovely against the cold outside. All the windows are fogging over."

"If you call that cold, come to Poland."

"I'm freezing right now. See?"

"Your hands are cold."

"Your cheek's so warm and bright as a peach."

"So is yours."

"Your eyes a beautiful. A pond of water lilies."

"Trickster."

"That taste of your lips."

"Try again?"

"I'm craving for them."

"I like how you're biting my lip."

"I like how your hands are feeling their way."

"Yours are better than mine. Not cold anymore."

"Oh, I was seeking the radiant warmth."

"What did you find?"

"A fragrant, delicate wonderland."

"I'm yours. Oh, Duke, I'm all yours."

"Under palm trees, I found paradise."

"There's more to come," she said taking his hand, pulling him towards the exit.

It had been but half an hour since they'd entered the Royal Botanic Gardens. When they walked back out, the woman in the ticket window stared at them in disbelief. It must've been unimaginable to her under what circumstances anyone would leave a place this beautiful after such a short period of time.

The humming of the juiced up 912 engine reverberated through Angie's body, making it sing in unison with the song playing inside of her head. Focusing was hard. Duke knew this. Not once would he try striking up a conversation along the ride.

"Here we are," he said pulling into the driveway, not cutting the engine just yet.

"Nice home," Angie said popping the door open. Duke gently reached out for her hand, stopping her from getting out. Their eyes met. "I'm sure. Oh, I've never been this sure in my entire life."

Her naked body on the bed curved beautifully, like snowcapped rolling hills early in the year, when you could smell melting snow and growing grass and rotting leaves from last season, all mixing into the scent of next summer. The tips and valleys moved gracefully with her breath. Duke traced the line of her hips with his fingertips, barely touching her silk skin but doing plenty.

"You're giving me goosebumps," she said without turning around.

"It's talent."

"Jerk."

"You've been missing out on something. It's better to give than take. Taking is for the feeble-minded."

"There's a problem I'm having with him."

"Tell me about it. If you'd like to, of course."

"I'm not sure if I'm ready."

"It doesn't have to be today."

"But I'm impatient."

"You've come so far in such short time. You should be proud of yourself."

"Actually, it'll have to be today."

"I heard of him."

"Did you? How?"

"Through the grapevine."

"Grapevine?"

"You know how these things go. You know enough people, you hear enough."

"Enough nonsense."

"Without a doubt."

"Would you explain to me then how you're telling fact from fiction?"

"I got my experience and common sense to rely on. That's it. I swore to myself never to give too much credit to somebody else's view on things."

"There's no way you could always know everything for yourself."

"I wasn't judging, only confiding you in the fact people have been talking."

Playing with a strand of hair, Angie took her time to deliberate. Duke appreciated it. If there was any quality in a person he favored over others, it was the ability to think and contemplate first before speaking.

"What is their gossiping to me," she continued. "After all, it's not them deciding who I want to be with."

"I second that."

"I don't care if you've heard he's a violent person."

"Fine."

"I don't care either if you've heard he's a boozehound and unfaithful and a liar and living off of his father's money and generally not to be trusted."

"What is it that's bothering you?"

Again, she paused, contemplating, planning her words.

"He's got some kind of strange tastes."

"A fetish."

"That's the word."

"Don't tell me he's into wearing diving goggles and flippers in bed because then I'll lean back and yearn."

"He's a sadist. Only goes off when he's inflicting pain."

"Did he beat you?"

"No. Not really."

"I saw those marks on your thighs."

"Those are bite marks. He calls them his love bites. It didn't bleed."

"Gosh, it must be painful."

"Yeah, but it didn't do the trick for long. Says he doesn't want to hurt me but must to."

"To fulfill his desire."

"To live a life worth living. Those were his words."

"Did he ever hurt someone really bad?"

Angie shrugged.

"I never asked him about it," she said looking at the white sheet, Duke still lying behind her, stroking her neck, her head, her shoulder blades. "I have no idea what he's doing when he goes to Sierra Leone or the Philippines or Middle America."

"Are you sure about him?"

"Other than that, he's a gentleman. At least to me. He drinks an awful lot but it's all good fun. And he can take care of me. Provide me with a lifestyle I'd otherwise never be able to have."

"I'm not one to lecture others."

"I know."

"In the end, it's none of my business if you're okay with him. But let me assure you, I make it my business the second he oversteps that line you, and only you draw right in front of him. I'm serious. Should you ever need me, I'll be there for you."

"Only one call away, huh? I don't even know you."

"I give you my word."

"I feel like I can trust you. But I've felt that way with people before that never really cared for me."

"Other than myself, there's nothing else really I got to offer."

There was a doubtful glance on her face when she turned around looking at Duke. It quickly vanished.

"I wish it was you, Duke. Please, love me again."

When it was done, they sat at the kitchen table, drinking tea. Angie looked gorgeous, wearing his t-shirt and nothing else.

"You think you could get a hold of a liter of pig's blood?"

"Yes."

"Is something wrong?"

"I suspect where this is going. Part of me isn't quite sure if I want to know. But I promised you something."

"He's talking about blood a lot. About drinking it, you know? If all he really needs is simulation, there might be a way."

"There's one catch to it."

"What is it?"

"Same as with porn. It'll suffice. For a while. It's not the real deal, though. It caters to the craving. Help it grow."

"Until reality is the only thing that will help."

"Yes."

"I'm willing to take that chance."

"A friend of mine is raising cattle, sheep, chickens and pigs."

"How long would it take?"

"Tomorrow morning, if I call him right away."

"My roommate won't be in tomorrow night."

"Okay."

"Okay."

"I'll go make that call. Want me to drive you home afterwards?"

"Please drive me home tomorrow morning on the way to your friend's place."

34

Natalie eyeballed Duke as he was staring down that tiny cup of Earl Grey tea, with nothing to do with his hands after refusing that slice of Austrian pie she'd offered him. They were sitting at her apartment, right at The Meadows, after Duke had declined meeting her at a café in fear they might be seen together. It was a much bigger concern to Natalie than to him, and yet she preferred testing him from time to time. To see if he still had that sharp edge she lusted for so badly.

"What's bothering you?" she asked. "It's got nothing to do with you but after a hard workout, I– "

"It's not that, never mind."

"Trouble with another customer?"

"Hush-hush. You know well enough I'd never confide you in any details whatsoever."

"Whatsoever, yeah."

"Did they review your application? That law firm you've been talking about."

"They did."

"What'd they say? Disco?"

"They'd love having me. Which is quite self-evident, isn't it?"

"Let me make an educated guess what you said."

"I'm rather bored with offers these days."

"To me, they seem like a step in the right direction."

"Only if you're headed for Boringtown, Average Joe County."

"Are you still in that arts phase of yours?"

"Here we go again. Artist at night, pauper the rest of the day."

"That's a drastic paraphrasing of what I said."

"It reflects what I heard."

"People hear whatever they want to hear."

"It speaks volumes of them, doesn't it?"

"Sometimes. And please, don't raise your voice."

"I'm not raising my voice."

"Maybe you didn't notice, it's alright."

"It's not okay. I don't like how you seem so unfazed of what I'm saying."

"Are you admitting to trying to start a fight?"

"Yes. And no."

"I'm not one of your college friends. Leftists taking daddy's money, preaching water to the world when they're buying wine for themselves."

"Did it ever occur to you it's revenge when you're spending it on yourself?"

"Only in the most cynical, nihilistic think pattern imaginable."

"You know how to throw your punches, I give you that."

Natalie fished a cigarette out of the crumbled pack she'd brought back from last night out on town.

"Can I have one?" Duke asked.

"Sure," she said passing the cigarette she'd lit for herself, making sure it had a neat ring of burgundy lipstick on its filter.

"Are you still into street art?" Duke asked, exhaling smoke.

"Shifted towards pop art lately."

"Warhol and Basquiat?"

"Yeah, that circle."

"It's not corny when you like them."

"Maybe not. But I wonder if I really like their art."

"Or?"

"Or if it's their times that got me hooked. 70s and 80s vibes. The way they lived."

"Spending money, snorting coke."

"Sounds good to me."

"What about canned soup?"

"Is that a test?"

"Maybe."

"Maybe, huh? And maybe the soup can is many things, yet one more than all the other ones combined."

"Flipping the bird at the world with a big, fat grin on your face."

This produced a grin on Natalie's face.

"I tried making art like Warhol. Not that anyone these days would care, least fork over a bushel of money for a copycat. It was more a study of his style. When I paint, it's a lot more like Basquiat or Haring."

"I never knew you were painting. Oil on canvas? Or urban materials?"

"Poplar boards."

"Nod to the Renaissance."

"Where'd you learn all those things?"

"I read a lot."

"Bullshit. I know a scam when I see it. Come."

Barefoot in a silk house suit and smoking, she walked him through the spacious apartment, past the bedroom, to the farthest corner, where Duke had never been before. The walls were lined with contemporary art. It wouldn't evoke any feelings. All it did was look chic in a place like that.

"You have an ashtray back here?"

"Use that rumpled old olive oil can over there," Natalie said carelessly dropping ash to the floor.

"The red is intense," Duke said. "Thick as a Jackson Pollock."

"I wasn't thinking at all when I put it on."

"Thinking is the arch enemy of creativity."

"Formal education. Orson Welles. But nice try."

"It has rhythm for sure."

"What do you see?"

"There's a woman. Very feminine."
"What type is she?"
"Caucasian. Does it matter?"
"What does she wear?"
"Nothing. She's naked. The man isn't."
"He's wearing clothes."
"There's disparity."
"Disparity?"
"Of power."
"He's got power over her?"
"No. She's got power over him. Because he has what he wants."
"Very good."
"There's a prize to having it. And to giving it. But to me, she's the one in charge."
"Why?"
"Because she's allowing it. The things he's doing to her."
"Letting him live out his fantasies."
"That small room. It's hers. She doesn't have much."
"What about him?"
"He seems like a noble man. It's his mask."
"A mask she couldn't wear."
"You'll always see where she's from. Made it from the ground up. It doesn't matter, though."
"It has to matter."
"No. She's too beautiful. Smart and charming. But her beauty sets her apart. You can't buy it. Can't fake it. You either have it or you don't. If anyone's going to try and replicate it, they're bound to fail miserably."
"Nature made her beautiful."
"Even in her most abstract form, covered in layers of different shades of red, you can't deny her beauty."
"It's gotten her into trouble."
"It'll still get her out of it."
Suddenly, Duke turned away from the painting.
"Are you alright?" Natalie asked putting her hand on his shoulder.
"One last thought."
"Yes?"
"The man. He's not a man. He looks like one. Feels like one. At least on the surface. But he's not a man."
"How did you know?"
"Whatever you tried and did to emasculate him, you did it well.
"It's a universal, masculine fear. Women could only pretend to understand."
"Does that universal fear apply to me?"
"There's exceptions to any rule."
"Right," he said sliding his hand into her house suit, grabbing her fullness, making her moan. "Fear is like water."
"Yes."
"It flows."
"Where does it flow?"

"Wherever you let it flow."
"Yes."
"It seeps into any crack in the foundation."
"Oh."
"You can't run from it."
"No. Oh Duke."
"If you climb to the top, jump right at it, just like water, it's going to kill you."
"Faster."
"It's going to kill you fast, faster, right away."
"Yes, Duke."
"Because water won't ever be compressed."
"No."
"Like fear, you have to drink it up. With your lips."
"Those lips."
"Let me take you."
"Take me."
"I'll show you my fears, Natalie. You'll learn them all."

35

"Care for another beer?" the waiter asked Duke, who was dipping his last fries in mayonnaise.

"Three for dinner are plenty, wouldn't you say so?"

"You look like you need another one."

"I'll have to work on that look then."

"Going on a date later on?"

"So to say. And none of your business."

"Sorry, I was just trying to converse with you."

"You're doing fine."

"Another beer, then? Don't worry, the double cheeseburger's going to soak it all up."

"Okay, another beer."

"I'll be right back."

He was working his way around the restaurant with the efficiency of either the young and delusional or those refusing to ever bow to reality. The cheeseburger was on the raw side, oozing beef juice even before Duke bit into it. The sight made him somewhat sick to the stomach, but he knew the feeling would pass.

"Who's gorgeous sitting over there?" Duke asked cocking a thumb at the back of the restaurant.

"The attorney?"

"No, the other one."

"The cop?"

"Yes, the cop."

"That's Joe."

"Joe Doe?"

"Joe as in Josephine or something."

"It figures. Is she a regular?"

"Uh-huh. Even though she sure doesn't look it, but that lady's got a healthy appetite for red meat."

"You got an appetite as well, huh?"

"Hey, we're all human, alright? Wanna get acquainted?"

"No, thanks. She's got my curiosity, not my attention."

"Never tangle with the law, gotcha."

Duke paid up his bill, tipping the waiter twenty-pound sterling. Something about the pretty police officer sneaking peaks at him whenever he turned his head looking out on the street told him it was time to leave. The car was still parked a block down from Angie's flat, a nice walk through the cold night, bringing him back to life after the burger and fries and beers had done their work. Not enough to eradicate the effect the beer had on his system, and that he knew he needed still.

When he popped the trunk open, the whiteness of the plastic bucket screamed right at him. The clear lid allowed a look inside. But there was nothing there to see, really. Even in the yellow shimmer of the trunk's light bulb, the contents looked utterly black. Duke grabbed the bucket by the handle, then got the tarpaulin he'd bought from a hardware store along the way. Last chance to punk out, he thought feeling the weight dangling from his arm. Something didn't feel right. The promise he'd given popped back into his mind. As much as he despised what he was about to do, Duke decided he'd do it anyway. The light bulb was cut when he closed the lid, leaving only darkness.

A group of students passed him on the stairway, squeezing past him and the bucket without wasting any thought on it.

"Cheers, mate," one of them said for no particular reason.

At Angie's door, Duke took a deep breath. The beer had gotten to him, slowing his head, speeding up his heart. It didn't feel fantastic. Eventually, he knocked on the door before changing his mind.

"Hi, Duke," she said opening up wearing a plain white bathrobe that looked like ten quid a pop.

"Hi there. I schlepped myself all the way up this murderous staircase. My apologies for panting some."

"Come in."

Once the door clicked shut behind them, she threw her arms around him, kissing him, eyes closed.

"Nice to see you, too," Duke said.

"It's been hours only. But I missed you."

"Sorry to say this, but you shouldn't get attached too much."

"Let me have some fun, okay?"

"Where's the bedroom?"

"I'll show you. Come."

At first, she wouldn't comply when he wanted to put up the tarpaulin. It was impossible to her imagining what two liters of pig's blood would look like soaked into carpet. Duke wondered how this could end well in the first place. Concealing the evidence once they were done seemed increasingly unlikely.

"We'll relax for a while," Angie said pulling the plastic cork from a cheap bottle of wine. "I want to wind down with you."

"What about your roommate?"

"She's not going to be back until next week."

"If we're out of luck, it'll take some time cleaning up the mess afterwards."

"This isn't the best wine money can buy but I like this one. It's from Hungary."

"I prefer Rioja, but Hungarian wine isn't half bad. Oh, it's actually quite good."

"Never judge a bottle by its plastic cork."

"You're funny."

"Aren't you curious what's underneath this bathrobe?"
"Suspense is something I've come to cherish over time."
"I'm still too young and greedy for that."
"Did you have some wine before I arrived?"
"A bottle. Maybe one and a half. I didn't go to class."
"You said you'd attend."
"Gosh, are you my father? I didn't feel like it."
"I'm sorry."
"Don't be sorry."
"Just understanding?"
"Why's it that few men always know what to say?"
"Instincts," he said moving closer, knowing his call sign. "There's things you can't learn."
"That's what you always say, don't you? You try your lines until they work and then you stick with them."
"Never change a working system."
"Know what's funny? Even though I believe I got you figured out, I want you either way."
"It's not funny. It's natural. Mature."
"Shut up and kiss me."

The routine took about fifteen minutes before they ended up in the bedroom. They wouldn't even take notice of their prior preparations. As if they'd never existed. Whatever physical attraction they had going between each other was stronger than most feelings.

"You've done this before," Angie said when she was lying in his arms, both of them panting and sweating.

"Anything you care to be good at takes practice."

"You say this without shame."

"I believe you know where I'm coming from."

"Let me show you something," she said reaching under the bed. What she pulled out puzzled Duke for the briefest moment.

"Looks real," he said. "Typical hunting knife. But it's a prop. You could easily scare someone away in a dark alley, though."

"Friend of mine, she works at a theater in Glasgow."

"Let me guess, it's one of those squirting blood."

"To make it as real as possible."

"I don't know," Duke said getting up from the bed, the tarp crackling underneath his bare feet.

"You're so beautiful."

Staring out the window, Duke was trying to clear the fog out of his mind. But there was no concise reasoning lying behind it.

"We'll do this now," he said to the reflection of himself in the window pane. "We'll do this and we'll make it look real. Make it feel real. We'll slaughter this beast right here, right now. And once we've accomplished that, there's nothing more to be feared."

"Duke?"

"Huh?"

"Promise me you'll hold me in your arms when we're done."

"I'll love you again one last time when we're done. It's not giving me choices."

Duke slipped into Angie's cheap bathrobe, the rough cotton cloth itching on his skin, giving the impression of being dressed. When she handed him the prop knife, he instantly tested the bluntness of its blade on the palm of his left hand. It produced a thin line of fake blood.

"It's so red," Duke said, staring at the imaginary cut in his hand.

"It has to be much more intense than actual blood. Otherwise, it wouldn't look real in the bright, cold light of the theater."

"Okay, then," Duke went opening the bucket of pig's blood, prying the rim open with the plastic knife. It smelled like an iron girder covered in layers of rust.

"I'm ready for you," Angie said leaning back on the bed.

"Any safe word?"

"Lotus," she said blinking at him. "Get into your part now. Don't worry, I know it's not you."

The only part fitting Duke could imagine was Jack the Ripper from a movie he'd seen as a kid, maybe too young for it. All the details had washed out over time. The impression remained, though, and the explicitness of violence, the subtle, nuanced play with what was shown, what was obscured and what's omitted altogether. It was plenty, he discovered, to get him going all the way through that farce.

His hands around her neck. Choking off her screams and pleas. Making it harder and harder to breathe. The knife. Its pointy tip only inches from her beautiful eye. Tears rolling down her cheeks. Tears he sucked up with his lips before delivering the first cut. Right underneath her left eye. A shade of blue paler than the left. Tears mixing with blood. A vampire, devouring it all with great lust.

"You're not going to like this," he said still choking her, running the edge of the knife from her neck all the way down her body. "Not a bit. But I'll enjoy every moment of it. Should you scream, it won't help you. It'll only turn me on."

The bed was layered in shades of red. One line after the other. One splash after the other. A cut down her arm. On the inside of her firm thighs. Until all the blood inside of the prop knife's reservoir was used up. Duke wasn't thinking when he jumped out of the bed, picking up the bucket of pig's blood. Dumping his hand in the blood, he could feel its texture. The thickness of it. The iron smell intensified. And then he pulled his submerged hand out, splattering blood all over Angie. A strike to the left, one to the right, red dots and lines flying through the air, flying until they splashed onto skin, cotton, wallpaper alike. Like an artist, spraying thick acrylic paint on wood or canvas.

Eventually, all the blood was used up. Duke's heart was racing with ecstasy, blood rushing to his head, hammering in his temples with every beat of his heart. Angie didn't move on the bed. She was trying to catch her breath as well. The empty bucket dropped to the floor when Duke regained his composure. Jack the Ripper slowly faded from his mind's eye, walking into a sinister London East End back alley, dimly lit by gaslight, soon mingling with the darkness, but not before turning around again tipping his hat at Duke, the one who was sentence to stay behind in the mess they'd made together. The bathrobe had sucked up the blood like a leach close to exploding. It was hard to make out Angie, the human being with all that redness, dots and lines and stains. But there she was, alright. Her beautiful, magnificently blue eyes beaming through redness like headlights in a sandstorm.

"Angie," Duke said dropping to a knee right next to her, taking her hand. "Angie, is everything alright?"

"Be quiet and hold me."

Duke climbed into the bed, taking her into his arms. The wet feeling of thick blood was unpleasant, but soon became manageable. The other side of the room was normal, untouched from their display of theater violence, supposed to nurture the needs of a sadistic lunatic. There was nothing, really, Duke could think of. For the time being, his head was empty space.

"We need to clean up this mess," Duke said without looking. "It makes no sense washing ourselves before we've made due with this."

"We're not done yet. You promised me something."

"Of course. After we're done cleaning up."

"Forget about it. It's his mess. I consider it his mess. He wants to see me anyway. I'll tell him I'll come if he sends someone over to clean this up."

"Are you sure?"

"Yes," she said breaking from his embrace. "I look worse than you. Join me in five minutes or so."

The red bedroom painting felt like unattended business. Duke couldn't look at it anymore. It gave him a sense of powerlessness he hadn't felt in many years. Like being a teenager all over again. That was clearly something he'd left behind, presumably for good, and he couldn't afford a relapse. Hearing the water running in the shower, he imagined Angie's body. How the redness came off. One layer after the other. One drop at a time. Disappearing in swirls washed into the drain. To reveal the perfection it had masked and disguised.

Duke took off the bathrobe and stuffed it into the bucket, together with the tarp he folded up neatly, making sure not to spill any more blood to the floor. There was no way he would leave this bucket. Joining her in the shower felt like reanimation and being baptized simultaneously.

"I've been waiting on you," Angie said.

Duke had nothing to respond verbally. Angie dug a fingernail into his shoulder, cutting him like a blade. A thin line of blood appeared, washed away with the water, creating a misty swirl as it washed down the drain.

Once they'd said their long goodbyes, he went back to the car, throwing the bucket in the trunk, driving for a while, aimlessly around town wherever the road was free, stopping behind a butcher's shop he knew, where he disposed of the bucket and tarp and bathrobe in a dumpster stinking like hell even in winter from the animal cuts nobody wanted, before getting back into the car and driving some more until he found he couldn't go on.

Angie called up the madman right after she'd dressed and put makeup on that made her more attractive for him but never did her beauty any justice. Two henchmen were sent over to take care of the mess while Angie was already on her way to his Old Town apartment. But they were running late. Police cars were already lining down the block in front of the building.

36

The windscreen wipers were squeaking from left to right, right to left, taking off the rain prickling so hard against the Lotus' fiberglass body you could barely hear the engine running. It was quiet inside the car, though. For the first time ever, Duke could make out a monotonous, squealing noise of a fan. It was driving him insane. Worse, he knew if it wasn't for the complete silence between him and Emily, the fan noise would've remained a secret forever.

"You need time," Duke said, his tongue heavy as lead, his mouth sticky as maple syrup. "I know you have nowhere else to go than my place. I'll leave it to you for as long as you want it."

"What does that mean?" she asked in a lifeless voice that brought Duke on the verge of tears.

"I have a house on Loch Fyne. I'll leave Edinburgh for good. Once everything is set up there, I'll give up the house in Edinburgh."

"Okay."

"Emily, I want you to come with me."

"Come with you and do what?"

"Share a good life. Listen, you need time to think. I understand that. Take all the time you need. Once you know what you want to do, and you want to talk about it, you call me."

"Okay."

"You have to know that I– "

"Huh?"

"I care a lot about you."

Emily sighed.

"Thank you for telling me everything you needed to get off your chest. But there's nothing else I could say tonight. I'll get my stuff from your house and check into a hotel."

"Please, stay at the house. It's all yours. I'll take you there and drive out to Loch Fyne."

"You're going to leave me alone?"

"I'll never leave you alone unless you ask me to. No, I'll give you space. To think things over."

"Think things over, yeah," she said with her head hanging low.

Duke wanted to take her in his arms. Kiss her. Pet her forehead. Her neck. Anything. Instead, he did nothing. Then he did the only thing he could think of. Put the car in gear and race through flooded streets. Rain had always brought out his prime driving skills, and even though he was going much too fast for comfort, Emily wouldn't say a word.

At the house, she got out into the rain, and Duke rolled down the window, hollering against the wind: "Call me when you know, okay? Emily! Emily! I– "

But his voice was drowned out by the piping wind and the noise of rattling shutters and rustling leaves.

It was a three-hour drive to the house in good conditions. Duke managed it a little quicker than that despite the rain. The roads were free, because nobody was crazy enough to drive, and he knew what the car could do. When the tires would lose grip. When to brake into corners, slam down the accelerator without spinning into the ditch.

The house lay in utter silence and darkness when he arrived. It was the first time in two months he'd gone out there. Everything had been tidy and clean when he left but a layer of dust had already settled over everything again. There was a good supply of canned and frozen foods but he wasn't hungry at all. The only craving he felt was for distraction.

With a cup of Earl Grey tea he didn't want, Duke went to the upstairs study, pulling the cover off his desk. The desk was his own creation, a solid oak piece designed to be the home of his electronic music equipment. Learning how to produce music had been his goal for a while and within the solitude of his house on Loch Fyne, he felt it was the only thing he could do. It occupied him all through the night, submerged in white noise, blue noise, the random sounds he produced, listening through headphones hand-built in Brooklyn, New York he'd bought on a trip with Rachel.

Rachel. The thought of her name revived all those memories inside of his head. The need to phone her up was quickly followed by doubt. It didn't seem like a good idea. Nothing did anymore. Checking his phone, Duke was devastated. No word from Emily. But then again, what had he really expected?

"Keep yourself busy," he told himself, listening to his faint voice blocked by the cacophony he squeezed out of the analog and digital circuits.

No sign of fatigue. Sometimes, he got up looking out the window, out on the lake. Whatever he hoped to see wasn't there. The calmness, the solitude, they'd attracted him to this house in the first place. But that had been before he'd known the void inside of his chest. He hoped to spot a monster, a giant sea serpent or plesiosaurus, like Nessie, anything really that would take his mind off the issue at hand. Dragging the extra-long headphone cable after himself like a snake, Duke paced up and down the study, only stopping as not to yank his equipment off the desk.

It was a very nice setup, a blend of vintage and brand-new sound making tools. Some classics from the 80s and 90s he'd seen at a shop as a youth but never really understood what they were doing. A genuine Roland TR-8 drum machine that had cost him a fortune even though he didn't know how to operate it and if it was worth as much as the seller was asking. The blue Korg Electribe EMX, a machine he'd admired since he was sixteen but never really understood how it produced sound. They gave him a good feeling. Just looking at the gear he'd amassed over the course of the last two years gave him a sense of reassurance. After a while, the vibe started seeping into his fingertips. Cacophony became something remotely resembling electronic music.

When he needed a break, he listened to the masters of Detroit Techno without feeling inferior, honoring their skill and creativity instead, admiring how they turned limitations into art. It wasn't a competition. Here was finally something he didn't need to excel at. The thought crossed his mind again when he saw the sun coming up over the loch, the beautiful colors it conjured out of darkness.

Two days no sleep. No word from Emily. No fresh air either, since Duke preferred staying inside, sometimes opening a window just a crack so he could poke his nose out and inhale the scent of Highland grass and loch water. The more he familiarized himself with the equipment, the better he navigated menus, diving into the sound presets, tweaking them the way he wanted to. Taking classes had never been for him. Luckily, he was a quick learner. The phone woke him after he'd fallen asleep on an ancient wooden chair he kept around in the kitchen.

No word from Emily.

Were two days enough? No, it had been three days already. How long to make up your mind, darling? Duke wondered. When he tried putting himself in her shoes, he failed. If only he knew. For better or worse. It'd free his mind. But it wasn't giving him choices. All he could do was wait.

What if he got back in the car, raced it all the way to Edinburgh, bringing it to a sliding stop in the driveway, taking her into his arms, telling her everything would be alright, and what if she fell for him for good, requiting his feelings. It was a pretty prospect, straight out of a corny summer romance, where you cut out the unwanted bits. Like unrequited feelings.

Life was not a movie, he decided, and there was little to gain from pressuring Emily into something she didn't want.

The fourth day was okay. The fifth turned into a stretch. Whatever progress Duke had been making with his music was slowly eradicated by madness, seeping into his mind. Melodies he'd been fond of suddenly sounded dreary, bad, bland. They were driving him insane. He unplugged the Korg Volca FM, raising it so he could hurl it against the wall and destroy it, stopping just shy of releasing it. Duke had caught a view of the loch in the corner of his eye again. It wasn't clear to him what he saw there. It was enough to reinstate some sense of sanity.

Sitting at the kitchen table, he produced a pack of cigarettes he kept in a drawer for emergencies. This clearly felt like the type of emergency they were meant for. The smoke did something. What it didn't do was work miracles. After his third straight cigarette, Duke felt a very unpleasant dizziness kicking in.

"Bloody fool," he said cursing himself.

The confines of his home wouldn't serve him well any further, he came to understand. The weather was nice, with mist hovering over the water. Duke decided to go for a walk. The cigarettes and a can of beer would accompany him. With his duck boots on, he didn't have to pay attention to the ground beneath his feet. After a while, he finished another cigarette out of the pack, lit it, took the last drink of beer from the can. When he turned around and looked at his house, the red Lotus Excel parked in front of it, he barely recognized it at all. It felt like the end of the world. Which was foolish, of course. But he couldn't see a way out of this self-imposed predicament.

Something had changed over the course of the past five days. Walking back to the house didn't seem right anymore. It was an empty shell he'd tried to fill with something so clearly not him, setting himself up for failure deliberately.

And then the phone started shaking in his coat's pocket.

"Duke?" Angie said, hearing him breathing heavily.

"Angie?"

"Where are you?"

"Loch Fyne."

"Where's that?"

"North-west of Glasgow. Where are you?"

"Piccadilly Circus."

"Hope the clowns are coming out soon."

"You said you'd come for me any time I needed you. Remember?"

"I remember."

"I need you now."

"Don't cry, it's going to be alright."

"Can you come?"

"I won't make it before tomorrow morning. I'll have some miles to crunch to London."

"Okay."

"Can you hang on in there?"

"I'll try."

"I'll get in the car. Text me a meeting place. I'll give you an update when I stop for fuel."

"I don't know what got into him but he lost it from one moment to the next."

"Is he alone with you?"

"His entourage isn't here."

"I'll be with you soon as I can."

"See you here."

Duke was wide awake. He quickly walked back to the house, changed into the clothes he'd worn in Edinburgh and floored the Lotus.

Driving through the Highlands and Lowlands of Scotland happened almost as if in automatic flight mode. It got dark soon, with few cars on the road. When he crossed the English border, Duke didn't feel alright. Head aching. Stomach cramping. Neck hurting. Back killing him. It was the first and only time he remembered feeling this way behind the wheel of his beloved car.

Despite all, he carried through, stopping for fuel between Manchester and Liverpool. Angie had sent him another message, naming a café close to Piccadilly Circus as their meeting place. Duke knew he could be there around five in the morning at the earliest, which wouldn't get them anywhere, so he texted her back to meet at eight am. The Snickers bar he'd bought trying to fight his cramping stomach only made matters worse, so he threw it out the window carelessly. Only Highland water helped, touched up with an occasional aspirin.

London was slow when he approached it. The lanes turned narrower, narrower, almost like cooked-through spaghetti stretched out in front of him. It was hard keeping the car in lane. At one time, he almost crashed into a truck he hadn't seen. It had him worried.

The last time he'd been to London, on a business assignment, he'd been driving around town at night, enjoying the empty streets, accelerating, decelerating, revving the engine, sometimes racing against cars and guys on café racer motorcycles, all for the hell of it. None of this made sense this time. A guy in leather jacket on a vintage Norton gave him a thumbs up. All Duke could muster was a quick, fake smile on his sweaty face. It did nothing to deceive the man, who turned the throttle and sped off into the night.

At another gas station, Duke filled up the Excel, buying himself a sandwich he didn't want and some more Highland water before parking the car in the back of the compound falling asleep quickly. He had about two hours. But then again, he thought, what difference would it make if he was a bit late for once?

Sleep was bad, filled with the type of dreams he usually only had when he was running a fever. It was an analogy to the tale of Sisyphus, taking him back to Ben Nevis, where he'd failed making it to the top thanks to being ill-prepared, overheated, sweating though his clothes, getting cold at the gravel field, only to turn around in defeat. To fall sick the following day, running a fever that would come and go for the next five consecutive days. Duke assumed it was the punishment he deserved. Exactly why he deserved it was still beyond him.

When he woke up, he was sweating hard. All the windows of the car were fogged over. And he was cold. He quickly gulped down another pint of Highland water, then forced four bites of sandwich into his upset stomach, knowing he'd definitely need it.

"Look like shit," he told himself when he checked his face in the mirror.

Pomade was running down his forehead and right cheek, and with his entire scalp soaked with sweat, there was nothing that could've been done about his hair anymore. Duke started the engine, rolled down the windows, cranked up the heater to full blast and drove out into London's commuter traffic jam.

The café was at a non-parking zone, prompting Duke to stop at a taxi rank. It wouldn't bother him much. As long as he stayed in the car and returned before they could tow it, he was good. You could see the full length of the café, which was busy but not buzzing yet. Angie was nowhere to be seen. Now, all he could do was sit and wait, making sure this wasn't a trap or set-up of any kind. Thinking things through, feeling sick as a dog, Duke was still caught unprepared when the passenger's side door popped open.

"It's been a while," Joe said, getting in. "But something told me I'd see a red Lotus Excel here. Hi, Duke."

"Hi, Joe."

"Oh, you know me?"

"I remember you. Caught my eye once when I was having a burger."

"I can't remember seeing you."

"But you saw me at university."

"Yes, I did. Back then, we couldn't know we were looking for you. Funny thing, a perpetrator, returning to the crime scene. So cliché."

"What did she tell you?"

"What didn't she tell me would be a better question. You look terrible. Is everything okay?"

"Heard you handed over your badge."

"Seems you hear a lot around Edinburgh. Didn't help you much when you were red-listed, though."

"How's it possible that you're here right now?"

"I'm a good soul, sent by an angel to look after poor little Angie."

"When die she call you?"

"Yesterday, around midday. Said that bloke she was gutting like a Christmas goose was losing his bearings or something. Lucky coincidence I was in London already."

"It never occurred to her you weren't a cop anymore."

"Not until I told her. When she asked me for a colleague's phone number, I kindly refused."

"But you knew the hotel was somewhere around Piccadilly Circus. Further, you knew she'd be calling me."

"You were her last resort. Then it all started adding up. Some basic calculations and killing a couple of hours on the watch."

"Are you mad I never turned myself in? Not even after being cleared from all charges? I was a suspect at best."

"And yet you behaved very much like a guilty man. Duke, are you okay?"

"I'll have some water."

"I asked myself one question. Over and over again."

"What would that be?"

"What's got a man to be ashamed of if he's done nothing he could be tried for and still prefer going into hiding, mingling with the lowest scum of the city, just so he wouldn't have to answer some, admittedly, unfavorable questions."

"I thought it'd be fun if the rozzers were running around town like headless chickens trying to outsmart me."

"Horseshit."

"What about you, sitting in my car, all high and mighty? Let's talk about it."

"At any length you'd like."

"What did you see when you were trying to find me? When you dove into the world of shadows, not the upper crust, rather the underbelly. What did you see that scared you so much you wouldn't want to be a cop anymore?"

"I wasn't scared."

"Beg your pardon. What tasted so good?"

"Oh, come on."

"The bright lights?"

"You're making a fool of yourself."

"The smell of expensive perfume and cheap tobacco?"

"Duke, please."

"Was it the scent of sweating people, pheromones airborne and plenty, beautiful people without souls and hearts and qualities that you want nevertheless, and that want you too, exploit you like you exploit them back, build you up and strike you down until you're doing the same in retaliation? What was it, Joe? Money? The drugs? Sex? Or simply a yearning for adventure in your dull, meaningless life making sixty-thousand pounds a year? What?"

"You," she said with tears welling in her eyes. "I wanted to feel what it was like, being you. Being in the life of this man I've seen before but never connected to, and now was forced to hunt down for a crime never committed."

"I didn't mean to tease you."

"It's only natural you're upset."

"I still had no right."

"You know," she said quickly destroying the evidence of crying, "before I said it, I didn't even know it for myself. Somewhere deep inside of me, I knew. But not consciously. If it weren't for you coming to London today, I'd never have known."

And when he leaned over, taking her into his arms, it came naturally. So naturally. Duke petted the back of her head, feeling a sensation rushing through him like a tidal wave.

"What did you learn from it?" he asked her.

"That I don't know how you did it. You must be much stronger than anyone ever suspected."

"I'm not strong."

"Yes, you are."

"You're strong."

"Not in the same way."

"Then maybe it's okay. It's how it's supposed to be. Complementing strength."

"I don't know what I'm doing right now."

"Me neither."

"I tried living out those ideas I've had in my head for some time now. I nurtured these notions of who I could be, if only I was free. If I didn't have all these obligations."

"How did it turn out?"

"It all felt like shit."

"Same for me."

"Something was off."

"You couldn't put your finger to it."

"There's one thing I know for sure," she said looking him right in the eyes, drowning him, and drowning herself in his gaze staring back at her: "Angie's found the self of hers that looks like an angel but plays like the devil. Opportunism is her driving force. I feel it. If you go into that café, she'll play the part. She'll tell you how much better a man you are than that lunatic. She'll tell you, oh, wouldn't it be pretty imagining the two of us together? How sweet it could be. But I tell you, even though you're quenching a lot of her thirst, there's nothing you could do about the rest of it. She'll soon feel like walking the desert on a dry mouth. And then she'll dump you, like trash, going back to that sicko or any other benefactor, creeping back to you once they run dry or raise their hand or verbally abuse her. It's going to be the game on her rules and she'll waste you."

"You don't want to see me wasted."

"No."

"I don't want to see you wasted, either."

"I could tell you now how much I'd love throwing that abusive pig's ass to jail. But the truth is, there's too many like him out there and I've had my share of catching them."

As she sunk her face in his shoulder, trying to regain her composure, Duke saw Angie walking to the café on the other side of the road. She was wearing a short skirt, no leggings, despite the cold, fur coat, unbuttoned, as not to conceal anything, arms folded in front of her chest fighting the shivers. Hair done beautifully, flickering like diamonds in the early morning light. And an oversized pair of rhinestone sunglasses. A guy stared at her in passing, making her smile. When she walked in, she mingled with the crowd right away. Duke lost sight of her.

"Joe," Duke said starting the engine, which roared to live instantly. "I have a house on Loch Fyne. Quiet and Solitary. Would you like staying there with me for a while?"

"I've always loved Highland lochs," she said leaning back in the seat, ready to ride shotgun.

"We'll stop at your hotel, get your luggage and check you out."

"I'll guide you."

"Let's roll."

The tires squealed as they shot out into traffic, turning heads even in London, Piccadilly Circus. All the people ever saw, for the briefest of moments, was a red Lotus, gunning through traffic with lightness and ease, shooting flames out the stainless-steel exhaust pipe between gear shifts.

EPILOGUE

Hesitantly, Joe walked through the house they'd returned to in Edinburgh. It had been locked up, laying in utter silence. As if nobody had been there for quite some time.

"I'll go get the things I need," Duke said already on his way.

"Your father will love this house."

"I hope so. I wanted to make it up to him for quite some time. I'll be right back."

It seemed as if there was no connection between Duke, the man, and all the things he owned. Whatever it was Joe had expected, it wouldn't quite fit. It was a beautiful home, no doubt. But far from the stylish, James Bond themed apartment downtown anyone would've associated with Duke, the character.

And therein lay the issue at hand. Only few people knew Duke, the man, while at the same time, all the world seemed to know Duke. Joe peered in the garage, amazed at the workshop, fully equipped to do so many things she knew next to nothing about. A plaid on the sofa, lambswool with a unique pattern she'd never seen before and felt it must've been of Irish origin. The garden was small but nice, with a compact bamboo grove to the left fence. Trying to process all this, she couldn't wait to get back on the road.

Thinking a cup of tea would do them both good, Joe spotted an envelope on the kitchen table on her way to the sink. It was sealed. To Duke, was scribbled in hastily written letters on it.

"Okay, I'm ready," Duke said returning downstairs with two leather bags and a photograph in a self-built frame underneath his arm.

"Here's a letter for you," Joe said.

"Oh. Did you read it?"

"Why'd I read a letter that's written to you?"

"Please take it and let's get out of here, alright?"

"Doesn't feel like home anymore?"

"Edinburgh doesn't feel like home anymore. You can relate, eh?"

"Yes."

Duke dropped the letter to his father in the mail box on the other side of the road before returning to Joe waiting in the running car.

"I've had an idea," he said getting back in.

"What's that?"

"A farewell tour. Just a small one."

"To say goodbye to the city."

"Yes."

"I'm in."

They parked the car on the backside of Carlton Hill and climbed to the top. It was still early in the morning and few tourists had found their way to the vantage point. The skies were clear, the view magnificent. Joe took his hand and they walked to the National Monument, illegally, like everyone else, climbing the oversized stairs together, feeling like sitting on top of the world.

"I've always loved the view," Joe said, her head on Duke's shoulder. "From up here, it looks like a wondrous place. As if anything was possible."

"As if nothing bad could ever happen to you."

Duke felt the envelope in the chest pocket of his jacket. Like a lead paper weight, it hung there, heavy and unwieldly.

"I have a hunch this isn't the place for us anymore."

"We're tourists now."

Then he got the envelope out, ripping it open, finding a note written on heavy paper. Duke shook the envelope, and it fell out, the few letters written on it clearly visible. Even though Joe hadn't intended to read it, there was nothing she could've done about it.

"You know why," Duke read it out loud. Joe bend down to pick it up but he stopped her. "No, please. Leave it right there."

"I'm sorry."

"Don't be. There's nothing to feel sorry about."

"Let's go, then."

"We can stop for coffee along the way, maybe at Loch Lomond. What do you say?"

"That's a lovely idea."

"They have the best views for sure. Come."

They climbed down from the National Monument, descending Carlton Hill just before the tourists started flocking in. Duke let Joe take the wheel, navigating them down Easter Road, into Duke Street in Leith, just a short stretch going down memory lane, before they took Ferry Road leading them out of Edinburgh. It was a lovely day for a drive into the Highlands, and they were in no hurry. The modified 912 engine was just warming up to ideal temperature, so they could pick up speed once the roads became narrower, more twisted and deserted.

Printed in Dunstable, United Kingdom